KING OF THE SEVEN LAKES

A B Endacott

ISBN-978-0-6481875-3-0

Books by the same author

Queendom of the Seven Lakes

King of the Seven Lakes

Coming soon

The Ruthless Land

Dark Intent

Dark Purpose

Dark Heart

Untitled (First Country)

On the auspicious occasion of his 90th birthday,
I dedicate this book to
my Grandfather,
Whose moral code is strikingly similar to Gidyon's.
And of course, without his lifelong companion,
my Grandmother,
This would be only half a dedication.
Therefore, this book is dedicated to her, too,
Because they are not simply husband and wife, but
friends,
And the most beautiful stories are those about friends.

A
woman of hot temper – and a man the same –
Is
a less dangerous enemy than one quiet and clever.

-Euripides, Medea

THE FAMILIES OF THE SECOND COUNTRY

The Royal Family

For centuries, the Royal Family have overseen the stability of the Second Country underneath the firm hands of their queens. Following the sacrilegious murder of Queen Latana, in a complete breach of custom, her son Gidyon ascended the throne. Despite his gender, those who have observed him have commented on his intellect, sense of duty, and political nous. Guided by his uncles, Kaine, Silius, and Nikalus, in the first year of his reign, Gidyon ruled over a country divided. While some supported him, others were less enthusiastic in their willingness to be ruled by a man, and others still saw an opportunity to further their own power.

The Aadran Family

Presided over by their formidable matriarch, Arlena, the Aadran family possesses enormous wealth. They have had longstanding familial and business connections with the Tak family, which has entrenched their position of power. However, were it to become known, the illicit romantic relationship between one of the Aadran sons, Zekken, and the late Queen Latana, would see them shunned by even the steadfast Taks. Their social, and ensuing economic, ruin would be complete were it also known that Zekken believed himself to be Gidyon's father. The only thing worse than a queen conducting an enduring love affair with a member of the Seven Families would be if she knew who had fathered her child, decimating the neutrality her position was supposed to enshrine.

The Rasatan Family

One of the lesser of the Seven Families. Their fortunes were ruined when Erek Rasatan killed Queen Latana. Few know that underneath his unusually handsome visage lurked a deeply unstable mind. Erek's instability was preyed upon by his cruel mother, Keela, who despite her outward timidity, was best described as a masochist. Upon Erek's death in a struggle following his murder of Latana, Keela apparently killed herself. While Zekken and Latana may have considered themselves Gidyon's parents, at the first Season – the events at which royal children are conceived – Erek also made himself a contender for Gidyon's paternity. Following the scandal of Erek's regicide, the Rasatan family have become shunned by polite society and much of the power they held has been lost.

The Katan Family

Despite their powerful wealth generated by the spectacular ceramics spun from the clay within their lands, the Katan family have always been greedy for more power. The remoteness of their lands made marrying Latana's sister into the family seem like a good way to remove her as a direct challenger to the throne, as well as being a Royal gesture of goodwill to the Katan family. But the move also produced a girl now being touted as an alternative heir to the throne. Serenah's claim is especially strong now that a man sits on the throne in contravention of tradition. The patriarch, Halen, aggressively advocates his granddaughter as the rightful queen of the Second Country and will use any opportunity to put her on the throne. In the instance of her being placed on the throne, he would be adviser to her, and strongly encourage her to implement whatever policies he desired. Certainly, this likelihood makes a compelling case for the current system and the impartiality it ensures.

The Bertak Family

A lesser family, and famously resentful of that fact. While they mine precious gems from the mountains of their estate, they lacked the foresight – and now the capital – to establish master artisan workshops to cut or set these gemstones, and thus the wealth that enables true power eludes them. The Bertaks' manners are almost as minimal as their willingness to do anything that even vaguely promises them power is strong.

The Haree Family

Making their money from the timber of the forest that lies across their land, the Harete family is perhaps the most enigmatic of the Seven Families. The bitter enmity between husband Timet and his wife Janyce (by birth, a Katan) is a poorly concealed secret. Like all of the Seven Families, they seek to further their power and have demonstrated a certain breed of unscrupulousness in the pursuit of it. Their most recent attempt was to instruct their daughter, Rania, to try to seduce Prince Gidyon when he visited them prior to his mother's death. Were it not for intervention, Rania's charms might have succeeded, too. Certainly, it did not endear them to the Prince.

The Tak Family

Historically allying themselves with the Aadran family, the Tak make their fortunes from livestock. Their wealth offers them the luxury of being able to claim neutrality in a great many circumstances so that they can always side with whoever ends as the victor. Led by Serek and Karan, the Tak family would be a powerful political ally.

The Veertak Family

A family of scholars, the Veertaks have always been more interested in books than politics – just. Their leaders, the aged but sharp-witted Varlena and Varl, have steadfastly put their support behind the Royal Family. They alone know the true identity of Gidyon's mysterious companion, Elen-ai, but have vowed to maintain this secret.

The Family of Assassins

Some may dispute their place on this list. However, the Family of Assassins was formed in the infancy of the Second Country following the great wars of the Godskissed Continent. The Family takes in children only a few months old and its Mothers and Fathers train them to become masters of every weapon, as well as disciples of the arts gifted by the Shadow God. If someone's name is on a contract taken out by the Family, their death is all but assured. No fighter alive can match the skills of the Family. Their one rule: they will not take the life of any member of the Royal Family. The Family's loyal daughter, Elen-ai, was contracted by Queen Latana not to kill but to protect Gidyon following her decision to name him her heir. Initially reluctant to accept the contract, Elen-ai's reservations seemed to be confirmed by the Prince's distaste for her origins. Yet, somehow, she and the Prince became friends, and she returned to the Palace following his coronation in an unofficial capacity to assist him. While she might have the blessing of some of the Family, acting as a sort of informant for them, this arrangement is not unanimously supported within the Family.

ONE

Pulling her scarf more tightly around her in a valiant fight against the cold, the assassin hurried toward the Palace. She moved with lithe grace, habit pushing her to stay close to the shadows. The inclination to remain in the darkest, most unobtrusive part of wherever she went arose from the training instilled in her from the youngest of ages.

Elen-ai passed barely anybody as she ascended the hill to the Palace, where it occupied the highest point in the capital. Even now, despite months of living there, it felt strange to be climbing the broad street to the sprawling complex rather than winding her way through Herran's lanes to the Family's home. Opulence was all very good and well, but nothing could ever compare to the familiarity of home. But the information swirling in her head took precedence over any sense of being out of place. Despite the prowling sense of urgency in her stomach, she paused at a shrine to the Divine One decorated with coloured ribbons and flowers. It was the fifth shrine she had passed since leaving the Family's home. A year ago, there had been no such shrines in the Second Country, only the temple to the Divine One in the heart of the capital. Now, it was almost impossible to walk for five minutes without seeing one. Tensions between the Seven Families and the Royal Family had not yet led to any true instability within the Second Country. The roads through the Second Country were still reasonably safe to traverse, and there were no shortages of any food or material, but people were worried.

Some of the Seven Families, like the Veertaks, remained steadfast in their loyalty to the crown, but others had taken advantage of the recent political instability to try to subvert the authority of the Palace and increase their own wealth and power. Of course, while those seeking to gain – or at the very least not lose – power always had enough to eat and trained fighters to keep them safe, the lives of most others were less secure. Problems wrought by the squabbles of the powerful always affected those who lived at the pleasure of the wealthy. The lowborn were keeping a sharp eye on what transpired between the powerful families of the Second Country, and it was obvious that they were worried by what they saw. The concern the shrines represented in turn worried Elen-ai. People often turned to faith in their gods when faith in their leaders faltered, and when people no longer had faith in their leaders, they were often not particularly averse to seeing those leaders leave. Often bloodily.

It was one of the reasons the Family of Assassins would accept a contract on anybody of high or low birth, provided the client was able to pay: the Family did not discriminate. The only strict exception to that neutrality was an unwillingness to touch a member of the Royal Family. Their deaths would cause too much instability, and the Family liked being situated in a prosperous, war-free country. It was good business. The Family's home was in an area that straddled the less dangerous parts of the poor district and the residences of individuals whose wealth offered them some measure of comfort, where the buildings ceased to be made entirely from timber and the more sturdy construction of stonework crept into the designs. In some ways, the Family's home was situated in a space of perfect neutrality between the high and low born, echoing the Family's apolitical nature.

As Elen-ai progressed through the wealthy district, each shrine was grander than the last. Those erected by the poor were all hastily made from whatever materials could be spared – a sun clumsily carved from a piece of scrap timber, a wooden sphere painted yellow or orange, even a simple cloth banner with a sun symbol embroidered or crudely drawn on it. Not so the one outside the fencing arena of the Artisans Quarter. Some fortunate woodcarver would have received a handsome commission for the work. Even the arena, which was easily distinguishable by the height that enabled many people to crowd in to watch the match, was of better construction than those arenas in poorer parts of the city. This one was built mostly from stone and had a fresh coat of paint on the door. Elen-ai could easily imagine the wealthier members of Herran's society cheerfully coming here for an evening's entertainment. One of the favourite pastimes of the Second Country's residents was to watch several fencing bouts across an evening. A night's entertainment would start with matches in which contestants fought with dulled blades and were limited to touches, then progress to first blood as the determinant of victory, and then finally to unrestricted fighting when victory was only determined when one fighter yielded – or died. Those final matches were the most eagerly anticipated. Many a lowborn citizen had made a comfortable fortune from their prowess with a blade, especially those lucky few to be sponsored by one of the Seven Families looking to add a champion fencer to the things about which they could boast. Elen-ai wondered if the shrine was visited by the competitors before they came to fight. Not that a simple shrine to the Sun God would protect any of the contestants from a well-aimed strike, but people liked to believe that something larger than themselves watched over them. Elen-ai personally preferred to place her faith in quick wits and rigorous training.

Predictably, the Katan family's shrine to the Divine One outside their city residence was taller, wider, and more splendid than all of the others combined. Despite her desire to be out of the bitter cold, Elen-ai crossed to the other side of the street so

3

she could better regard it. She snorted in amazement at the gold that covered the orb at the centre of the sun symbol and the gems embedded in the point of each ray emanating from the sphere. Such an extravagant display of wealth did not surprise her in the slightest. Halen, the leader of the Katan family, had aspirations for his granddaughter to be put on the throne. It didn't matter to Halen that Serenah was woefully inadequate as a potential ruler. He did not care that a ruler who had not been trained to possess the neutrality and even-handedness that was crucial when managing the delicate politics of the seven ambitious families, could be disastrous. The presence of a man on the throne following the brutal murder of Queen Latana was reason enough for Halen to justify the even greater instability he risked unleashing by trying to make his granddaughter queen. Though Elen-ai had only met the man once, it was a genuine pleasure to despise him. That vehement dislike was only compounded by what she had just learned about his actions. The rage that left a sick feeling in her throat fought with tense concern at what Halen's ambitions might mean. Taking one final look at the vulgar statement to Katan self-importance, Elen-ai continued on her way.

The ascent up the hill to the Palace offered progressively lovely views of Herran and the harbour around which it had been built. As she climbed higher, the city's rooftops fell together in a curiously harmonious patchwork of reds, greys and blacks, regularly interspersed with curls of smoke hanging softly in the cold air. With distance, even the ramshackle timber houses of the city's lowborn areas were beautiful. Elen-ai paused to turn and look back to the city. She swept her gaze along the crowded streets to the stone blue of the water in the harbour. In sunlight it would sparkle with unparalleled radiance. Today, however, the colour of the overcast sky was mirrored in the grey waves. She couldn't help but think that it suited her current mood.

Finally, she reached the Palace gates. Nearly the height of three people, the Palace's walls were an imposing sight, only rendered plain by the magnificent structure that rose behind them. Made from pale stone that glowed even in the lowest light, the immense complex was home to the Royal Family. Since the formation of the Second Country, its queens had resided within the Palace walls where they had managed the delicate power balance of the country's seven wealthiest families. Glimpses of the Palace could be seen from almost anywhere in Herran, but up close, there was something awe-inspiring about the elegant buildings.

Elen-ai wasn't sure she would ever become accustomed to so brazenly passing through the main gate. Her preferred method of entrance and egress was always the least noticeable one. Assassins who were spotted were not particularly successful in their trade, nor were they particularly long-lived. It was odd to realise that she even recognised the guards who stood on either side of the gates, nodding a quick greeting to them as she passed and receiving one in return.

For a moment, Elen-ai contemplated entering through the servants' door. The entrance was far less conspicuous than the grand doors of the Palace through which people of high birth, or high importance, entered. However, to enter through the servant's door would be more cause for attention given her place by Gidyon's side was well known. So, in defiance of every instinct she had ever cultivated, she gritted her teeth and ascended the stairs to the grand entrance. The door was opened for her and she walked out of the cold into the grand foyer. The foyer was its own testament to the wealth and power of the Royal Family. Several stairs and doors led away from it, hinting at the expanse of the Palace beyond. The foyer itself was huge. Every part of its walls was covered in murals painted by the most skilled artists of the time. Even the ceiling was painted: a blue sky, complete with clouds. Elen-ai had always found it odd to simulate the open sky while inside, but most people seemed to think it a stroke of the painter's genius. The first time Elen-ai had been in the space, she had been too curious as to why a member of the Family had been summoned by the Queen to actually notice the magnificence of where she was. Now, she had seen the foyer so many times that its splendour was almost lost on her.

Elen-ai made her way through the maze of breathtakingly beautiful corridors with a comfortable familiarity born from months of living there. Sadly, the stone out of which the walls had been built, despite the beauty it offered, held in the cold, encouraging swift passage through the building. Once more, Elen-ai thought wistfully of the Family's home. A clever system spread the heat from a fire throughout the home's walls. It meant that the whole building was a sanctuary from the chill of winter, unlike the Palace where one had to all but run from wing to wing in order to stay warm.

She was struck anew – as she always was – by the strangeness of being greeted by servants as she passed them. Never before had she been so recognised. Indeed, when she reached the council chamber, the guards at the door simply moved aside for her as they saw her approach. While there had initially been some element of novelty that made the experience somewhat enjoyable, she had never managed to shake the discomfort that such special treatment evoked. Anybody who was given immediate, unrestricted access to the most senior members of the Royal Family was uniquely privileged as well as uniquely conspicuous. It went against everything she knew to be at the centre of such attention.

At the opening of the doors, the room's occupants halted their conversation. Maps and charts pinned to the walls, with no regard for the plasterwork, all spoke of warfare strategies. However, the well-groomed and well-dressed men who were conferring inside seemed totally incongruous with war and fighting.

"Well?" The youngest of the group, handsome and authoritative despite his lesser years, seemed to recover himself first. He strode across the room to greet Elen-ai, who was privately delighting in the room's warmth.

Most people in Elen-ai's position would have bowed, faced as they were with their monarch. She did not. Gidyon and Elen-ai had been through too much for such formalities.

Every time she saw Gidyon, it seemed there was a further ageing in his face. At seventeen years old, it seemed hardly fair that the burden of ruling had been thrust upon him, let alone the burden of being the first male to sit on the throne of the Second Country.

His advisers, also his uncles, looked at her expectantly, waiting for the news that she had promised to bring. She remembered the hostility with which they had opposed her presence when Gidyon's late mother, their sister and queen, had engaged Elen-ai to protect Gidyon prior to the public announcement of her decision to make him her heir. Fearing violent reprisal for her boldness to go against centuries of tradition, she had engaged the Family, reasoning that an assassin would know best how another may try to take Gidyon's life. Elen-ai could still recall the suspicion and unease with which the Queen's brothers and advisers viewed the decision to have an assassin protecting the Prince. But their hostility toward Elen-ai had melted away in the face of Elen-ai's obvious loyalty to Gidyon. Perhaps a slight reserve remained, but she could hardly blame them for that. A member of the Family within the Palace was unprecedented. Then again, they were living in unprecedented times.

"The news is not good, I'm afraid," Elen-ai said. She made no effort to hide the grim tightness in her voice, or on her face.

A look of weary resignation flashed across Gidyon's face. He must have been very tired. Normally trying to discern what he was thinking or feeling was impossible. The duties and obligations of the throne not only robbed him of hours of sleep but weighed heavily upon him, too. Even Elen-ai, who was accustomed to very little sleep, would often take herself to bed long before him. It wouldn't be untrue to say that she worried about him.

"Let's have it then," Gidyon said. His face was totally impassive once more.

Elen-ai reported what she had learned at the Family's home: "From all accounts the Katan family is training a small army." She linked her hands behind her back while she observed the reactions of the men.

Silius, the oldest of Gidyon's uncles, displayed his anger in the tightening of his face and the flare of his nostrils. His two brothers, however, were less restrained, expressing their anger and dismay with muttered oaths and profanities. For his part, Gidyon absorbed the news with no visible reaction. After a moment, he let out a slight sigh.

"So it's for what we've been preparing," he said, his voice utterly even. He walked back to the table, Elen-ai falling into step beside him.

For a while, the five of them stood there in silence as the implications of her information were fully considered. During her walk to the Palace, Elen-ai had arrived at the conclusion that Gidyon and his uncles were no doubt drawing now: if Halen Katan would not be given the throne, it seemed he was willing to take it by force.

TWO

Almost all coronations are undertaken with a certain undertone of unacknowledged sadness. In most instances, this makes sense, as the coronation is taking place due to the previous monarch's death. Gidyon's coronation, however, had been characterised by overwhelming grief and confusion, if not also the muted undertone of outrage. The murder of Queen Latana by the deranged Erek Rasatan had plunged the Queendom of the Seven Lakes into a profoundly shocked mourning. Gidyon's mother had been beloved by her subjects, even though she hadn't yet produced a girl to one day take the throne from her. The fact that she had named Gidyon her heir and had been planning to do so for some time left her people in a tricky position: accept the decision of their unjustly murdered queen, or look upon this as a move that destabilised the political balance of the Second Country while ignoring generations of history and tradition. At first, the grief and shock had meant that not much thought had been given to who succeeded Latana. But as time wore on, it seemed most people had arrived at an uneasy middle ground: not violently opposed to the prospect of a man on the throne while remaining deeply uncomfortable with it and what it may mean.

What people didn't know was that Erek might have been Gidyon's father and he had killed the Queen in a jealous rage following his discovery that Latana had, unbeknown to anyone, been conducting an affair with Zekken Aadran for several years. The only thing that made this worse was that Zekken considered himself Gidyon's father, as Gidyon had been conceived during the Queen's first Season – the only time that Latana had actually adhered to protocol and taken more than one man to her bed. Had this been public knowledge, support for Gidyon would have fallen away entirely. It was of the utmost importance that the Royal Family remain neutral. That was why the Season theoretically ensured that the father of any child produced from the liaisons between the queen and eligible male members of the Seven Families during the few days of feasting and socialising was never known. It meant that the queen's children were not obligated to any one of the families. Fears over whether as a man Gidyon could keep the Royal Family's neutrality intact would boil over into infuriated rejection of him were the Queen's lapse in judgment ever known.

However, shock had still been the dominant emotion on the day of Gidyon's coronation. He had walked through the streets, taking practically the same route of his mother's funeral procession, all the way through Herran until he arrived at the Temple of the Divine One where he was officially blessed by a Priest and Priestess before making his way back up the hill to the Palace. However, unlike Latana's funeral parade when he had been surrounded by his uncles, Elen-ai, and the heads of the Seven Families, this path he had walked alone, still wearing the silver mourning colours underneath the purple and gold cloak that fell from his shoulders. The streets were no less crowded than at Latana's funeral, as the people lined up to lay their eyes on the man who dared take the throne.

In truth, Elen-ai could think of nobody better to rule. She had accompanied Gidyon through the Second Country following an attempt on his life, orchestrated as it turned out, by Erek Rasatan. He had undertaken the journey to both gain the support of the Seven Families for his claim to the throne and try to determine who was behind the attack. Following her initial impression that he was a brat, Elen-ai had arrived at the realisation that in fact he had the makings of a great ruler. It was why she had helped him to discover that Erek Rasatan was behind the attempt on his life. It was why she had returned to his side, even after he had tried to send her back to the Family.

That hot, late summer evening on which she had scaled the wall of the Palace and crept through the grounds was inscribed on her memory. She could still taste the scent of the night-blooming flowers in the garden that she had used to gain entrance to the Palace building. Guards patrolled at very commendable intervals, but Elen-ai moved past them, invisible to anyone, even if they were looking directly at her. The Family's devotion to the Shadow God gave them skills that less enlightened individuals might term magic. The Family had always termed them forgotten skills, capabilities that might once have been possessed by all in the time when the divide between gods and humans had been less clear, but had been forgotten when the veil between divine and mortal had grown almost impermeable, and most people in the world simply viewed their god as an oath to be used in emotional moments.

She effortlessly remembered the way to Gidyon's room, even though the number of days she had spent in the enormous, complex Palace had totalled only a few. She entered through a window that had been carelessly flung open to allow the scant night breeze in to cool the room. Given that Gidyon's chambers overlooked a sheer wall that no ordinary person could climb, Elen-ai hadn't been particularly outraged that the window had been left open, although she was certain whoever had opened the window had not ever considered that it may invite danger to Gidyon's side. She found the room empty and settled herself in a chair to wait. True to form, when he had finally come in, he didn't seem surprised in the slightest to find her there.

"What are you doing here?" he had asked calmly, blue eyes fixed on her as he shrugged off the ceremonial jacket, sighing slightly in relief to be free of the restrictive garment.

"I want to help you." Elen-ai remained seated. The formality of standing at her ruler's entrance, let alone bowing to him, was already long behind them.

Gidyon arched an eyebrow. "I told you that your contract was fulfilled." He crossed the room and poured himself a measure of something from a tall bottle. He didn't drink it, though. He merely swirled the liquid around in the glass vessel as he gazed into its depths.

"I..." Elen-ai faltered, uncertain of what to say, of how to convince him that she should be by his side. So she said nothing, allowing her silence to speak for itself.

Gidyon did not immediately say anything. "Are you certain?"

There was a certain tightness in the way he asked that gave the question a weight and meaning it otherwise would not have had. Gidyon had his uncles, but being the ruler of a country, especially the first male ruler, left him apart from everybody else, and perhaps the only person who knew that, along with his other secrets, was Elen-ai.

She hadn't even heard the end of his question before she was nodding. "Gidyon, I am yours to command." She was surprised by how seriously she meant it.

He took a sip of his drink. Elen-ai knew the action wasn't because he had any great fondness for liquor. She had once nearly killed him by making him drink ale. She would have bet that the action was to mask some emotion that he didn't want her to see, to give him time to compose himself. "You are free to go at any time—"

"I am here, Gidyon," she interrupted him, her voice firm.

"I will have rooms made up for you. Sleeping in my room is perhaps not appropriate." His voice was rough with emotion and his eyes perhaps a bit brighter than normal, but Elen-ai pretended not to notice either of those things.

"It's a good idea. Although people will still probably assume we're lovers," she said, the slightest hint of mischief in her voice.

"And you will need a new wardrobe," he continued, as though she hadn't referred to the assumption that had been made about them in the spring when they were travelling through the Second Country. He had been mortified by that assumption, even after Elen-ai had pointed out it hid both their purpose and her position as a member of the Family. It seemed he was still mortified by it now.

"What?" Elen-ai made no attempt to mask her horror at the prospect of a new wardrobe. She was perfectly comfortable in her own clothes

"Well, we need an explanation for you to be here. Given you are lowborn it would be plausible to say that I have taken you on as a special adviser."

Elen-ai nodded. What he said made sense. Only those born into the Royal Family or the Seven Families had an unbroken first name. It meant that the moment they introduced themselves, it was clear they were someone to be treated with appropriate respect – or disrespect, depending on your attitude. Indeed, all lowborn women had the suffix -ai or -am at the end of their names, while men were given the suffixes -et or -en. From the second that she was introduced, everyone would be aware of the station of her birth. Yet that was advantageous, as it meant that she could easily claim credibility within the Palace as Gidyon's liaison to the people, something he most definitely was in need of given the complicated mix of feelings with which he was viewed by most of his subjects.

Gidyon continued, sounding completely serious. "Well, if you are to take such a title, you must look the part. That means a new wardrobe full of beautiful clothes."

"I regret coming back," Elen-ai said. The idea of being fitted for a variety of clothes, or even of being forced to be the subject of a discussion about the fabrics and colours that best brought out "the depths of her dark eyes" and "complemented the colour of her skin" (phrases she had heard used in several tailors and been thoroughly grateful that she was merely passing through), seemed the most awful torture that she could ever envisage for anybody, let alone herself.

Gidyon nodded as he came to sit next to her. "Oh yes, a beautiful collection. An abundance of clothes for you, in fact. And many, many dresses." He sounded so sincere that for one horrifying moment, Elen-ai believed that he would force her into a dress.

"Well played," she muttered as she took the glass flute from his hand and drained the expensive vessel of its very fine contents. The feel of the cool glass against her fingers was a shock. She had only ever held glass drinking vessels on a select number of occasions – most of them during her time with Gidyon. "I am yours to command, my King," she repeated her earlier statement, although the false sweetness to her tone undercut the gravitas of the comment. "And I can't imagine a better way to use my many skills than putting me in a dress," she added, dropping the sickly sweet tone and adopting one of most fervent sarcasm.

Gidyon chuckled. "I've missed you these last weeks," he admitted, leaning back into the cushions of the couch. He seemed too tired to pretend he didn't want her there any longer. His expression sobered as he put his hand on hers for the briefest of instances. "Thank you, Elen-ai." The emphatic gratitude had brought unexpected tears to her eyes.

Now, standing in the council room, considering the implications of Halen Katan's actions in his attempt to take the throne, that summer evening seemed an age away. If Gidyon had seemed tired then, it was nothing compared with the fatigue that constantly seemed to weigh on him now. The escalating belligerence of the Fourth Country, who seemed disinclined to curtail the border raids resulting from their own political instability, the hostility within the Second Country to a man on the throne, the actions of Halen and his allies to destabilise Gidyon, and of course, the normal requirements of being a ruler, had aged Gidyon far beyond his seventeen years.

Gidyon leaned on the table at the room's centre. He looked down at his hands as he spoke. "All right then, let's have it."

Elen-ai spared a moment to share a glance with Gidyon's uncles. They all looked as though they were bracing themselves to be severely beaten.

"As we know, the Katan estate is one of the most remote in the Second Country. It seems Halen has been using that to his advantage, training a small army without anybody noticing."

"How is he arming those people? We control where weapons are made," Silius asked. His features, which naturally fell into a disapproving expression, had arranged themselves in a look which was even more unimpressed than usual.

Gidyon answered before Elen-ai could. "The Fourth Country is trading directly with him. His land shares a border with them, after all."

"Of course they're trading with Halen." If Silius' lips were pressed any more tightly together, they would disappear.

"What do we know about this?" asked Kaine, Gidyon's youngest uncle.

Gidyon shrugged as he turned to look at the war charts on the wall. Elen-ai wondered if he was thinking about how he would fight Halen on a battlefield. The thought perturbed her. War had not touched the Second Country for centuries thanks to the manner in which power had been divided and the impartiality of the queens. It need not touch the land now but for the small-mindedness of certain people.

"I only know that there are discrepancies in the trade reports they have been providing us," Gidyon said. "I thought they were incompetent or being deliberately vague..."

"I know a trader from the Fourth Country who is often in Herran," Elen-ai volunteered.

Gidyon remained looking thoughtfully at the charts. "Would she know anything?"

"Would it hurt to ask?" Nikalus, Gidyon's other uncle, asked.

Taking Gidyon's lack of further comment as an approval, Elen-ai said, "Next time she's here, I'll speak with her."

"Where would we be without you, Elen-ai?" Of Gidyon's three uncles, Kaine had taken to her the most. Given to mischief when the situation permitted, he winked at her across the table, gesturing with a small inclination of his head toward Silius who was clearing his throat in preparation to voice an objection.

"We do have our own informants who can find out the goings on within the Seven Families, and beyond," Silius pointed out to his brother coolly, apparently playing right into Kaine's verbal provocation.

Elen-ai swallowed a smile as she again caught Kaine's eye and saw the satisfied twinkle there.

Gidyon, who had seemed to be lost in his own thoughts and had missed the baiting of Silius, turned back to face his uncles. "Yes, but we have something they do not. An Elen-ai." He glanced at her, a tiny smile on his face. It brightened him, made him almost look his age. All too quickly, the smile was replaced by the solemnity that had become customary for him.

"And Halen?" Kaine prompted.

"The Council of Families will take place in a few days. I will wait to decide how we act until after I see what he does there," Gidyon said.

Silius gave a satisfied nod.

"We were just about finished here before Elen-ai came in. Is there anything else pressing?" Gidyon looked at his three uncles, his family. They shook their heads.

"Good. I believe I have a mathematics class that I should attend. My poor tutor, Gled-am, has come here for the last three days and each day has been sent away not having seen me because I have had to attend to something else. I am determined to see her today. Elen-ai, will you walk with me?"

Every so often, it was almost possible to forget that Gidyon was in charge, that he could end or start meetings as he pleased. Then he would decisively conclude matters, and the absolute certainty with which he conducted himself made it impossible to ever doubt his authority.

As Elen-ai walked out of the room with Gidyon, she was curious, not for the first time, how his uncles felt that he confided in her above anyone else. But the thought was driven from her head by her friend's slight frown.

"How worried should I be?" Gidyon asked as they walked.

"How worried are you?"

He chuckled without mirth. "Oh, very good. We'll make a statesperson out of you yet." He slipped his hands into his pockets. "Do you think we can get away without war? I really would prefer not to be known as the king whose reign saw the first war in the Second Country since the modern state's inception." It did not escape her attention that Gidyon had waited until there were no guards or servants nearby who might hear the question before he asked it.

She looked at the beautiful tiles they walked past. The gentle geometric arrangement was curiously meditative. "I honestly don't know. Perhaps we may be able to corner Halen so that he feels he cannot march against you."

Gidyon made a sound that suggested he was not optimistic. "Where is he finding these people who are willing to march against me, anyway?" He sounded curious more than anything else, but Elen-ai knew that frustration lurked underneath his voice.

"I'm not so certain that they're willing to march against you as much as unwilling to resist the lure of his coin," Elen-ai said.

"Are people that untethered to the throne?" Gidyon sounded genuinely shocked.

"The throne on which your mother sat, no. The throne on which you sit..." She let the unfinished sentence complete itself. It was not necessary for her to say that the people did not love him as they had his mother. Few monarchs could be loved in the way that Latana had been adored. But Gidyon's sex made it even more difficult for the people to come close to loving him with the adoring fidelity with which they had regarded Latana.

To Elen-ai's amusement, Gidyon cursed under his breath. It was not something he did often.

"Are you sleeping enough, Gid?" She asked the question even though she knew what the answer would be.

Gidyon threw her an amused look. "Of course I'm not," he replied. "Divine One, it's cold," he added, pulling his jacket around himself more securely.

Without thought, Elen-ai unwrapped her scarf and offered it to him. He waved her offer aside. "I'm all right, but thank you."

With a shrug she draped the garment back around her neck. They were nearly at the room where Gidyon's mathematics tutor was waiting. He had ordered that every effort be expended to make the poor woman comfortable while she waited for him to find a spare moment in which he could see her.

"Do you really think we're going to end up at war?" Elen-ai asked, unable to resist asking the question that had preyed upon her mind since she had learned about Halen's actions.

Gidyon stopped and looked properly at her. As was his custom, he did not answer her question immediately. She could almost see him choosing each word.

"Honestly, I don't know. But I'll do everything I can to try to stop it."

She could see the weariness in the shadows smudged under those violently blue eyes and the tiny lines that had worked their way into the smooth skin of his face. She worried that among the spun gold of his hair she would soon be able to see streaks of grey. However, none of that marred his beauty. If Erek was his father and not Zekken, Gidyon had definitely inherited the man's good looks. Erek Rasatan had been the most attractive man Elen-ai had ever seen. In some ways it was sad that he had been so tormented by his unassuming yet cruel mother to the point that his own sanity was so tenuous.

Elen-ai wanted to take her king in her arms and hold him close, lift the burden of everything – the question of who his father was, grief for his mother, worry about his position, and everything in between – for just the slightest of moments. But despite their closeness, he was still her king, and that was one line she could not cross. She kept her arms at her sides as he walked away.

THREE

Twice a year the Council of Families was held. It was the occasion on which the heads of the Seven Families would come to Herran and meet with the queen – or king as the case now was. It was first conceived as a mostly ceremonial occasion when the families would formally present their taxes to the queen in a demonstration of their fidelity to the crown. However, over the years it had also become a time when the Seven Families would convene with the queen to negotiate over administrative and political matters such as rates of tariffs or the maintenance of roads through various parts of the Queendom. It was also considered a forum in which the power politics of the Seven Families were exercised, for allegiances to be subtly displayed, or challenges to be made to one another. This was Gidyon's second Council as king, but the first had been so soon after the death of his mother that all of the families had maintained a certain respectful restraint. In the intervening months, that decorum had apparently fled and the power games had returned with vengeful intensity, amplified by the underlying knowledge of the Katan desire to usurp Gidyon's authority.

The leaders of the Seven Families and Gidyon sat in a room of understated magnificence at a large circular table. The varnish on the table's wooden surface reflected the flickering light of the fire that fought the chill trying to make its way into the room. Elen-ai stood against one wall, nearly invisible among the shadows. Nobody had made any comment, although she was certain her presence was not entirely unnoticed. She had met all of the family leaders the previous year, when she had been introduced as Gidyon's companion and assumed lover. It was the monarch's prerogative to allow an adviser into the room, although this convention was more observed in not being exercised. Her lowborn status made it less affronting than had it been one of Gidyon's uncles, especially as she had never once opened her mouth to yawn, let alone utter some comment that might upset the delicate political construction of the discussion.

This was the third, and thankfully final, day of the Council and the second day Elen-ai had quietly observed the proceedings. She had blessedly managed to avoid attending the first day of the Council by going down into Herran to determine when her merchant friend from the Fourth Country would be docking. She had taken her time, ensuring that she missed almost the entirety of the day. The other two days, she had not been so fortunate, and could find no excuse in the face of Gidyon's request that she observe, as perhaps she might notice something he missed. She could hardly wait for the Council to be concluded.

"Your Majesty, I'm just not certain that we should be made to subsidise the instruction of teachers. After all, the mandatory education of our people in letters and numbers is an edict that does come from the crown," Karan Tak said. She was a broad woman whose firm demeanour left no doubt of her competence, and while Elen-ai normally quite liked Karan, she found herself disagreeing with the Tak stance on this particular matter.

"So how do you propose teachers are paid, then?" Gidyon asked calmly, his fingers interlinked on the table in front of him. He did not appear to be particularly put out by the understated aggression with which Karan had challenged him.

"Well, the Veertak family could always—"

Valena, the matriarch of the Veertak family, used her advanced age like a battering ram to commit the otherwise unforgivable act of interrupting one of the other family heads. Almost as ancient as her husband, she nevertheless had one of the sharpest minds that Elen-ai had ever come across.

"Are you proposing that we pauper ourselves to pay those who teach your people to read and count, Karan?"

"Well, not exactly," Karan said, but she was again interrupted, this time by the woman to her right, Arlena Aadran. Another frighteningly competent woman, her family were the Taks' traditional ally.

"That's not what she meant, Valena, and you know it."

Not easily goaded, Valena stared down the Aadran matriarch. "What exactly did she mean then, Arlena?"

To Elen-ai's dismay, Gidyon spoke before anyone else could. She had been looking forward to an escalation between the three women. Her money would have remained on Valena, and it would have been very entertaining to watch the old woman put the Taks and Aadrans in their place, especially given how accustomed they were to getting their way through combining their wealth and power.

"The benefits of having people able to read and count have been well established. I think all of the families here have profited from their people's knowledge with sums. To name one example, being able to make an inventory of any commodity means you can keep track of your livestock, or grain, or ceramics not only when they are sold, but wherever they are. My great-grandmother's edict regarding the education of our people was a good one and there is no reason to remove it. The Veertak scholars are the best positioned to instruct teachers for all the families. As it stands, no alternative funding method seems viable. I think perhaps it is best if the existing way remains: all families will pay a set sum to the Veertaks for the instruction of teachers."

At this, Halen cleared his throat ever so gently.

"Something to add, my lord Katan?" Gidyon asked politely.

"Oh my King, it is nothing," Halen demurred.

"I welcome any contribution from those whose longer lives than mine may offer some unknown experience." Gidyon's courtesy masked that he was throwing words at Halen that the man had once said to him. Elen-ai swallowed a smile.

"Well, if you insist, then. I just wonder whether, given that the Veertaks themselves pay nothing for the training of teachers, if it wouldn't seem to the uneducated observer as though you were displaying a certain favouritism toward them?" The ingratiating demeanour with which Halen suggested Gidyon was playing favourites had Elen-ai all but reaching for the many blades concealed about her person. It was undeniably true that the Veertaks were the closest to Gidyon of all the families. It was also undeniably true that the Veertaks had never demonstrated a significant desire to expand their power, merely an impulse to protect what power they already had, as well as the knowledge that resided within their estate. As scholars, they controlled the Second Country's institutions of knowledge. All members of the Veertak family were bookish to some extent, less concerned with politics and power than the acquisition of knowledge. Varl and Valena were unquestionably two of the most formidable scholars of the time. Although, they could be as skilled at political games as anyone else in that Council room, if the need arose.

Gidyon might have pressed his lips together in rage, or he may simply have been musing on Halen's words. Elen-ai knew it was the former but nobody else would have.

"My lord Halen, you are very kind to be so concerned with perceptions of my position. I am so fortunate to know someone is so interested in my welfare. I will certainly weigh your words carefully, but I would not want to make too hasty a decision. For now, I think things should stay the way they are."

A muscle tensed in Halen's neck. It really must have galled him to be verbally outmanoeuvred by a boy young enough to be his grandson, Elen-ai thought. She delighted in that fact. The small victories were just as important to relish as the important ones, she told herself.

The meeting dragged on. Petty issues were raised and resolved, and everybody vied for just a little more power, to prove how much more important they were than anyone else in the room. Even the Veertaks, who Elen-ai adored, at times were more competitive than was strictly necessary. But perhaps that was her view as an outsider. Nobody else seemed to think the subtle assertions of authority or wealth or cleverness were unusual. Elen-ai realised how commonplace and relatively minor this sniping was because she saw how the room's occupants reacted when the true power move of the afternoon took place.

The weak afternoon light was valiantly trying to illuminate the room and Elen-ai was preoccupied with the desperate hope that the talks might soon draw to a close when Julyana Bertak shifted her enormous bulk, making the chair creak ominously, and spoke. "My King, what is this about reforms to the judicial system?"

Everybody stilled. Halen couldn't resist a smile of smug satisfaction. Elen-ai thought it stupid that he would reveal the Bertaks were so closely allied with him, but perhaps that was in itself a certain show of power on his part.

Julyana Bertak was not by any description a good looking woman. Perhaps once she had been, but any attractiveness had been lost under a mound of fat and years of snide superiority that had distorted her features. The only remotely lovely thing about her appearance was an unexpectedly delicate nose, but that only served to emphasise the ugly vastness that was the rest of her. Perhaps her physical enormity was her inner twistedness made manifest. Certainly, Elen-ai knew a number of people whose generous girth was not accompanied by such a foul personality. Julyana had received Gidyon and Elen-ai during their spring travels in a manner that was unpardonably rude. Upon their departure, Elen-ai had offered Gidyon her skills as an assassin to exact vengeance upon the woman. To her regret, he had declined. It was an offer that she resolved to remind him about once this infernal meeting was over.

"What do you mean, Julyana?" Gidyon asked. It was the first time that he had not addressed someone by their title, indicating she had crossed a line. Arlena Aadran straightened; the imposing woman's gaze was darting between Gidyon and Julyana with an almost predatory focus.

"Well, my King, the manner in which you plan to separate the different types of cases to be heard, and the changes you propose to the local magistrates are very ambitious," Julyana said. Her tone was so sweet that it could only be interpreted as false pleasantness.

Elen-ai wondered if the roll of flesh that bulged over Julyana's collar would impede the progress of a blade. As far as she was concerned, Julyana would make an exemplary test subject for that question.

"But they're good changes," Gidyon protested. "As it stands, more often than not, the challenge to a decision by a local magistrate costs lowborn more than they would stand to win or regain. And the courts in Herran have weeks of waiting time to hear cases due to the lack of differentiation."

"That may be, but people can only take so much change and you are imposing a lot of it," Halen interjected gently.

As much as Elen-ai hated to admit it, the odious man had a point. Gidyon evidently recognised that fact, too. After a very unpleasant moment of silence, he said, "Once again, my lord Katan, you have given me something to think about. Thank you for bringing this to my attention, lady Bertak, lord Katan. I would still like to implement the changes, but perhaps over a longer period of time, and only once I have considered suggestions from all of you, of course."

And there Elen-ai saw the brilliance of how Halen had played the meeting. His comment about the Veertaks had pointed out that Gidyon possibly was closer to one family than the others – breaking the monarch's requirement of impartiality – but it had been made in such an obvious way that Gidyon would dismiss it and the accompanying request to reconsider his stance on the matter of funding for teachers. But had Gidyon rejected his second, far more reasonable point, in support of another family too, Halen could have plausibly claimed that Gidyon was being a pigheaded child who would not listen to wisdom when it was offered to him and was ignoring anything that Halen said because of the well known – if not openly discussed – acrimony between Gidyon and the Katan family. There had been no choice but for Gidyon to heed Halen's suggestion.

The meeting was finally concluded about an hour after Halen's victory. The attendees left to prepare for that evening's feast to celebrate the conclusion of the Winter Council of Families. Elen-ai fell into step with Gidyon as he made his way back to his rooms. Finally alone, he allowed his frustration to show.

"That was stupid of me," he said quietly.

"Don't feel bad about it." Elen-ai valiantly tried to console him.

"I should have known that he had something else planned. Now he looks like he can best me. Which he can."

"So best him next time," she suggested.

"No. I have to best him every time," the King snapped. "This is not about who wins the best of three. This is about whether or not I am his monarch, whether he kneels to my authority. He cannot do that some of the time. He has to do that all of the time."

There was no response to that, really. "I'm sorry," Elen-ai said eventually.

"I am sorry, too. It is wrong of me to take my anger out on you," he said with a sigh.

"I'm here to help you. If being the target for anger you can't express elsewhere helps, I suppose I can manage that," she said.

They reached Gidyon's rooms. He nodded a greeting to the guards outside his door who stood to attention at his approach. Shadows from the enormous fire in his sitting room danced across the small mountain of papers had been placed neatly on his desk. At the sight of it, Gidyon groaned. "Two hours until dinner commences and I am going to be spending them reading."

"Anything I can do to help?" Elen-ai asked.

"Do you want the throne?" Gidyon offered in jest as he used a taper to light the candle sconces above his desk.

"I think I'll pass on that one," she muttered. "Don't want to take all the fun away from you."

Gidyon laughed. A genuine laugh this time.

"You know that offer still stands for me to take care of Julyana Bertak, by the way," Elen-ai added. "At least Halen has the stomach to try and take you on directly. She's just wallowing around with whoever she thinks will give her the most power."

Gidyon made an amused sound as he read the first paper. "Don't tempt me," he said distractedly.

"I was trying to figure out if her bulk would act as a sort of shield," Elen-ai commented conversationally.

Gidyon looked up, amusement written in the arch of his eyebrows and set of his lips. "I dare you to say that to her tonight."

"If I do it, will you give me her lands?"

"You would almost certainly do a better job of managing them than her. Divine One, she's a right terror."

"How do you think her husband faced the prospect of procreating with her? Carefully?" Her lips twitched at the thought of Julyana's slender husband approaching her bed with timidity if not outright fear for his life.

Gidyon tried and failed to look disapproving. "There are a great many things about her to mock other than her size," he commented.

She threw herself onto the couch with a sigh and propped her feet on one of its high sides. "Yes, but I hate her so much, that I don't feel she deserves my effort when it comes to insulting her."

Gidyon glanced at her, evidently giving up on his point. "Shouldn't you be doing something assassin-y?"

"I'm too tired after that boring meeting." She gave an exaggerated yawn.

"Here I was thinking the life of an assassin was all discipline and rigidity," Gidyon muttered, lowering his eyes back to the document in his hands.

"Nope, I think you were mistaking it for your life," Elen-ai told him cheerfully.

Making a noise of disgust, Gidyon paced as he read.

"What's this?" She plucked several drawings from the table in front of the couch. "Fancy." The pages were of vellum, normally reserved for important or official documents, rather than the paper pulp or cloth scraps that were used to make pages of lesser quality.

"Oh, they're proposed drawings for a new wing to the Palace," Gidyon said distractedly.

"Another wing? The Palace has so many wings that I can't remember them all."

"Apparently it's the thing to do when you want to be impressive. Build something," Gidyon said.

"Yes, but where are you going to build it?"

"Mm, it is a problem. I was thinking that I would tear down an existing wing. Maybe this one."

"But there's nothing wrong with this one," Elen-ai protested.

"I have been in these rooms since I was ten. I think it is time for a change."

"So pick one of the other five hundred rooms that nobody sleeps in."

"I really think we should rebuild this wing. It is very old."

"So? There's still nothing wrong with it. It's a perfectly good wing." Elen-ai held up two of the drawings side by side. Both designs certainly looked grand.

"Nonsense." Gidyon's tone was condescending. "Apparently the foundations of the wing are in need of modifications. And haven't you noticed that the corridors here are tiled, not painted? It's so outdated. Anyone who sees it will think that we cannot afford to stay up to date. As silly as it sounds, these sorts of perceptions do matter."

"So fix the foundations and slap a few paintings in the corridors. You don't need to tear down the whole thing." Elen-ai couldn't understand why Gidyon was so adamant about this.

"We already have one room in the Divine-cursed wing that can't be used." It wasn't quite an exclamation, but Elen-ai heard the slight edge of distress in Gidyon's tone and immediately understood her error. Gidyon's mother had been killed only a few rooms away. Nobody had entered the chambers since her funeral. It seemed the worst form of sacrilege to disturb the site of such a gruesome and unnatural crime. It was little wonder that Gidyon wanted to tear down the wing in which his mother had died before his eyes.

"I like this design with the curly bits on top." There was nothing else Elen-ai could say. Unless he specifically referenced Queen Latana, she never discussed the matter with him. She did not ask anything further about the Queen's murder. She knew Gidyon wished to speak no more of the subject.

"Curly bits, really?"

"As well you know, I am neither a designer nor mathematician," Elen-ai pointed out.

"I will keep in mind your preference for the curly bits." Gidyon smirked at the term, then returned to his reading.

Elen-ai rested her head against the couch's arm. As she reposed, she thought back to the meeting. Halen's play concerned her more than she had let on to Gidyon. While the man might have been contemptible, he was also clever, and he had his sights set very obviously on the Palace. He was even clever enough to use the fact that he wasn't particularly well liked to his advantage. That was troubling. She ruminated on what she had learned in the Family's home. The fact that he was buying himself an army was worrying, especially given the belligerence he had demonstrated in the Council. While every family was expanding the size of their household guard under a variety of pretences, this was something else entirely.

When she was certain he wasn't looking at her, Elen-ai sneaked a glance at Gidyon. He seemed to have shrugged off the anger at Halen's behaviour and the anger at himself for falling into the man's trap, but she knew that he was readying himself for the evening's social activities and the traps Halen may have set for him there.

FOUR

Of all the things about the royal life that Elen-ai loathed – and there were many – she despised the social events the most. Very rarely were there any truly inconspicuous places for her to unobtrusively skulk, and inevitably someone would seek her out. Since Gidyon had announced that he would marry a lowborn woman from Herran to ensure that any child of his would be as free from political obligation as any of the Second Country's heirs were supposed to be, the world had simply assumed she was the King's lover, currently being groomed to marry him. That meant that at social functions, she was viewed as a potentially sympathetic and useful ear. She was regularly accosted by any number of people with an ingratiating smile etched into their faces, and a request that she appreciate the importance of something near and dear to their heart swiftly following their introduction. This torment was compounded by the fact that she was inevitably forced to wear some ridiculous garment or another. Gidyon had yet to coerce her into wearing a skirt or dress, but he had bet her if he could convince Silius to dance at the upcoming midwinter festival, she would have to wear a skirt to the next social occasion. While she was confident Gidyon would not be successful, she nevertheless feared he may miraculously accomplish the impossible. Elen-ai might have been an assassin of the Family, trained in the art of being invisible, of winning any fight in which she might find herself, but the prospect of being put into a dress left her terrified.

Tonight she wore a dark green tunic over a pair of grey trousers. Gidyon really hadn't been joking about a new wardrobe for her, as Elen-ai had ruefully discovered. The material was so fine and soft that she imagined the value of her clothes would easily buy at least one of the houses in the lowborn district outright. The thin fabric and beautiful cut of the garments made them totally impractical and as such, something she would never have chosen for herself. However, as Gidyon had pointed out when they had chosen which clothes would become part of her new Court-appropriate wardrobe (he had actually taken time out of his schedule to inflict this small torment upon her), if she didn't have fine clothes she would look totally out of place. And that would raise further questions about who and what she was. Adding to tonight's frustration, one of the Palace tailors, skilled in everything from repairing a torn garment at the last minute to the artistry of makeup and coiffure, had tried to do things to her face and hair as she had prepared. Elen-ai had restrained her impulse to pull one of the blades concealed on her person and brandish at him and settled for swearing at him until the man had fled in terror.

The evening began with two fencing champions duelling for the enjoyment of the gathered families. Men and women across the Second Country competed in arenas every night for the amusement of high and low born alike. The Seven Families even sponsored certain fighters, taking a percentage of any winnings – and glory – that their swords might collect. Elen-ai herself almost never went to the arenas. She had never found much point in fighting for the entertainment of others. Yet she had no choice but to watch tonight's match. To add to her discomfort, Elen-ai ended up sitting next to Halen, whether by chance or his design, she couldn't tell. She made a valiant effort to watch the match and maintain an internal commentary on the silliness of such a functional skill being made into a spectacle so she could ignore the smugness that radiated from the man. He was sucking on the type of fruit lozenge often favoured as a means to sweeten the breath. Elen-ai could hear it clinking against his teeth.

"You know, lady Elen-ai, some say the art of swordcraft is much like the intrigue of politics." He spoke conversationally, but Elen-ai knew he was leading to some point.

"My lord Katan, surely politics is far more deadly than swordcraft," she replied, struggling to keep the venom from her tone.

Halen chuckled softly. The clash of metal rang across the room as the competitors engaged. "My lady, perhaps you should consider the merits of my analogy. Look at how the opponents size each other up before truly attacking. Even when they do engage, almost in every exchange neither swordsperson is injured. They retreat, regather and then wait for the next engagement. The fighter who can understand the rhythm of the other the best will see a weakness, and then practice and patience will give them the necessary edge to snatch victory."

Elen-ai looked away from the fight so that she could see him properly. Halen's face was flushed with some form of excitement. The light from the torches flickered across his features, making him appear alternately wreathed in shadow or bathed in harsh light. She thought about what a blade would feel like slipping into the delicate flesh of his neck.

"Well, my lord, when you put it that way, I see the persuasiveness of such a perspective," she said.

His smile was like a curved blade.

"Then again, others may simply interpret such a thoughtful analysis as someone attempting to draw a parallel when none exists in an attempt to sound unnecessarily dramatic," she added. If she wasn't to have the pleasure of killing this man, she would at least enjoy the slight puckering of his lips as he heard her insult. It was a truly exquisite feeling.

"You know, lady Elen-ai, you remain a mystery. Your origins, and why our King seems to trust you so much, have yet to be revealed to me." His abrupt change of subject was either because he had been stung by her insult, or because this was the real reason for striking up a conversation. She suspected the latter.

"There are a great many mysteries in this world of ours, my lord," Elen-ai responded coyly.

"I wonder how the people of our country would feel if they knew how close you were to him," he murmured.

"I imagine safer than they would with an inexperienced girl-child on the throne," she replied.

Halen laughed quietly. The sweet smell of his fruit lozenge wafted across the space between them. "An attack rather than a parry. I suspect my little comparison may have merit after all."

The blade on her left arm was so slender that she could have slipped it into the flesh of his side without anyone noticing. But she held the impulse in check. "The only problem with your analogy, my lord, is that it assumes both contestants will abide by the rules. In such a situation, I would likely throw a punch or kick to gain the upper hand. I can't help but feel you may be overtaken by a similar urge," she said. "Excuse me, I think we've missed the winning exchange," she added before he could respond.

Indeed, a round of applause filled the room as the young woman, panting heavily, held her blade aloft and bowed low to Gidyon.

"It seems tonight's loser may lose more than the match," Halen observed, gesturing to the defeated swordsman who was bleeding heavily from a wound in his chest.

"It seems a waste," Elen-ai commented as attendants ran from their place waiting at the side of the court and tried to staunch the bleeding.

"It is an unfortunate possibility when one plays such games," Halen replied over the applause.

Dinner was served immediately following the conclusion of the match. It seemed a callously gruesome thing to do, given the likely loss of the loser's life, but Elen-ai was grateful for any opportunity to get away from Halen. She feared her resolve to not stab him may falter. To her immense relief, Elen-ai was seated next to Varl Veertak. Halen was two to Gidyon's right, far away from Elen-ai. She had seen his granddaughter and would-be queen, Serenah, earlier in the evening, but the girl was so uninspiring that unless one was looking directly at her, it was easy to not see her.

"And what did you think of the sword fight, my dear?" Varl asked. He and his wife were the only two family leaders to know she was a member of the Family. Valena had discerned it almost immediately upon meeting Elen-ai, but they both had promised to not speak of it to anyone.

"Show fighting. If either were in a real fight they wouldn't have lasted a minute," Elen-ai replied around a mouthful of food. The food, as always exquisite, was served on delicate Katan plates. Each plate alone was worth a fortune. It was unfortunate that such a necessary display of wealth and status came from the family of the man who would remove that power and wealth from Gidyon if he got the opportunity.

Varl chuckled. "I do regret I'll never see you with a blade in your hand," he admitted in an undertone. "I've heard that skills like yours are unforgettable to witness," he added, avoiding any overt reference to her origin.

Elen-ai smiled and shook her head. The tiny man's thirst for knowledge was endearing. In his youth it would have been terrifying. "If you ever do get a chance to witness such a thing, my lord – Varl," she corrected herself when he made a noise of protest, "I'm not sure it will be an opportune moment to appreciate such a spectacle. My people aren't particularly interested in fighting for the amusement of others." Elen-ai pictured the triumphant face of the winner. By the look of her, the woman had been lowborn, which gave Elen-ai a small measure of solace. Many champion swordfighters came from families of people with at least some power. The whole exercise still seemed a terrific waste to her, though.

Varl shook his head, fluffy white hair quivering with the movement. Elen-ai saw his attention fall on Wenden Rasatan. Once possessing a reputation for being domineering and forceful, since his son's regicide and death, and the apparent suicide of his wife upon hearing of her son's act, Wenden had become a spectre of that image. To what extent he had been encouraged to present a blusterous persona by his cruel wife, Elen-ai was uncertain. Since the unconscionable crime of his son, though, trade with the Rasatan family, whose primary source of income came from fish in the estuary within their lands, had become a dirty task, undertaken only in the barest minimum.

"Poor man," Varl said softly.

Elen-ai did not know what to say. Wenden had said practically nothing in the Council, for the most part simply looking down at the table. Nobody was particularly surprised. Not only was the Rasatan family fortune being eroded by the diminished trade, but perhaps more crucially, the family's reputation was irreparably shattered.

"Do you think the Rasatan family will survive?" Uncertain how to tactfully refer to Erek's regicide, Elen-ai avoided mentioning it explicitly.

Varl considered her question with a slight tilt to his head. "I honestly don't know. It would be curious to see what happens to the land if the Rasatans were unable to pay the taxes on it, or be a sufficient political force to retain power."

It was with slight discomfort that Elen-ai realised the Veertak estate bordered the Rasatan lands. The Veertaks were in a position to make significant territorial and power gains if indeed the Rasatan family did fall. She wondered if Varl's interest in the prospect was born of such a realisation. As much as she adored the old scholar, he was still one of the Seven Families, and they were all ultimately invested in securing their own power.

Dinner finished and the plates cleared with a flurry of efficient servants. Guests were free to stand up from the long table and mingle, dance, or gossip. She excused herself and stood. Lively music started playing as she walked across the grand dining hall. Kaine appeared in front of her as though from thin air. His boyish good looks were emphasised by some clever artist's pattern on his face, Elen-ai could not help but notice.

"Lady Elen-ai." An ironic smile settled briefly on his lips.

"Kaine." She refused to ask him what he wanted.

"You captivate my eye, as always. Perhaps you would care to dance?" He held a glass goblet – the material from which it was made another marker of power and wealth – aloft as he spoke, as though he was toasting the suggestion they dance together.

"I might decline," Elen-ai said. She wondered if he was intoxicated.

"A shame." He gave her a look that seemed to linger, or perhaps it was her desire to be out of the room's centre that made it feel protracted.

"One day, perhaps, I'll get a yes from you." He bowed slightly and winked at her with his bright golden gaze. He suddenly looked completely sober, and Elen-ai found herself fighting a smile at his charm.

Focusing her gaze on the check pattern of the tiles so that nobody else tried to invite her to dance, she made her way toward Gidyon. As she neared the King, she paused once more to speak with the emissary from the Third Country, Freyanna Kuch, known simply to her as Freya.

"Are you well, Elen-ai?" Freya asked, a smile touching her face.

Elen-ai gave a little sigh that caused the other woman to laugh. "It's a bit like that, isn't it?" Freya said kindly.

"Do you have anything like this in the Third Country?" Elen-ai gestured to the room full of people adorned with finery and ulterior motives.

The Councilwoman shook her head, her dark mass of hair swinging ever so slightly from side to side. "The Council members are not born into their positions. And wealth and prestige is not really maintained within a few families like it is with your Seven Families," she explained.

"I wish I lived somewhere like that," Elen-ai muttered.

"It has its own problems," Freya noted. She was certainly correct. She had been a part of the religious Pious community who had overthrown the Kade governance, who themselves had overthrown the previous regime several years earlier. The Third Country was more like a city-state than a country, in the middle of nowhere but on the way to everywhere, so the political turmoil had been of interest to many. The woman, who Elen-ai considered a friend of sorts, was a legend amid the stories of that time. Rumours of her ability to heal with her mere mind were woven into the mythology that surrounded her. The fact that those rumours were correct – much like the skills of the Family, Freya had capabilities beyond many others – was in some ways incidental to what Freya represented. Not that those skills were useless; Freya had healed Gidyon in the spring when Erek Rasatan had orchestrated an attempt on his life and nearly succeeded.

"I still think I'd prefer a different set of problems sometimes," Elen-ai said.

Freya gave her a sympathetic pat on the shoulder.

Elen-ai would have liked to linger and talk longer with the foreigner, but she felt she should check on Gidyon.

By the time she reached him, he had gotten to his feet, a polite smile on his face that gave no indication whether he was actually enjoying himself.

"Are you all right?" he asked her, a slight frown of concern flashing across his face. Her expression must have been more troubled than she realised.

"Yes. I sometimes forget that everybody is here for their own benefit," she mumbled.

He gave her arm a light squeeze. Most would dismiss the unusually intimate gesture as the King being foolish enough to parade his affection for her in front of anyone who cared to look. She appreciated the comfort he sought to offer.

"I sometimes forget that it is not like this for everybody," he told her softly.

She gave a tiny shrug. "In a way I guess it is, but the stakes here are so much higher."

"I am sorry," he said. "If it helps, you have been quite magnificent. You are quite magnificent."

His sincerity touched her. Coming from him, the compliment meant a great deal.

"My King," she teased, smiling despite the profound sadness that had made its way into her heart at the realisation that Gidyon inhabited a world in which even the sweet Varl worked to fulfil his own purpose. To anyone who did not know, she and the King must have looked like a couple caught amid the throes of adoration for one another. In some ways, that was correct.

"Would you care to step outside for a little while? I wish to speak with the dear Rania Harete and I would very much like an escort." The request was an unexpected one.

Elen-ai raised her eyebrows. The daughter of the Harete family had been pushed by her parents to try to seduce Gidyon when they had visited them. Only Gidyon, Elen-ai, and Rania knew that she had very nearly succeeded; Elen-ai had found them before anything serious had transpired. Gidyon's fury upon learning that Rania was trying to better her family's position still made Elen-ai shiver. With a terrifying calmness he had outlined every action he would take to ruin Rania's family if what had transpired between them ever came out. Elen-ai had no doubt that he would fulfil his word.

"You want to talk to Rania?"

Gidyon deliberately ignored Elen-ai's surprise. "Yes, she may be of some use."

"As you command, my King," she said, causing him to snort in amusement.

She met him and Rania by the door to the garden outside the dining hall. In the summer, flower beds were overflowing with beautiful displays that guests could look out on as the light lingered long into the evening. Of course, the high bushes and trees also made the garden perfect for a discreet moment away from the eyes of those in the hall. Rania had her left arm hooked through Gidyon's right, a look of disconcerted unease on her face. Her long tresses hung free in her preferred style, swirling around her blue dress. Naturally pretty, someone had done something to her face that meant someone who had never seen her before might think her beautiful.

The King and Rania strolled through the garden, Elen-ai keeping a polite distance behind them so that Gidyon and Rania could converse naturally. It would have been almost possible for Gidyon and Rania to forget she was there. Almost.

"And what have you been reading of late?" Gidyon sounded as though he had never been more interested in anything than what her answer would be.

"Oh, nothing that interesting, your Majesty," she replied hesitantly.

"Come now, there's no such thing as an uninteresting book," he cajoled.

"Well, I'm reading the most recent book by Har-ai of Her-ran," she admitted.

Gidyon let out a warm laugh. Har-ai of Herran was an author whose fiction was very popular, if not a little puerile at times. Elen-ai had chanced to read one or two volumes herself. The stories had been commendably engaging.

"There is no shame in reading Har-ai of Herran. I wish I had the opportunity to read for enjoyment," Gidyon told Rania kindly.

"You don't have any time now?" Rania asked, seemingly encouraged by Gidyon's warm demeanour.

"Sadly, no. Being the king is a time-consuming business, Rania," he said. "And your parents, they are well? I was saddened that Janyce was not in attendance at the Council."

"It's very kind of you to say. My parents are very well. Mother is still recovering, though. The baby's birth was a very difficult one," she said.

"Mm, I heard," Gidyon replied.

Elen-ai was sceptical about the truth behind Rania's claim. The acrimony between Janyce and Timet was clear for anyone to see. She had even eavesdropped upon a violent argument between the two of them in which they had hurled the most vicious insults at one another. If she had been betting, she would have put her money on the fact that the birth of their most recent child was a convenient excuse for Janyce to seclude herself, away from her husband and the family into which she had married and had been made to feel she did not belong.

"Are you well, my King?" Rania asked after they'd taken a few steps in silence.

Gidyon took a moment to reply. "My health is perfect, if that is what you were asking," he said slowly. Then he took a breath and continued. "However, the fact that some individuals – and I am sure you know who they are – seek to take the throne from me leaves me disquieted."

Rania's body stiffened, almost as though she was waiting for Gidyon to turn and hit her. While Elen-ai didn't know exactly what Gidyon had planned, she knew that something perhaps worse than a mere blow was about to follow. It surprised her that she felt a stab of pity for the girl.

Gidyon stopped and pulled Rania to a halt. "Rania, have you heard any talk in your home of a plot against me?"

"Surely nobody would dare," the girl said breathlessly, as though shocked by the mere prospect. Her pretence of surprise was not convincing.

"Do you remember that evening at your home, Rania?" Gidyon's voice was suddenly quiet. He did not need to specify to which evening he was referring.

She nodded.

"Have you heard of any talk in your home that may suggest your family will move against me?" Gidyon grasped Rania's arm, his fingers digging in.

"Your Majesty, my arm—" Rania said, fear choking her voice.

"Your arm is the least of your concerns if you do not answer me truthfully, Rania." Gidyon's voice remained soft. He didn't need to raise it. "Now answer my question, please."

"I don't know." The beauty loaned by the artistry on her face was tarnished by the way her features crumpled with fear.

"Rania, if you are lying to me, I will destroy you and everything and everyone you care about." Gidyon's voice was quite even.

Fear gave way to outright terror and Rania made the tiniest movement to jerk her arm out of his grasp.

"You are right to be scared. Even if the throne is taken from me, if I find out that you have misled me, I will ensure that your family is ruined. That is a promise, Rania." He was clutching her arm so tightly that Elen-ai was sure he would leave bruises.

"I know of no plans, I swear before the Divine One," Rania gasped.

Gidyon held onto her a moment longer, staring into her face. How he could see anything by the feeble light cast by the yellow moon and the intermittent braziers throughout the garden, Elen-ai had no idea. He did not have the skills of the Family to provide clear sight in the dark. Yet it appeared as though he was seeing through to Rania's very mind. Finally, he released her arm with a slight sigh. "Go inside, Rania." He sounded tired, even fed-up. "And do not forget my promise."

She stayed where she was for a moment, then walked swiftly back toward the Palace, not even appearing to notice Elen-ai as she passed the assassin.

Elen-ai joined Gidyon. "Was it really necessary to be that hard?"

He looked at her in surprise. "Maybe not," he admitted.

"Is this because you didn't realise she was only pretending to be interested in you?" Elen-ai had no compunction about asking such a brutal question. She felt he deserved it a little bit.

With the skills of the Family, Elen-ai was able to see his face clearly. The slight tension in his jaw gave away the fact that she was right.

"I learned something," he said, ignoring her point. She decided to let it slide. She couldn't expect him to be perfect in his conduct and self-restraint all the time.

"Oh?"

"The Harates are likely to move against me if it comes to siding with me or the Katans." Gidyon tried to sound nonchalant, but he couldn't quite manage it. Smugness warred with tension in his voice.

"You discerned all that?" Elen-ai didn't bother to hide her scepticism. It wasn't as though he could see her raised eyebrows, anyway.

Gidyon snorted in a most unregal manner. "I have heard rumours from our spies in their household about some of the conversations occurring between members of the Harete family. Besides, as much as he may hate her, Timet is married to a Katan. That sort of marriage does not occur for fun. There is a tie between the two families that he cannot deny out of hand."

"It almost feels as though Halen's been planning this for a long time," Elen-ai commented.

Gidyon exhaled, his breath a long stream in the cold night air. "It certainly feels like it, doesn't it?"

FIVE

It was a relief when the families left Herran the next day. Even though they had all stayed in their city residences, simply knowing how close the lot of them were to her left Elen-ai with a somewhat unpleasant taste in her mouth.

With Gidyon taking the morning to meet one of his tutors, Elen-ai roamed the Palace, feeling slightly like a caged animal.

She went to the stables to see the kittanae. Fascinated by the giant cats, she went there as often as she could. At her approach, two of the five beasts raised their heads to regard her with the natural insolence of all felines. Having regarded her with sufficient hauteur, the two heads were lowered, and Elen-ai approached the animals, all curled up in a tangle in their pen. She often came here simply to regard the animals. Knowing her by now, they permitted her to vault lightly into their stall and place her hands gently on them.

Kittanae were owned only by the most wealthy of individuals. They were notoriously difficult to find in the wild, and often rejected anyone who tried to train them whom they deemed unworthy of their affections. They were highly valued, though: if they consented to bear people, they could cover the same distance as the Fourth Country's most popular beast of burden, the hearat, in less than half the time. Elen-ai had been fortunate enough to see kittanae a few times when slipping through the homes of the wealthy on a contract, but she had never ridden one. Most people never even got the chance to see them up close.

Elen-ai stepped lightly into the pen and allowed her hand to sink into a cat's silky coat, marvelling at the softness of the fur. The russet-furred animal purred its appreciation as she stroked it. She could not help but smile as she moved around the animals, admiring the different colours of their coats, or the tenderness of the manner in which they curled together. She would deny ever thinking it if directly asked, but she had to acknowledge that there were some benefits to living in the Palace.

Following a whim, when she left the stables some time later, she made her way into the library. She had only taken a few steps into the room where she almost stumbled over Kaine sitting cross-legged on the floor. He was surrounded by a mountain of books, far too many to fit on any of the library's reading desks.

He brushed the curls out of his eyes as he looked up at her, then smiled mischievously. "Ah, our resident assassin."

Uncertain if it was a comment or an insult, Elen-ai walked forward so that she was standing directly in front of him. To look at her, he had to crane his neck. It might have been slightly petty of her, but she took her enjoyment where she could find it. "What are you doing?" she asked.

"Building a fortress." His response was immediate and deadpan.

"You'll need a few more books." She glanced down at the titles of the considerable stack in front of him. All of them were legal texts of some form or another. "Researching Halen's – sorry, Serenah's – viability to claim the throne?"

He laughed at her biting joke with a lack of restraint that suggested his initial greeting had not been intended as an insult after all. "Quite correct," he said once he had regained control of himself. "Now if only I could prove that Halen would put Serenah on the throne as his puppet, then we may have a way to completely disqualify her."

After hesitating for a moment, Elen-ai sat down, sinking to the richly patterned carpet in one fluid motion.

"Divine One, sometimes I forget what exactly you do, and then I see how you move like that." Kaine shook his head in amazement.

"I just sat down." Elen-ai protested, awkwardly remembering the way he had complimented her on the evening of the feast.

He shook his head. "You didn't 'just sit down'. The rest of us lumber to the ground like a falling tree, but you gracefully sink down."

She laughed. "If you did the exercises I do every day, you probably would fall less like a tree and more like a feather too."

"But then who would read all this?" He made an exaggerated gesture to the piles of books surrounding him.

Elen-ai leaned forward to pick up the closest one, the motion bringing her close to Kaine. He grinned mischievously. Kaine was the youngest of Gidyon's uncles, and the most handsome. Not for the first time, Elen-ai wondered whether or not any of Gidyon's uncles had lovers. She knew that if they wanted to marry and have children, they had to renounce the name of the Royal Family and leave the Palace, but she imagined that the convention when it came to taking a lover was less rigid. The image of Kaine winking came back to her.

"You smell of cat," he said.

"I've just come from the stables," Elen-ai said, feeling uncharacteristically self-conscious.

"Admiring the kittanae?"

She nodded.

"Do you like them?" His pride in them was obvious and merited. The Palace beasts were in obviously superb condition.

"They're magnificent," Elen-ai said, the words almost falling over themselves as they left her lips. She became uncomfortably aware of the unusual effusiveness with which she spoke and dropped her gaze to the book she had plucked at random from

Kaine's small mountain of books. "*Conventions of Legal Heritage,* volume one of fourteen!" The last word became an exclamation of horror at the prospect that thirteen more books of such dull material had been produced by some poor person who likely considered the collection their masterpiece.

"It's my favourite bedtime reading," Kaine told her seriously, breaking into that mischievous grin again at the last moment.

"Oh, mine too," Elen-ai said.

He laughed. "Divinity, this is the most boring task I could possibly think of. Why did I volunteer to do this?" He threw his hands up in the air, casting around at the books that surrounded him.

"I have no idea what notion overtook you," Elen-ai told him. "Don't you have a life of your own?" Her earlier thought prompted the question and she asked it before realising perhaps it was too personal.

"The uncles of the queen – or king, I suppose – live in service of the Second Country." The cadence made it clear he was reciting an oft-told maxim. Despite her worry, he did not seem at all offended.

"And in the three minutes of each day when you aren't living in service of the Second Country?" Elen-ai prompted.

His face went blank for a moment, either concealing a thought or trying to comprehend the idea. "All I have ever been taught to do is to serve the throne. No part of my life is not affected by that."

"Don't you ever want to do something else?" Elen-ai persisted.

"Why, did you have something in mind?" The gentle teasing in his tone was at once deflection and flirtatious invitation. Elen-ai had to admit, the invitation was a tempting one. Kaine looked unfairly good, especially considering he was sitting on the floor, surrounded by the world's most boring books.

"It's your life." Elen-ai held up her hands, fingers spread wide.

He reached forward and captured one of her hands in his. Dangerous, given what she could do with her hands if she so chose. "You are certainly interesting to have around, Elen-ai," he said, kissing her hand.

"What's that supposed to mean?" Her skin vibrated with phantom tingles where his lips had brushed. She told herself to cease being foolish.

"Exactly that," he told her.

From somewhere within the library, a bell marked the hour. According to history, that on a day of the Council of Families several generations ago, a queen had been so engrossed in a book that she had completely lost track of time. The heads of the Seven Families had been forced to wait for several hours, unwilling to leave their seats in case they might be absent when she arrived. While nobody had disgraced themselves at the Council table, almost all requested that they briefly take their leave of her to relieve themselves as soon as she had arrived. This caused more upset as nobody wanted a mass exodus that left the queen alone and might inadvertently cause the perception that they were in some way colluding to offend her. After that hilarious but uncomfortable incident, a bell was installed in the library so that people did not lose themselves in the pages of whatever they were reading. Not that Kaine's choice of reading matter seemed to be in danger of doing such a thing to anyone.

"Gidyon's lessons should be done by now, I'll go and find him," Elen-ai said, rising swiftly to her feet.

"See? Ridiculous." Kaine gestured up and down at her.

Shaking her head at him, although feeling nonetheless replete with flattery, she left the library and made her way to the room where Gidyon had told her to find him. She knocked on the door then immediately entered, assuming he would be alone. He was not.

The priestess of the Divine One who chanted over his kneeling form was the last person Elen-ai expected to see with Gidyon. The woman's raised hands glowed softly in the dim room as she spoke the final words of the prayer of light.

Elen-ai closed the door behind her and leaned against the wall. The priestess had her back to the door so she may not have noticed Elen-ai's entry. Gidyon, despite not having acknowledged her, almost certainly would have.

As someone whose path was dictated by the Shadow God, it was strange for Elen-ai to be around the rituals associated with a different god, especially a god that few people followed with any true devotion. She observed the glow around the woman's hands with cool curiosity, realising that the priests and priestesses of the Divine One, it appeared, had their own memory of the forgotten skills. That was not something the Family knew, as far as she was aware. The next time she went to the home, she would tell them. The priestess' hands glowed a little brighter, then she lowered them completely. "The light grows bright within you," she told Gidyon.

The King nodded solemnly. "You do me a great honour, priestess," he replied. "Until next time."

The priestess gave him a stern smile and turned to leave. She gave a sharp intake of breath when she saw Elen-ai, then turned back to Gidyon as though to say something about Elen-ai's presence. But she seemed to think the better of it and simply left the room, staying as far from Elen-ai as she could.

"That was odd," Gidyon commented, frowning.

"I'll say. What are you doing with a priestess?"

"I was actually talking about her reaction to you."

"Her reaction to me? It was hardly odd. I follow the Shadow God. She is an agent of the Divine One. The Divine One brings the sun, which is the opposite of shadow, if you hadn't noticed. I would have been surprised had she not reacted to me, really, especially with..." She trailed off, unwilling to note that people were turning to the Divine One in their uncertainty over a man being on the throne.

"Especially with people rediscovering their faith in the Divine One as uncertainty increases over the throne being held by a man?" Gidyon finished the sentence for her. He continued into her silence. "I'm not blind, Elen-ai. I know the hearts of my people, even if what I see I would rather not be there. Besides, you and I both know the power that faith can have." He absently rubbed his stomach where he had been gored in the attack on his life. Freya's ability to heal him was the result of her faith in her deity – the Goddess. It was the same when it came to Elen-ai's own skills. "What faith can do is quite amazing. We barely understand it."

"How long have you been reading about what faith can bestow?" Elen-ai wondered how Gidyon had managed to hide this interest from her.

"Since the attack," he said. "I never realised you were so devout, by the way."

"Oh?" Elen-ai went over to a chair and flung herself into it.

"To be bestowed with the gifts of the gods one must not only believe, but believe with a deep conviction," Gidyon said.

"I am aware," she said dryly. Only members of the Family who had profound belief were allowed to be assassins. Her instruction about the Shadow God had begun at the same time as her combat training, before she could even walk properly. "I still didn't realise you were particularly devout," she persisted, mildly uncomfortable with the subject of her faith.

"Of course I am." He sounded surprised that she didn't know.

"You've never talked about it, though."

"Conviction does not need to be shouted for everybody to hear in order to exist," he replied.

She shrugged, discomfort and uncertainty robbing her of an immediate response. She wondered how often he conferred with the priestess of the Divine One, and why she had not discovered it sooner. "I just didn't think that you thought much about the Divine One, or the gods. Faith isn't for everyone."

Gidyon gave a small laugh and came to sit next to her. He looked tired. He always looked tired. The bright blue of his eyes practically jumped out from the shadows on his face. Perhaps he had lost weight; he looked a little gaunt.

"Elen-ai, I have to have faith," he said softly, clasping his hands together and resting his forearms on his knees.

"Nobody has to have faith," she countered.

"I do. When the modern state of the Second Country was formed at the conclusion of the great wars, it was decided that no man should be entrusted with the throne. So the land was divided among the eight strongest warriors, with the strongest of them, Latana the First, being given the throne, and that is the way things have been for centuries."

Elen-ai nodded when he paused for breath. Every child was taught this alongside their numbers and letters.

Gidyon continued. "As time progressed, the regard in which men were held waned, then grew again. As you know, there was even a time when no man was permitted to hold property. And now we have me. The first man on the throne. Perhaps the only man to ever take the throne if I do not do the best I possibly can. Elen-ai, I cannot believe that I am here due to some accident. I have to believe that I am part of something bigger, something greater than myself. I cannot think that I am here on my own for no real reason."

The intensity of Gidyon's gaze was like the point of a knife. His knuckles were white from the strength with which he gripped his hands together. "I have to be a part of some greater plan," he concluded softly, almost more to himself than to her.

For a moment, silence stretched between them.

"And that's what you honestly believe?" she asked.

As with any question of weight, Gidyon did not answer immediately, choosing the correct words for his response. "I do not think that I have a choice except to believe it."

She scrutinised him, the handsome face, his blue eyes, the way his broad shoulders were set with such tension. The fact that he was driven to overcome fatigue and uncertainty through sheer willpower had not escaped her. He certainly shouldn't have been able to possess the energy that he did with the meagre sleep he got each evening. Now she saw how desperately he was clinging to the belief that he had just confessed to her. It wasn't just that he believed he had some divine part to play. He needed to believe it in order to keep going, to keep fighting.

"Do you want glory in the name of the Divine One?" Elen-ai asked.

It gave her some comfort that again, Gidyon did not answer immediately. "I just want to know that my life, what I am, what I did, that it meant something more."

It was a good answer. "And where does being allied with one who follows the Shadow God fit in with being an agent of the Divine One?" Knowing how Gidyon felt, she could not dismiss the priestess's reaction to her with simple amusement.

Gidyon gave her a look of incomprehension. "You are my friend," he said, as though it were the most obvious thing in the world.

She thought about arguing with him, about pressing the point that he was unable – or unwilling – to see, but she thought better of it. He did not need yet another worry on his shoulders. So instead, she gave him what he did need: levity. "And have you found divine enlightenment, yet?" She forced a teasing note into her voice.

"Oh yes, just last week the world and all its mysteries were revealed unto me," Gidyon said. "That's why the priestess was blessing me just then, and why I was still receiving religious instruction from her."

"You might have been instructing her," she said innocently. "The ways of the Divine One and its followers are a mystery to me."

"Perhaps you could do with a bit of religious instruction yourself," Gidyon said, his tone prim, leaning back. His shoulders had lost their tightness and his face looked a little less pinched.

"You wound me, my King." Elen-ai put a hand to her chest, recoiling with mocking exaggeration.

"You should remember that I have this power to wound you, my assassin," he said, his mask of seriousness marred by the fact that the lines around his eyes were, for at least that moment, crinkled with amusement rather than worry.

"My life is yours to do with what you will, your Majesty. Wound me, maim me, kill me, I am but your loyal subject." Elen-ai bowed her head, the very portrait of a subjugated servant.

Gidyon snorted. "Unless you disagree with me," he said. "Come on, you can be my loyal servant in the petition hall." He rose to his feet, straightening his jacket as he did.

Elen-ai shadowed his movement, albeit without the perfunctory straightening of her clothes. Nobody would really look at her, or care if her clothes were slightly rumpled. As ever, she would stand in a shadowed part of the hall and watch almost completely unnoticed, as those petitioners who had been granted an audience with Gidyon would speak to him of their grievances and he would listen with a completely genuine sincerity. From the petitions that he heard, he would often make notes to which he would refer back when later considering other matters of state. Gidyon was a ruler who did care, and for that, Elen-ai would follow him to the end of the world.

She and Gidyon walked through the Palace, both hunched slightly against the chill that seeped through the walls.

"I wish your Divine One would warm the day up," she said.

Gidyon laughed. "Somehow I suspect it does not work quite like that."

"Seems to me it should," Elen-ai grumbled.

The King laughed again, the sound echoing in the tiled corridor. "Next time I'm praying, I will be sure to throw that request in for you."

The ease of the exchange between them went some way to wearing away at the tension that had knotted in Elen-ai's stomach. It was perfectly understandable for Gidyon to have faith, to be faithful, and to find meaning in faith. Many did, even though until recently it was not a widely practised part of life in the Second Country. But the fact remained that she was not an agent of his god. She worshipped the shadows as he worshipped the sun. Perhaps she was being silly. She tried to allay her concern by telling herself that some of Gidyon's tension was seeping through to her. However, she couldn't quite shake the sense that something of a fundamental difference between the two of them had been pointed out. Now that she knew it was there, she couldn't dismiss it from her mind.

They reached the petition room. Gidyon turned to her, the intimate smile of a private joke on his face. "Maybe if I work hard enough people will think the sun shines from my arse. I keep trying to make it happen, but it never does."

With that crass joke, the thoughts that were chasing themselves around Elen-ai's head fled as she struggled to keep her composure. "Only if they know you like I do."

SIX

When he had been just the son of the queen, not her heir - certainly not the king - every week Gidyon would go to the great market of Herran. There, food was laid out with care and carelessness, people were harangued by stall owners promising their wares were the best, and deals flowed like water. The marketplace truly was a spectacle of life in the Second Country at its most vivid. But Elen-ai thought it was the docks that were the true heart of Herran. Far removed from the ordered quiet of the Palace, the docks offered a jumble of sounds, smells and people which tumbled over each other in a chaotic sort of order. The excitement of travel and exoticisms created an intoxicating atmosphere that could not be found in any other part of the city. Not the fencing arenas, not the market, not the beautiful district of the highborn nestled underneath the Palace walls. Crates were unloaded and loaded under the supervision of beady-eyed traders who screamed orders or encouragement to the workers straining underneath the weight of whatever goods were contained within the boxes. Deals were quickly made between individuals who shook hands and slipped away, both parties feeling as though they had netted a bargain. And on beautiful days, the water glistened. Even today, despite the stone-grey sky, the docks were vibrant. One could hear half a dozen dialects while walking only a few paces. There was even a ship in the harbour from the notoriously xenophobic First Country, a relatively uncommon sight. The only known way to get to the First Country was by a treacherous channel, so one of the few places on the Godskissed Continent outside the First Country to see its inhabitants was at a port. Even then, few came ashore. To her chagrin, the vessel was too far out for Elen-ai to make out any clear details of the people on deck.

Of course, a place where so many people congregated also meant that crime flourished, but Elen-ai knew how to avoid trouble. She ignored the offers of the women and men selling their bodies, and dodged the girls chasing each other through the chaos, who would slip a hand into the pockets of anyone they passed quick as a breath, and stopped at the berth she sought. A relatively small but sleek-looking ship from the Fourth Country was docked there, gangplanks down crates in the process of being unloaded by men whose every scrap of skin was covered from sight. Several carts were waiting to receive the crates. From a glance, Elen-ai thought that the crates were filled with spices, but she was not close enough to verify her guess.

An entrepreneurial individual had set up a food cart close to the wharf and was conducting a roaring trade. Perhaps she had been in the Palace too long, for Elen-ai shuddered to imagine what meat the man was cooking over the brazier which belched black smoke into the cold air. Cats, the smaller cousins of the kittanae, prowled around with an equal mixture of haughtiness and hopefulness. There seemed enough of them to dispel Elen-ai's concern that they were the filling of the street vendor's food.

She had to admit, it did smell delicious. After a moment of contemplation, she joined the line where the order of arrival only loosely dictated the order in which they were served, and held up two fingers. The man deftly flicked the just-cooked meat filling into waiting parcels of thin pastry and handed them to her. Taking a bite from one of the little parcels, Elen-ai grunted in satisfaction. To say that the food within the Palace was divine was no understatement, but there was something peculiarly reassuring about the taste of the type of food she had eaten her whole life, even if its contents were dubious. But that too, was part of the familiarity.

When she'd finished the first parcel, she ambled over to the wharf where a beautiful woman supervised the unloading of the ship's cargo with a beady eye. The woman barely regarded her as Elen-ai came to stand beside her. Wordlessly, she held out the second parcel of food.

"You can't bribe me with that dubious offering." The trader's voice was heavily accented, her vowels drawn out to the point that they were almost unrecognisable. But she took the proffered food and bit into it, her red-painted lips parting to allow sharp, white teeth to sink into the unidentified meat.

"How have you been, Ziziana?" Elen-ai asked.

"The wind was not fair on our journey, your boy-king has made the market unacceptably volatile, and my favourite *elui* has issues with his ... performance."

"All grave problems," Elen-ai responded solemnly.

"The worst of course being Hanan." Ziziana was perfectly serious. In the time that Elen-ai had known the formidable trader, she had often grumbled about her slave-husbands.

"Of course," Elen-ai said.

Ziziana barked out a command to her slave-husbands in the language of the Fourth Country. Although Elen-ai knew only a handful of phrases, the sharpness of Ziziana's voice was clear enough to understand. The men did not reply – to do so would have been an unforgivable breach of their station – but their pace slowed and they appeared to take more care with their burdens. Custom demanded that men of the Fourth Country, other than those who were in the midst of fighting, cover themselves from head to toe so that only the merest amount of skin was visible. From time to time, the movements of the men under the ownership of Ziziana would reveal the suggestion of their form – the broadness of the shoulder here, or the curve of a hip there – but for the most part, they were simply cloth-covered pillars undulating with human-like movement. Elen-ai always found the Fourth Country's practice of veiling men profoundly odd, even off-putting. Many of the Fourth Country's customs perplexed her, though.

"Look at them," Ziziana said to Elen-ai, a patronising affection in her voice. "They'd be utterly hopeless without a firm guiding hand."

"Yes, where on earth would they be without you?" Elen-ai's sarcasm turned the trader's head.

"You seem unusually serious, my dear. You know, a cohort of *elui* would do you the world of good. Your every whim would be taken care of, emotionally, spiritually..." her voice dropped to a seductive bass, "...sexually."

Personally, Elen-ai did not see the appeal of having several husbands who were bound to her by a slave contract. "Maybe when I grow old and tired of this life," she replied lightly.

Ziziana cackled, the bangles on her arms jangling as she gestured effusively. "You really don't know what you're missing. All of my husbands are from the finest families."

The assassin shook her head, amused. "I was wondering if you could help me with something."

Her comment elicited a theatrical sigh. "Darling Elen-ai. You never want to see me simply because I'm in your lovely city. Always it's because you want some thing or the other from me."

"Now don't be like that, Zizi," Elen-ai protested. "You know that the Family loves you for your wonderful wares."

"Don't flatter me with business talk – it's cheap." Ziziana mock-pouted.

"Must I buy you more food?"

The woman wiped invisible crumbs from her fingers. "I'm not sure my stomach could take it. All right, what do you want to know?"

"Halen Katan," Elen-ai said.

Ziziana made a derisive noise in her throat. "He certainly pays well," Ziziana said, a dismissive slant in her voice. "Ridiculous man. Now there's someone who should cover himself. Then nobody would see that unfortunate bald spot."

Elen-ai almost choked as unexpected laughter took hold of her.

Once she had recovered, she asked, "So you've traded with him?"

Ziziana blinked deliberately. "On occasion."

"May I ask the nature of your exchange?" She worded the question carefully so as not to offend Ziziana. The people of the Fourth Country were a proud lot.

"It sounds as though you already have some suspicion of what items changed hands." Amusement gave the woman a little, full smile. "I'm not much use to you. As you know I normally travel by boat, here and to the First Country. Especially given the current issues that plague my home country, I increasingly prefer to avoid land routes. Ship is much safer, if not a more expensive way to travel." A dismissive wave of her hand accompanied the comment. Elen-ai suspected that the woman was covering a deeper sadness at seeing her country wracked by constant infighting. Ziziana was a handsome woman, her features strong, her skin smooth. She was also a rich woman, hailing from one of the Fourth Country's most powerful families. As a trader, she was somewhat insulated from the instability that plagued her home. But given the fractured nature of power in the Fourth Country where a family could be invaded by another and lose their power in the blink of an eye, she lived with the knowledge that her power and wealth were only as secure as she could make them with trade and guile. It seemed an impossible way to live, to Elen-ai's mind.

"Don't your *elui* dislike being covered?" Elen-ai asked after watching one of the men stumble.

Ziziana shook her head. "For them, to be without their robes would be as though they were naked."

"Why veil them, though?" Elen-ai persisted.

She received a blank look. "Men are little better than animals, my love. They must be restrained, for their own good, as well as ours. Surely you know that."

Elen-ai said nothing, not knowing how she should respond. "So what sort of weapons is Halen buying?" she asked, diverting the conversation away from the awkwardness she felt at Ziziana's prejudice.

"Oh, anything and everything. Whatever I could get my hands on, he bought."

"And you never thought to ask why?" Elen-ai couldn't help but sound a little frustrated. The woman's lack of concern about Halen's purpose for wanting a significant number of weapons seemed irresponsible.

"Now, now," Ziziana cautioned. "I'm not bound to your king." Her lip curled at the word, making it perfectly clear what she thought of a man on the throne. "I have to make an honest living. I have husbands to support."

"You're right," Elen-ai relented, knowing she had overstepped.

"Hm." Ziziana's red lips pressed together.

"I had better be off." It was clear that no further information would come. "Take care, Zizi," Elen-ai said, turning to leave.

"You too, Elen-ai. Are you all right?" The question was oddly gentle, coming from the formidable woman.

Elen-ai turned back. "Of course. Why do you ask?"

Ziziana tilted her head slightly and scrutinised Elen-ai before she spoke. "You seem different to when last I saw you. Worried, perhaps? No," she answered her own question. "Well, yes, worried, but also ... different."

Elen-ai gave her a bemused look. "I'm the same as I always was."

"Maybe I have too many things on my mind." Ziziana's shrug was an elegant dismissal.

"Like I said, take care." Elen-ai gave her a brief smile before leaving the dock and its bustle behind her.

She hadn't realised how cold it had been on the docks out in in the wind that had blown in straight from the sea until she returned to the meagre cover offered by the buildings which ringed the docks. Those structures housed a variety of places where one could buy food, a drink, somewhere to stay and a warm body to offer companionship, and shops to restock the essential items – at a price which reflected the convenience of acquiring the items so conveniently close to the docks, of course. Some of those operations were even properly licenced, too. For a moment, she stood in the cobblestone alley between two buildings as she considered the fastest way back to the warmth of the Palace. A ripple of air at her side told her that a member of the Family had appeared next to her.

"Mari-am." She smiled as she turned to face her Sister. Mari-am was her favourite Sister. In their younger years they had done absolutely everything together, much to the amusement of their Mothers and Fathers. That closeness had remained as the two girls had become women, although, for the past few years, Mari-am had sought contracts in other lands, often leaving the Second Country for months at a time.

"Elen-ai." Her sister returned the greeting with a taciturn demeanour.

"How are things at home?" Elen-ai asked.

"As ever," came the reply. "Have you learned anything the Mothers and Fathers may deem of interest?"

"Is that the only reason you came?" Elen-ai could not help but feel slightly disappointed. A bloom of joy had spread through her at seeing her Sister. She missed home, and the sight of Mari-am made the ache of feeling out of place in the Palace, slightly less acute.

"I am a loyal child of the Family, simply undertaking their bidding." Her comment sounded like it could have been a rebuke.

"We are both loyal children of the Family, Mari-am. I re-turned to the Palace at their behest." Elen-ai hated the defen-siveness in her tone. She had done nothing she should feel the need to defend.

"Of course."

"I just spoke with a trader from the Fourth Country. Halen Katan is buying weapons from anyone there who is willing to sell them to him. He also challenged Gidyon in front of the Council."

"Things do not look good for the boy-king," Mari-am commented.

"Well, when everybody's arming his enemy with no concern for what that may bring, of course they don't," Elen-ai said.

"You are too involved, Elen-ai." Mari-am made no effort to hide her disapproval.

There was no good reply that Elen-ai could give. She could not deny Mari-am's accusation. "I didn't realise you were such a traditionalist," she said instead.

"The Family's neutrality is everything, Elen-ai. Everything. For one of our own to be a part of the power games played by the Seven Families and the throne is..." Mari-am trailed off with a shake of her head in place of an end to the sentence.

"The Family is as old as the Second Country," Elen-ai re-torted, a defensive anger uncurling inside her. "For as long as it has existed, so have we. The Family was founded alongside the Second Country. Or have you forgotten your lessons?"

"What's your point?" Mari-am folded her arms across her chest.

"We have always been involved in the power games of the Second Country, but we've merely done the bidding of whoever happens to be able to pay." Elen-ai fought to keep her growing anger out of her voice.

"Are you doubting your place in the Family?" There was a challenge there, a note of disgust, even.

"I want to come home. I can't yet, though." Elen-ai wished she could explain to her Sister what was occurring inside her head. She wished she could show her the conflict she felt. The Family's neutrality was a cornerstone of its identity and its place within the Second Country, and it was true that she had cast that neutrality aside in her fealty to Gidyon. But she would not have gone back to the Palace had the Mothers and Fathers forbidden it.

Mari-am snorted. "You can come home whenever you want."

"We don't live in ordinary times, Mari-am. Perhaps you've been away from home too long to realise what's going on. Do you think Halen and his ilk on the throne would be good for anyone? For us?" Elen-ai took a step toward her Sister, looming over her by half a head.

Mari-am gave an angry laugh. "There's a delightful irony in you telling me that I've been away too long."

"Do you speak for all the Family or just for yourself?" Elen-ai snapped out the question, tired of being made to feel as though she should be ashamed.

Her sister's lips pursed. "There are many at home who view your actions with some consternation. You put us at risk, Elen-ai."

"Nobody outside the Royal Family knows I'm a member of the Family." Elen-ai chose to overlook Varl and Valena's knowledge of who she was. They were close enough to the Royal Family for the sake of this argument.

"Ah yes, you're the King's mysterious lover."

Something in Mari-am's tone made Elen-ai pause. "You think he and I are actually lovers?"

"You speak about him as though you're blinded by lust for him."

For a moment, Elen-ai was speechless, her mouth hanging open. "That's a disgusting thought," she thundered.

"You don't need to tell me that. A man on the throne. You'd be tainted." Mari-am's lip curled with distaste.

"Did you come here just to pass judgment on things of which you know nothing?" Elen-ai had heard enough. Anger, now free from its restraints, crackled around her body.

"You're very defensive." Mari-am's calm only served to infuriate Elen-ai further.

"You're very blind," Elen-ai retorted. "Please deliver my information to the Mothers and Fathers."

Without waiting for a response, she stomped off, rage and hurt pulsing under her skin. The cold swirled around her, but she didn't notice it. She moved through the streets quickly, trying to leave her hurt behind. She did not want to think about Mari-am's words, the accusation, the rejection. If she were calmer, she might have come to the conclusion that Mari-am herself might be feeling hurt, believing Elen-ai had left the Family for the King. But her own turbulent emotions left no room for such charity.

The narrow streets with their jumble of shops promising a variety of wares - some reasonable, some enticing only to the naive - passed by in a blur. Elen-ai dodged carts, people, stray animals, as she made her way to the upper areas of the city. She did not even see the shrines that she passed, despite the fact that she normally made a point of counting them. She was completely lost in her focus on simply getting to the Palace and leaving Mari-am's cruel words outside its walls.

Tiny buildings that housed up to four families as well as shops gave way to houses for one family, then to the grand residences of the city's rich. But Elen-ai barely noticed. When the streets emptied of people, as they did in the most luxurious parts of the city, Elen-ai broke into a sprint, craving the release and distraction of movement. She moved almost too fast to see. A part of Elen-ai wished she had hit Mari-am, but she knew her Sister would likely have dodged the blow and received only the satisfaction of knowing she had upset Elen-ai.

She reached the section of Palace wall she knew to be on the least inhabited street and, after a cursory glance around, Elen-ai flung herself at the wall, scaling its massive height with ease. Once she was over the top and in one of the Palace's gardens, she stopped for a moment, her breath only slightly heavier than usual. She looked back up at the wall. Nobody other than a member of the Family would have been able to do what she had just done. The wall was far too smooth and far too high.

"Always a member of the Family," she muttered, feeling the hard edges of her shock and hurt slide down her throat and into her chest. Then she walked into the Palace to tell Gidyon what she had learned from Ziziana.

SEVEN

Following her exchange with Mari-am, Elen-ai spent several days in a very poor mood. Gidyon was busier than ever upon learning that Halen Katan had been buying weapons, and while Elen-ai could give him the benefit of her extensive knowledge on any weapon in existence, she could not tell him how to stop such trading. He exchanged several communications with the Lord Protector of the Fourth Country, sent by messenger birds for speed. Before each reply, Gidyon spent hours on end in consultation with his uncles on how exactly he should word his messages. They could all read and write the language of the Fourth Country, although Kaine apparently was the most proficient when it came to speaking it, which was why he had been chosen as an emissary to them the year before.

Unfortunately, Elen-ai could not offer any counsel on how to most diplomatically word a letter, so she was left to roam the Palace with a certain aimlessness. She could have gone down into Herran, perhaps even consulted with the Family, but following her altercation with Mari-am, she was distinctly disinclined to do that.

One midmorning, as Gidyon composed another letter to the Lord Protector, Elen-ai curled herself up in one of the library's chairs and immersed herself in Har-ai of Herran's latest tale. Ever since Rania had mentioned the author, Elen-ai had been overtaken by a hankering to read more. This story was particularly gripping – a tale about a merchant boy erroneously accused of stealing a cargo of precious gems. She was reasonably certain she had discerned who the true culprit was, but enough doubt was left in her mind that she was pulled inexorably on to the story's conclusion.

Kaine strolled in. She barely registered his entrance, so enthralled was she in the book. He stood directly in front of her and bent down to see what she was reading. She ignored him. But. at his surprised chuckle, she felt it necessary to put the book aside.

"I honestly would never have expected lady Elen-ai, fierce assassin, to be absolutely absorbed by Har-ai of Herran," he said, his voice full of amusement.

"I do things other than stab people, you know," Elen-ai responded peevishly. She had endured a similar conversation when she had tried to discuss poetry with Gidyon the previous year.

"The fault is mine for being ignorant," Kaine said, his golden eyes dancing with laughter. He remained leaning down, his face close to hers.

"Shouldn't you be helping Gidyon?" Elen-ai asked.

He shrugged. "If you truly want to distinguish between the slightest nuances of two written words, Silius is your man. I'm better at charming people with my tongue." The laughter in his eyes turned wicked at the double entendre.

Unable to resist smiling in reply, Elen-ai leaned forward. "Has it ever occurred to you that you aren't as good as you think?"

Kaine's smile broadened. She almost lost herself in his golden gaze. Just as with his late sister, when he properly looked at a person, it felt as though they were falling into the very depths of his being.

"Perhaps one day I'll be fortunate enough to have you arbitrate on the matter," he told her in a voice so nakedly seductive that an unstoppable thrill ran along Elen-ai's skin.

Sadly, that exchange was the only notable moment in the lead-up to the midwinter festival of the Second Country, and Elen-ai had struggled to put thoughts of her confrontation with Mari-am from her mind.

Traditionally, the celebration of midwinter – the shortest day in the year – took place in the streets of Herran. Unlike on other days of celebration throughout the year, queens by custom would participate in the festivities alongside any of the city folk who wished to join her. Gidyon had been warned of the danger he may face in taking to the street due to the danger posed by the myriad of overhanging roofs, entrances and exits, and shadowed doorways. But he ignored the risk of attack, adamant he would take to the streets like the queens before him to celebrate. Low-born who wished to celebrate with the king mingled alongside the Royal Family and the Palace servants, laughing, joking, sneaking a glance at their king. The celebration was the people's bid to prove to the Divine One that they had not forsaken the sun during the short winter days. As excuses for a festival went, it was quite a good one to Elen-ai's mind, even if she was not a devoted follower of the Divine One. She had always joyfully participated in the carousing. One of the contracts she was most proud of she had conducted under the cover of the midwinter festivities, slipping a poison into the woman's drink and gently escorting her toward the water so that it looked as though she had stumbled into the water thanks to the befuddling effects of too much ale. After she had ensured the woman's demise, Elen-ai had returned to the festivities with the satisfaction of a job well done, making that year's festival even more enjoyable. So Elen-ai allowed herself to be dressed in garb of deep crimson rather than the muted tones she preferred, and accompanied Gidyon to the street upon which the king's celebrations were to take place.

The wide street was lit by a long line of tall braziers, and at one end, an enormous fire over which several meals were being prepared. Elen-ai felt sorry for the guards who were ensuring that not too many people came into the street where their ruler celebrated, but they were being well compensated for the duty, and the ambience over Herran was one where even someone who was working felt a certain lightness in the task. The midwinter festival was a time of joy and merriment that nobody could properly escape, regardless of the cold weather. One year, it was said, the festivities were held despite the presence of a terrible storm. The legend surrounding that story also said that the following year brought unprecedented prosperity for the Second Country.

As more and more people came into the grand road leading to the Palace gates, music began to sound, and revellers began to dance. Elen-ai suddenly found herself face to face with an unfairly handsome Kaine.

"Would you care to dance?"

His customary mischievous grin almost split his face from ear to ear. He wore clothes of flaming red and orange that offset the liquid gold of his eyes, which had been further accented by the dark blue pigment set around them. He looked very good.

When Elen-ai hesitated, his smile widened. He leaned in close to her and whispered, "I didn't realise assassins didn't dance."

"I can dance perfectly well," Elen-ai snapped, slapping her hand into his proffered palm.

He laughed as he led her to the ring of dancers.

To her right, Gidyon gently swung around a girl who could not have been more than twelve. She looked caught between delight and amazement that her king was dancing with her.

Elen-ai lost sight of the King and his partner as Kaine twirled her around and around, completely sure of himself as he moved to the music.

"You dance well," she told him.

"And you aren't even slightly out of breath," he protested.

She laughed, tipping her head back as they whirled around, looking up at the night sky as it turned end over end before her eyes. "Does that really surprise you?" she asked once he had pulled her back upright and she was staring into his beautiful eyes once more.

"No." He laughed again, pulling her even closer. She could have resisted. She could have had him lying on the ground, winded and with a broken arm. There was something endearing about the fact that he too knew that, and yet he still pulled her to him.

"I heard about your bet with Gidyon," Kaine said in her ear. She was most aware of the way his lips brushed against her as he spoke.

"About Silius dancing?"

He nodded, moving his hands to her waist. He might not have been as physically fit as her, but he did dance very well.

"Gidyon swears he'll goad Silius into dancing with someone tonight. I think he said something about finding the prettiest lady," Elen-ai said. "I must admit, Gidyon does have a way of convincing people. I'm a touch worried."

Amusement seized hold of Kaine's features. "You needn't be, unless Gidyon finds the prettiest man here to entice Sil to dance."

Shock almost had Elen-ai missing a step. She thought of the prim and proper Silius, his slightly balding head, the cheekbones so high that they had doomed him to a haughty air. His austere demeanour did not seem to fit with the other men she knew who slept with one another. Of course, the men who sold their bodies were always overt with their sexuality. The sensuousness with which they carried themselves made it easy to envisage them yielding to the touch of another man. The men of the Family who preferred men were simply quite comfortable and natural with that part of themselves. But Silius with his reserve and somewhat dowdy manner just seemed so incongruous with the idea of ever taking someone to his bed, man or woman.

As he watched her contemplate this new piece of information, Kaine grinned wickedly.

"Gidyon doesn't know?" Elen-ai asked, her lips close to his ear as another song commenced.

Kaine shook his head, his hair brushing against Elen-ai's cheek. "I don't think it's ever occurred to him," he yelled over a sudden crescendo in the music.

As the song became even faster, conversation became impossible, and they danced for several more before Kaine relented with a wry grin. "I admit, I'm weak. I must rest," he told her, panting slightly.

"I was just getting warmed up, too," Elen-ai said. She was disappointed. Dancing with Kaine had been fun. He was lively, and she was willing to admit that being so close to him offered a certain thrill.

Gidyon appeared by Elen-ai's side. "Uncle, are you getting old?" He put his hands on his hips. Like Kaine, Gidyon was dressed in reds and oranges. Most of the people were, the burnt scarlet and yellow hues and of their garb chosen to emulate the sun. His blue eyes shone in the light cast by the braziers, emphasised by the black swirls that had been carefully painted around them.

Kaine mouthed an obscenity at his nephew that had both Gidyon and Elen-ai giggling.

"I bet I can outlast him – and I've been dancing already," Gidyon said.

"Are you sure about making more bets? I've heard on good authority that the likelihood of Silius dancing is very low," Elen-ai challenged.

Gidyon grabbed Elen-ai's hand and pulled her into the stream of dancers. "Trust me, Sil will dance before the night is over."

Giving up the argument, Elen-ai instead set a tormenting pace for Gidyon. However, as the King always managed to find time among his many duties to practise fighting under Elen-ai's tuition every day, so he managed to keep pace with her now. Gidyon danced with a light-footed grace, his movements curiously beautiful. It was a pleasure to dance with him, and in the time that they danced he was not her king, she was not his assassin. They were simply friends dancing together.

As the final song before the evening's second feast commenced, Gidyon dared her with a smirk to dance as fast as possible. Never one to resist a challenge, Elen-ai moved faster and faster, the King matching her step for step. Finally, he faltered, no match for an assassin's quick feet, and Elen-ai caught him, the two of them collapsing into peals of laughter at the ridiculousness of their game. The pair were applauded by the other revellers and rewarded for the spectacle they had provided by being handed the first plates piled high with food. She wandered away from Gidyon, contentedly chewing on a wing of karrabal – a bird which was famed for its deliciousness. It had been cooked to perfection.

"To one who didn't know, you and Gidyon look very much in love." Nikalus' voice came from beside her elbow. It was unclear whether he was amused or disapproving.

Her mouth full of food, Elen-ai simply looked at him.

"It was not intended to be a disapproving comment," he said.

She shrugged, wiping her mouth with the back of her hand. He cringed at her lack of decorum. She delighted in it. "Gid and I are friends," she said simply, unsure what else she should say.

"I know that. He," he hesitated, "he trusts you. He can confide in you. It is good that he has a friend."

"I'll always be here for him." She found herself curiously touched by the comment.

"Hmm." He did not elaborate further on whatever the noise was supposed to mean. "The rumours about you two will continue to spread. It is good. Nobody will suspect the truth." His last words were spoken so softly that nobody else could possibly overhear.

"Can't have anyone knowing the truth, can we?" She swayed her hips at him suggestively.

At that moment, Kaine appeared by his brother's side. "Are you bothering Elen-ai?"

"Don't be ridiculous, Kaine," Nikalus snapped, although there was no bite behind his words.

"Come. Drink. Be merry. Once the music begins again, I believe I have recovered myself for another bout of the exquisite torment that is trying to keep step with you, if you'll indulge me, Elen-ai?" Kaine said.

She couldn't help but smile. "Are you sure I won't tire you out?"

"Almost certainly you will, but who in their right mind would resist an opportunity to dance with you?"

The music and firelight did cast a certain spell that anybody would struggle to resist, but she made a point of considering his offer.

"Oh, come on," Kaine pleaded, holding his hand out. "Tell me you don't want to."

She did consider refusing him. Truth was, she wanted to dance with him far too much. She made him wait until she had finished every morsel on her plate, then she handed the simple wooden item – no Katan finery tonight – to a waiting servant.

She had finished eating just in time. Music began to sound through the street once more, and Kaine took her hand in his, pulling her into a dance. His body was far closer to hers than was decent. However, tonight was midwinter festival. What was or wasn't proper was discarded in the face of the wine and food and the spirit of revelry that overtook the city on this night. Kaine's grip on her arm tightened suddenly. Her heart froze as she feared an assailant had appeared to threaten Gidyon.

"Divine One, how did he do it?" He shouted the question in her ear, incredulity across his face.

She turned to where Kaine was looking. There, his arms linked with a girl on his right and a slightly portly man on his left, Silius performed a surprisingly adept two-step dance with exuberant abandon. Elen-ai stared at the spectacle, aware of Gidyon in the background with a grin that showed all of his teeth.

Elen-ai excused herself and marched over to the King. "How?"

His grin widened, if that was possible. "The how is unimportant."

"Don't give me that rubbish. How did you do it?" Elen-ai gestured wildly toward the now twirling Silius. He practically bounced, bringing his knees up high with every step.

"I fastened a few cups of wine upon him," Gidyon admitted.

"You cheated!" Elen-ai accused.

"You bet I couldn't do it. You never said you bet that I couldn't do it without getting him drunk," Gidyon pointed out.

Elen-ai waved her hands at him in ire, but did not actually have a sufficient riposte.

"I'll send the tailor to you," Gidyon said, gloating.

"I hate you," Elen-ai told him vehemently.

"I still won."

"I definitely hate you." Elen-ai stalked back to Kaine.

"Happy midwinter," Gidyon yelled at her retreating back.

She seriously considered making an obscene gesture at him, but she suspected it might shock people too much to see her treating their king with such irreverence. She resolved to do it in private the next chance she got.

"I personally look forward to seeing you in skirts," Kaine told her.

"You do know where I come from and what I could do to you?" Elen-ai asked, pursing her lips in an exaggerated pout.

Far from inspiring fear in him, he laughed and drew her to him once more. "Our poor beleaguered assassin," he murmured in her ear, one hand caressing the small of her back.

The music stopped to rapturous applause. Everybody settled themselves on blankets or chairs as new musicians replaced their colleagues who had admirably kept such a lively pace for so long. Kaine let go of Elen-ai's hand and they stood together, watching as the new musicians set up their instruments. She was once more disappointed that she was no longer enjoying the thrill of being so close to Kaine, but this part of the evening, just like the break for feasting, was part of tradition. Over the momentary hush, Gidyon called out to his uncle. "Kaine, will you sing?"

"You flatter me, my King," Kaine called back.

Gidyon addressed the crowd, an easy, charming smile on his face. "My uncle Kaine has the finest voice I've ever had the good fortune to hear. I would love to share this with you all."

The street echoed with cheers and claps of encouragement.

"Go on," Elen-ai told Kaine, nudging him in the ribs.

"He knows I'll do it. But I can't capitulate too quickly. He has to think that he can't get everything he wants. You failed on your end," he told her in an undertone.

"I will stab you," Elen-ai threatened.

"Do you solve all your problems with violence?" he muttered as the calls for him to sing continued.

"Not all."

He laughed as he strode to his nephew's side. "As you command, my King." He bowed in a gently mocking manner.

"I only ask," Gidyon protested, making an exaggerated face of weariness, much to the audience's delight.

Kaine had a beautiful voice. Sonorous and pure, his first choice of song was a ballad about a man who sets out to find riches to make his mother happy. By pure chance, Kaine had chosen one of Elen-ai's favourite songs. The story ended with the man coming home poor and his mother, who was very old by that point, telling him that all she needed to be happy was her child near to her. It was far sadder than many of the other songs popular in the Second Country, but the composer had skilfully blended a beautiful melody with well-chosen words to make it linger in the minds of those who listened to it even once. Kaine's rendition was particularly moving. He was either a naturally talented singer, or someone had given him superb instruction. In addition to a beautiful voice, he knew how to sing with meaning, holding certain notes for a fraction of a second longer than strictly necessary, wrapping sorrow and bittersweet heartbreak around them. The song's conclusion was greeted with a cheer of approval from the audience and shouts for more. Clearly enjoying the attention, Kaine chose a love song. For the entirety of the song, he looked directly at Elen-ai. She appreciated his bold interest. It was a refreshing change from the allusions and layered meanings that characterised exchanges in the world of the highborn.

Kaine sang five more songs, the final one a bawdy tavern song that everybody cheerfully joined him in singing. Elen-ai sang too, swept along by the excitement of the gathered crowd.

As was the custom, the carousing lasted until the first rays of dawn began to peek across the horizon. A ragged cheer went up from the (mostly inebriated) crowd when the golden glow became apparent. At this signal, people began to leave the street that had for that evening, offered them food, dancing, music, and merriment. For the rest of the day, they would sleep, or at the very least rest, enjoying one of few days within the year that could truly be filled with nothing other than nursing the effect of too many drinks. Elen-ai walked slowly back up the hill to the Palace with Kaine, two guards following them. How he had contrived to leave with her, she did not know, but she did not protest. Their pleasantly fatigued strides brought them to gently brush against each other. There was a certain enjoyment to be found in the inadvertent yet deliberate contact. Kaine smelled of alcohol and wood smoke and sweat, and it was a curiously intoxicating combination. When they went inside the Palace and he pulled her to him and suggested they go to his room, she agreed.

EIGHT

Afternoon sunlight came in through the windows of Kaine's bedroom, falling onto Elen-ai's skin. With the heat of the room's fire and gently smoking braziers, the sun almost felt warm. Beside her, Kaine ran a curious hand along her body, making an inventory of the scars she had collected.

"This is the twenty-fourth and I'm only up to your waist," he said, lightly brushing a fingertip over the offending mark.

She shook her head at his dedication to the task. "I've spent my whole life around blades and fighting, what do you expect?"

"I honestly don't know," Kaine admitted, moving his hand to the small of Elen-ai's back and running it up and down her spine. She arched her back in pleasure at the sensation of his fingertips on her skin. "I've never been with an assassin before." His hand moved up to her shoulders.

"You've given up counting?" she enquired, turning to look at him.

"Too many to count," Kaine declared, placing kisses along the wake of his hands. His lips felt good on her skin. Coming to his bed had been a good decision.

She rolled from her stomach to her side and he lay back down on the bed, his hand coming to rest on her waist.

Kaine looked very appealing like this: mussed up, tired, naked. "You're very charming like this."

"And I'm not always?"

She leaned forward to kiss him. He eagerly kissed her in return, slipping his hand down the slope of her back to pull her against him. As she pulled away from him, her glance fell over his shoulder to the table by the bedside.

"Oh!" She scrambled to her knees, eliciting a groan of dismay at her departure. She reached over him and retrieved the object that had caught her interest.

"Conventions of Legal Heritage, volume one. It really is bedtime reading for you."

He sat up and took the book from her. "It is a sad truth that I take books with me to bed more frequently than beautiful women."

"Do you take women to your bed regularly?" She feigned haughtiness, putting her hands on her hips.

"Not often enough," came the mournful reply.

She rolled her eyes. A sense of possessiveness when it came to her lovers had never been something with which she had ever struggled. Yet a tiny thorn of competitiveness pricked her side. Kaine would have been discreet, yet she was certain he would have had his share of people in his bed.

"You know, you're quite energetic," she told Kaine, the condescension of the comment causing him to huff, and her to laugh.

"Are you trying to goad me into something, Elen-ai?" he challenged. The point was somewhat lost as his eyes roamed hungrily over her naked body.

Darkness was falling when Elen-ai raised her head, fighting the pleasant drowsiness that had settled over her. Kaine lay beside her, resting his head against her arm.

"I should go," Elen-ai said.

"Mm." Kaine's sound of protest was tinged with fatigue. Neither of them had slept since the night before the midwinter festival. Elen-ai at least had been trained to require very little sleep.

"I should go," she repeated. "I'm sure Gidyon will be awake and doing something dull like reading a petition or a report, or studying shipbuilding to better inform how to redesign the harbour."

"And? Let him. It's the day after midwinter, nobody should do work, let alone anything as impossibly dull as any of those things." Kaine turned so that his face was pressed directly against Elen-ai's arm, muffling his words. The offhanded manner with which he spoke about the tasks of rule belied the sincerity with which Elen-ai knew he took his role as Gidyon's adviser.

"Still, I should go," Elen-ai said.

Kaine groaned. "I can't believe you're thinking about my nephew when you're in my bed. Naked."

"I live and die by the wishes of the king," Elen-ai responded glibly, eliciting another groan from him. She laughed as he moved his head to bury it in his own arms. "Not liking your duties, my lord adviser?"

"Being adviser to my sister was much easier than being adviser to Gidyon," Kaine lamented, raising his head.

"Well, nobody ever thought they would see a king in the Second Country."

"There's a good reason for that."

Something in his tone caused Elen-ai to raise herself up so that she could look at him properly. "What do you mean?"

Kaine's reluctance to answer was obvious. "I just ... men shouldn't be on the throne."

"Why?"

"Men have less suitable temperaments to rule. Think about the fact that the jails to Herran's west are filled with men who have beaten their women, or each other, or who have raped someone weaker than them. Women just don't do that sort of thing."

"How are you so certain?" Elen-ai asked.

"Like I said, look at who we imprison. It's only exceptional cases where we lock up women. Think about Meg-am the murderess. She was imprisoned six years ago for killing fifteen people with a blunt axe. Since her trial, maybe one or two other women have been jailed, whereas I can't count the number of men who have been locked up for violent crimes."

"Just because most women are not always as strong as a man doesn't mean that they can't or won't also be violent, or dangerous, or of poor temperament," Elen-ai countered. "I've seen women order a killing just as easily, if not more coldly, than any man."

His disagreement was apparent on his face. "Women might be cold, they may be capable of poor impulses or even violence, but they're just more temperate, more naturally suited to finding reason and rationality," he said.

"Surely that's just taught."

"Of course it's taught. But it comes more naturally to women. Sil, Nik, and I had years and years of lessons to teach us to be rational and logical, even in the heat of argument."

"So you've never wondered whether you would be a good king?" Elen-ai asked.

"I would never presume to think it appropriate for me to sit on the throne," Kaine said. "I mean, I love my nephew, but the second he's anywhere near the throne, we're facing down a war. When a woman sat on the throne, there was never even the suggestion of any divide within the country serious enough to lead to war."

"But that's just Halen Katan," she protested.

"Exactly. Another man. The Second Country should have a woman on the throne to counter that sort of tendency."

"So what do you think about Gidyon then?"

"I think him being on the throne is an accident of my sister's inability to bear a girl. He should not be on the throne, but he is, and given that he is, he's doing a magnificent job. But he still shouldn't be on the throne."

His conviction surprised her. Kaine's light-hearted preference for mischief suggested not much overly bothered him. The fact he was so certain about the flaws of his own gender belied that levity.

"Surely you agree with me?" he asked.

She opened her mouth to disagree but found that he wasn't entirely wrong. When Latana had first told her about the decision to make Gidyon her heir, Elen-ai had been furious. She had thought the decision a terrible one, and the prospect of a man on the throne nothing short of blasphemous. Her reaction hadn't simply been informed by a natural preference for tradition. It was the thought that a man would be on the throne rather than the moderate, cool, calm competence of the unbroken line of queens who had safely guided the Second Country through generations of prosperity and security.

Kaine knew he had made his point. "It's all an exercise in rhetoric for the most part, really," Kaine said. "We have to deal with the circumstances in which we find ourselves, and right now, the circumstances are that Latana is dead and Gidyon is on the throne." He took one of Elen-ai's hands in his and kissed it firmly, indicating he felt no ill will over their disagreement.

"Do you miss her?" Kaine had been on a diplomatic journey to the Fourth Country when the queen had been murdered. The message informing him of Latana's death wouldn't have even reached him by the time the funeral service was held in Herran. Elen-ai had always felt sorry for him, that he had never been given the opportunity to say goodbye.

Kaine shook his head slightly in thought. "She wasn't just my queen, she was my big sister. I still can't believe that she's gone. Reading on a page what happened just doesn't feel real."

"I'm sorry, I shouldn't have asked." Despite his honest answer, she felt as though she had pried beyond what was reasonable. And she knew what Kaine did not: Gidyon was the product of a relationship that broke the sacred rules of impartiality. In some ways Kaine was lucky that his memory of Latana was not marred by that knowledge as it was for Gidyon.

"No, it's fine. You understand better than most people." He squeezed the hand he still held in emphasis.

"I really should go." She slipped out of his bed, her skin prickling at the chill in the air that the braziers could not entirely dispel. She cast about for her clothes.

Kaine watched her with undisguised appreciation. She tugged her tunic over her head. As she checked her blades were all properly in place, she wondered whether coming to his bed had been a mistake. At the time, when she had been caught up in desire and slight drunkenness on the spirit and the atmosphere of the festival, it had seemed a good idea, but now she wondered what exactly it was that he wanted from her.

Kaine took a breath to say something then apparently reconsidered, the hesitation lingering on his still-parted lips.

"Yes?" Elen-ai paused midway through buttoning up her trousers.

"This doesn't have to happen again, if you don't want it to," Kaine said, waving his hand at the tousled bed. "I mean, I enjoyed today, but you understand that as adviser to Gidyon..." He paused, seemingly at a loss for words – the first time Elen-ai had ever seen him as such.

The uncertainty of the unflappable Kaine made Elen-ai smile. She strode over and leaned down to kiss him, long and sweet. His hands made their way up to her waist, pulling her back toward him, and for a moment she contemplated surrendering to his suggestion.

"I'm sure we'll figure something out," she told him before she left.

On her way to Gidyon's rooms, Elen-ai ran into Freya. The Councilwoman's face looked comically small amid the scarves, throws and handmuff piled around her frame.

"I know I look ridiculous," the older woman admitted. "It's so Goddess-cursed cold here. Oranis is always reasonably warm."

"It does seem as though you could get lost in there," Elen-ai said, stifling a laugh.

"I cannot wait until we get back home. All I ever wear on my feet in Oranis is sandals." The wistful note in her tone was unmistakable.

"You aren't leaving us, are you?" Elen-ai was saddened by the prospect. She liked the foreigner very much.

"Sadly, yes. More than time we went home. We stayed far longer than we expected, but establishing the treaty with the Fourth Country to get some guarantee that our people will be safe took longer than any of us expected due to the Queen's death. Honestly, we should have left weeks ago, but we stayed especially for the midwinter festival. It reminded me of the festivals of dance back home."

"Did you enjoy it?"

"Oh, very much. And by the looks of it, you did, too." The knowing twinkle in Freya's eye indicated she was quite aware of what had transpired between Elen-ai and Kaine.

Not knowing how she should reply, Elen-ai dropped her gaze to her feet, eliciting a laugh in response. "I will miss you," she said truthfully, ignoring the subject of with whom, or how, she had spent the day.

"And I you. I have enjoyed the time I have spent with you, Elen-ai. But I think it is time to go home."

"The Palace is beautiful, but there is nothing quite like home," Elen-ai agreed.

The comment earned her a look of surprise. "I thought you had left the Family," Freya said. She too knew of Elen-ai's origins.

Elen-ai shook her head. "I suppose you could say I'm on loan to Gidyon."

"Perhaps I'm wrong, but I thought the Family was politically neutral."

"We are. That's why I'm not here as a member the Family," Elen-ai explained. She uncomfortably remembered her argument with Mari-am. It had been the first day she had not been preoccupied with it, until that moment.

"Ah." The Councilwoman clearly did not understand. "Well, wherever ends up being home for you, I hope you get there soon."

"Thank you, Freya." Elen-ai moved on to find Gidyon.

The King was in his private rooms, writing. The document looked long and was almost certainly boring. He glanced up as Elen-ai came in. "I was wondering what time I'd see you."

"I was taking some rest, like you should have been doing," she said, walking over to peer over his shoulder.

"Is that what you want to call it?" Amusement flashed through his bright blue eyes as he glanced up at her.

"I have no idea what you're talking about. Have you eaten today?" She adopted a haughty tone that almost completely failed to be effective.

"I think you and Kaine will be good for one another," he said, ignoring her question.

"Um." Elen-ai had no idea what she could or should say in response.

"Oh please, I have seen the looks he has been throwing your way, not to mention the way you two were with each other last night. And you are wearing the same clothes as last night, too."

She hadn't thought about her clothes. On reflection, she probably should have taken the time to change. She saw no point in trying to pretend. "Are you certain it doesn't bother you?"

He made a nonchalant gesture. "Provided you do not start doing anything where I can see, I have other things to find far more upsetting."

She didn't bother repeating the question. If Gidyon said he was fine with it, he was fine with it. "What about you? Did you find a willing woman to take your innocence last night?" she asked, knowing full well that he hadn't. Gidyon had never said it, but she knew that he was afraid of caring romantically for someone after the trouble he'd had with Rania Harete.

At this, Gidyon spared her a withering look. "Like I said, I have more important things on my mind."

"Not many boys your age would say that," she commented, the teasing tone still in her voice.

"How many of them are the unwanted king of a country?" Gidyon asked distractedly.

"Good point. Tell me, do you think men have a more violent temperament than women?"

Gidyon continued his writing, suggesting that whatever he was doing, it was of reasonable importance. Or he didn't want to lose his train of thought. "It is not really a debate I have given a great amount of thought to. Why? What do you think?"

"I don't know what I think."

"You really are a terrible liar. You will not hurt my feelings if you say you think men are less suited to rule, you know."

"You say that now," Elen-ai cautioned.

"Yes, I do. I happen to think I am well suited to rule and I happen to be a man, as many people have noticed. I do not have a choice, anyway. I have to be well suited to rule. And regardless of your thoughts on the male temperament, you support me, so clearly the question is a theoretical one."

"You could indulge me in a little roundabout conversation."

"I indulged you last night with all the dancing and merriment," Gidyon said, not looking up from the page.

"What are you doing anyway?" Elen-ai asked.

"I am writing, Elen-ai. Honestly, all these skills of observation the Family supposedly have seem to be just a myth."

She had to fight not to laugh at his facetious tone. "I did indeed notice that you weren't dancing on the tabletop, Gidyon. I was wondering what exactly you were writing."

His serious demeanour returned. "I am writing a letter to Kar-am of Atak. She is the leading expert on warfare theory, and I have been receiving quite the education from her by correspondence."

"Do you really think that you need to know this stuff?" Elen-ai asked.

From her vantage, she could see Gidyon arch his eyebrow. "Would you rather I find out I need to know it and do not?"

As was often the case, Gidyon had a point.

"Do you need me to do anything?"

"What, you want me to give you something to do? Surely you could just go and enjoy not having to do anything. I am sure Kaine will be still in his room."

Ignoring the attempt to rile her, Elen-ai sighed slightly. "Yes, but I knew you would be working, and I didn't want you to be working alone."

Gidyon looked up at her with his full attention. "You know, Elen-ai, I could say that I have been fortunate in a number of aspects. But I think that your friendship is the thing in which I have been the most fortunate. You are a wonderful friend." He smiled.

Elen-ai made a noise of dismissal to dispel the weight of the emotion. "Just give me something to do," she said brusquely to hide how deeply touched she was.

He directed her to a stack of petitions, telling her to put aside the ones that she thought were of importance. Happily, she began, bored by the task reasonably quickly but nevertheless willing to do it so that Gidyon had one less thing to complete.

The letter from Halen arrived an hour later.

NINE

"I really hate to admit how clever Halen has been about this," Gidyon said after he had finished reading the letter for the umpteenth time. He had not sat down since down since he had first stood to take the missive. His unceasing pacing of the room as he read and re-read the letter had Elen-ai on the verge of snapping at him to sit down.

"Don't. Give the credit for his cleverness to someone else," Elen-ai suggested, drawing an embattled laugh from her king.

Gidyon glared at the offending document before he finally put it down. "You know, doing this the day after midwinter was just mean."

"He's just a mean man with pretensions of importance," she said scathingly.

"Yes. Well, he just declared that Serenah is the rightful claimant to the throne and demanded that I recognise it. I am not exactly sure that I would have expected anything less from him," Gidyon said. Fatigue hung heavily in his voice.

"Does he honestly expect you to abdicate?" She still hadn't got over her incredulity at the man's boldness.

"Of course not. That is not how the game is played, Elen-ai."

"The game is stupid." Elen-ai put one foot after the other on the low table, which was probably worth more than she could have earned for the Family in an average year.

Gidyon sighed. "I do not necessarily disagree with you, but unfortunately this is how things are done."

"I think you should throw him in jail," Elen-ai suggested unhelpfully. "And while you're at it, Julyana Bertak could join him."

"While the prospect of Halen in a jail full of murderers, thieves, and rapists does fill me with a sense of childish glee, do you not think that people may feel he has a legitimate case against me if that is my immediate response to this?" Gidyon picked the letter up once more and waved it at her, as though she needed some kind of reminder of its contents.

Elen-ai grunted.

Gidyon sighed and threw the page back down on the table near Elen-ai's foot. He sat beside her with a thud.

"Are you all right?"

He threw his hands up. "My mother was killed by the man who might have been my father. Nobody wants me on the throne because of something I cannot help, Sil keeps telling me I need to find a wife, and now Halen is suggesting that my younger cousin who is clearly ill-versed in matters of state should rule instead of me. But aside from all of that, I'm fine."

"Speaking of fathers, have you spoken with Zekken?" Elen-ai asked. "The Aadran family may be able to assist if you approach him."

Gidyon made a derisive noise and shook his head. "I want nothing to do with him. Besides, if the relationship between him and mother is discovered, I would be finished. It is best if I do not speak to him."

Recognising that he had a point, she did not push him further. "Fair enough."

"You know, I am so angry with mother for leaving us in this incredible mess," he confessed.

Elen-ai did not respond. Gidyon rarely spoke of those feelings. She figured it was best to simply let him talk at his own pace.

"If she had not carried on with Zekken, Erek would not have killed her, and she would still be here to ensure my claim to the throne was secure before I had to actually take the throne."

"You can't know that Erek wouldn't have killed her. He was infatuated with her, and he wasn't well. Infatuation and instability are rarely an ideal mix. If not that night, perhaps at some other time in some other way," Elen-ai said gently. "He'd already tried it once before." She reminded him of Erek's first attempt on both Gidyon and Latana's lives with a pointed glance at where his stomach had been gored.

"You're trying to make me feel better," Gidyon said.

"Is it working?"

"No."

They both chuckled. Silence descended for a moment.

"I am so angry with her," he said again.

"She did love you," Elen-ai said. "She wanted so badly to protect you from her mistakes. It was why she hired me." Elen-ai remembered the calculated way the Queen had let her self-control slip in that first meeting, revealing the depth of her love and fear for her son. At the time, it had felt profane to witness the emotions of a monarch, but also curiously intimate, and had in no small way pushed Elen-ai toward accepting the contract despite her revulsion at the prospect of a man on the throne.

"I know. But it does not change that she died with me angry with her," he said, his voice dropping low with the admission.

"Death is rarely neatly tied up," Elen-ai said.

"Is that your professional experience speaking?"

"Yes and no. I've often heard a great many meaningless or angry words which are unknowingly the last ones spoken to a loved one. Some of them have even been mine. You are not unique in this."

"Does it ever bother you that you took away that proper last goodbye for so many people?" Unlike in the past, Gidyon asked about her trade with no judgment; now he simply sounded curious.

"Not really. It was their time. And there's no guarantee that anyone will have the opportunity to say the right goodbye to their loved ones – if such a thing as the right goodbye even exists."

The King was silent, his forehead furrowed for a moment as he considered what she had said. "I miss her, you know." The admission was laced with pain.

"Of course you do. She was your mother." Elen-ai put her hand on his knee.

"I do not want to be angry with her, you know. I'm scared I will never stop being angry with her for that stupid, awful choice."

"I don't know if you will or won't." She didn't like not being able to offer him certainty, but she would not lie to him to make him feel better.

"She should be here, fixing this. She always knew what to do in response to this sort of thing. She would have known how to outmanoeuvre Halen." His hands fisted in his lap. "Divine One, she would already have had a plan by now."

Elen-ai said nothing, knowing that there was no way for her to salve this particular wound. Gidyon's grief was still too raw to be eased by a kind word or platitude. Instead, she gently squeezed his knee in a poor offering of comfort. "We might not have your mother, but we'll come up with something."

He sighed. "I know. I must say, though, I do not look forward to breaking the news to my uncles at supper tonight."

Supper, a light meal in deference to the excessive quantity of food that had been consumed the previous evening and the slumber that had taken up most of the day, took place only a little later. Elen-ai, after changing into fresh clothes, accompanied Gidyon into the intimate dining room where he usually dined with his uncles. Silius was already there, in conversation with Councillors Freya and Ashtyn from the Third Country. While everybody always looked tired the day after midwinter festival, Silius had somehow contrived to look as immaculate as ever. If Elen-ai hadn't witnessed his dancing with her own eyes, she never would have believed it had occurred. It was almost worth losing her bet with Gidyon to have seen it.

At Gidyon's entrance, Silius, Freya, and Ashtyn rose. He waved them to sit back down and took his seat with minimal ceremony. Only a few moments later, Kaine strode in. His gaze slid to Elen-ai immediately. Their eyes met across the room. Both smiled.

Gidyon, evidently seeing this, cleared his throat and rolled his eyes with the briefest of movements at Elen-ai. "Is Nik joining us?"

"I wouldn't count on it." Kaine chuckled as he slipped into his seat, then elaborated for the Councillors and Elen-ai: "He always overindulges at midwinter and is in a right state the next day. He's learned that it's easiest if he just stays in bed all day."

"I can see why one might be tempted to overindulge." Ashtyn leaned forward, his green eyes glittering in the light from the torches on the wall. "The festival was quite wonderful."

"We are so glad that you decided to stay for it." Gidyon's smile made it seem as though there could be nothing else bothering him. Elen-ai couldn't understand how he managed it.

Servants converged on the table with plates – Katan plates, of course – of food.

While they were perhaps a little overly formal to her mind, Elen-ai had come to quite like the dinners at the Palace. When not in service of some grand occasion, or to entertain some guest or another, the candid discussions among the family members was quite enjoyable to be a part of. It reminded her of home.

"Well, you both witnessed a never-before-seen feat," Kaine told the Councillors.

"Oh?" Freya's mouth quirked in anticipation of whatever he was about to say. Despite the deep love she and Ashtyn shared, it seemed she, too, was not immune to Kaine's charm.

"You witnessed Sil dancing." Kaine chuckled gleefully. His elder brother glared at him balefully.

"Oh!" Gidyon punctuated the exclamation by clapping his hands, inadvertently claiming the attention of the room. "I will have to determine the best occasion for Elen-ai to debut her skirt."

"They made a bet about whether or not you would dance, Sil. Elen-ai lost," Kaine explained.

Silius glared first at Elen-ai then at his nephew. In reply, Gidyon smiled back sweetly. Both Councillors were obvious in their fight against laughter.

"I'm sure you will choose the least convenient time for me to be paraded around looking ridiculous." Elen-ai couldn't resist pouting. The thought of anybody seeing her in skirts, let alone a room full of people, was horrifying.

"Nonsense, Elen-ai. I would never have someone associated so closely with me looking ridiculous," Gidyon said with a wicked grin.

"Just for that, I hope Serenah takes the throne and bans the wearing of skirts," Elen-ai informed him haughtily.

Gidyon simply laughed at her response. It was a light exchange that for one moment made it possible to forget Halen's letter, and the very real threat that it promised.

Once dinner was over and the Councillors had excused themselves, Gidyon broached the subject of the letter. There was something heartbreaking about seeing weariness and resignation replace the humour on the faces of his uncles. Even Silius, despite his ire at the wager on his dancing, had seemed relaxed for once.

After the moment of shocked silence following Gidyon's announcement, Kaine cursed extensively. Gidyon said nothing, merely watching his two uncles.

"Well, obviously we need to have a response to this within a legal framework," Silius said from above steepled fingers.

"I've read just about every legal book in the Second Country," Kaine said. "The Veertaks were kind enough to send me a small mountain of them several weeks ago." Kaine threw a tired smile at Elen-ai over their shared joke about his bedtime reading material. "I imagine I would be able to start drafting something."

"Should I get Nik?" Silius offered.

Gidyon made a noncommittal gesture.

As the conversation continued, Elen-ai rose silently from the table, her departure almost unnoticed. There was little she could contribute to the discussion among the members of the Royal Family. But there was something she could do instead.

She detoured by her rooms to pick up warmer outer clothes before she exited the Palace. Herran, the evening after the midwinter festival, was quiet. Its inhabitants were still recovering from the previous evening's revelry. The near emptiness of the streets was disconcerting. Elen-ai was accustomed to the city resonating with the sounds of life at any time of day or night. Walking through the empty streets in the cold night air was quite eerie, and Elen-ai hurried to the Family's home. On a whim, she chose one of the roof entrances, and scaled the building with practised ease. She enjoyed using her skills. For the briefest moment, it took the worry from her mind. The warmth of the home enveloped her as soon as she stepped inside. After the cold stone walls of the Palace, it was blissful. A Mother appeared by her side almost instantly.

"Was I so loud?" Elen-ai asked. She didn't think that she had been at all perceptible in her entrance.

"Are you worried that you are losing the finesse of the Family?" A slightly sardonic smile kissed her Mother's lips. Evidently she did not view Elen-ai's presence in the Palace with favour.

"I have news, if you will hear it," Elen-ai replied in an even voice rather than the snapped response she instinctively wished to give.

Without any word of acknowledgment, her Mother led Elen-ai through the house. Even if she might disapprove of Elen-ai's open support for Gidyon, Elen-ai was still a daughter of the Family. Whatever information she brought would not be heard standing in an entranceway.

In a small room, Elen-ai's Mother poured tea that had been left on a low table ahead of their entrance by unseen hands. The Family had no fine Katan ceramics, nor did they have any of the achingly beautiful but outrageously expensive glass tumblers of the Palace. Instead, she was handed a simple clay cup, which itself was a luxury. Many drank from crudely carved wooden vessels.

As she sat on the floor, Elen-ai wondered if this room had been chosen on purpose. Was the absence of any furniture other than the table a silent jibe, suggesting that she was growing soft in the Palace surrounded by finery and luxury? She told herself not to be paranoid. Perhaps she had grown too accustomed to Palace life, seeing political messages in even the most mundane things. She looked down at the still water of her tea as she raised the cup to her lips. When she had been very young, she had been required to drink tea without creating any trace of the cup's passage from table to mouth on the water's surface. It had been a difficult task to master and the hours she had spent practising it were still burned into her memory. Now, she didn't have to even think about it. Whenever she lifted any vessel to her lips, whatever was in it remained as still as if it was not moving at all.

"Now. Your news." Her Mother sipped the tea, the picture of composed serenity.

"Halen Katan has officially requested that Gidyon recognise his granddaughter's legal claim to the throne and abdicate immediately."

Her mother offered no reaction.

"You seem perturbed by this," her Mother commented after she had taken another sip.

"The girl has neither claim nor aptitude to rule," Elen-ai replied.

"What does it concern the Family if some incompetent girl sits on the throne? It is not our way to hold an opinion on the politics of the Second Country."

"Unless the politics of the Second Country endanger the Family," Elem-ai noted.

"And how might an unseasoned girl be a danger to the Family, exactly?"

"She has too many ties to the Katan family. Not enough people would accept her on the throne. Civil war could come to the Queendom. If it reaches the streets of Herran, who knows what damage could be wrought. Our children who are not of an age to defend themselves may be placed in harm's way." One of the main reasons that Elen-ai had been sent back to the Palace was so she could alert the Family to any possibility of warfare so that they could move their children to safety well ahead of time. The Family would always protect its own.

"Very true. While unsurprising, Halen Katan's move is an unfortunate one indeed." The Mother sipped her tea calmly, as though they were not discussing the possibility of a terrible and destructive civil war.

"We should—" Elen-ai began.

"We should do nothing other than protect ourselves," her Mother interrupted firmly, the first suggestion of emotion in her voice.

"But surely we protect our own better if we can affect the outcome of such a struggle," Elen-ai said.

Her Mother raised an eyebrow. "You do not speak as though you are a member of the Family, Elen-ai." There was definitely the edge of a rebuke in her comment now.

"I am a loyal Daughter of the Family, my Mother, but that loyalty does not mean that I do not question, do not disagree," Elen-ai countered. She paused, expecting a rebuke or retort, but when she met only silence, she continued. "I know that you may think I have misstepped in becoming close to the King, but that does not make my thoughts any less valid. We find ourselves in times when precedent and history have already been overturned. If there is sufficient threat to the stability of the Queendom then perhaps the Family may find neutrality is not possible to maintain. I think neutrality is a fine position to hold, but perhaps not in all matters, when the consequences are so..." She trailed off under the severe gaze of her Mother, worried she might have overstepped her place.

For what seemed like an eternity, there was silence in the room. Elen-ai sipped her tea to disguise her uncertainty. Finally, her Mother spoke. "You have raised a good point, my Daughter. I cannot say that it will lead us into battle on behalf of the boy-king, but it certainly is something that we must consider."

Relief flooded Elen-ai's body. She hadn't realised how afraid she had been of the response to her words. "All I ask is that the perspective which my place within the Palace may offer be heard."

Elen-ai hadn't long left the home when she came across two people huddled in a doorway. The sound of their hammering practically assaulted her ears in the deserted streets. The unusualness of someone out on the streets after midwinter, let alone someone doing any form of work, prickled along her senses. She took a few steps toward the pair. Despite the meagre illumination only offered by light spilling through the windows of surrounding buildings, she could easily see them thanks to the skills of the Family. One of the people was nailing a notice into the timber door.

Elen-ai's first thought was that it was an eviction notice, but to deliver such news on the evening after midwinter, particularly a bitterly cold one such as this, was unlikely. Plus, like many of the houses in Herran, it was built from a mix of timber and wood, the reasonably solid construction and well-painted shutters suggesting that it was a successful store. She reflexively pulled the shadows around her, further concealing herself from view. Within a moment, the pair moved on. One held a large stack of pages. Truly troubled, Elen-ai went over to read the notice.

What she saw had her biting back a yell of anger.

She ripped the notice down and ran to the Palace, straight to Gidyon's rooms by the shortest route: the wall. As she had known he would be, he was still at work. Two huge stacks of paper were placed on either side of him. He did not seem particularly surprised when she unlatched the window and climbed through it.

"I always enjoy the new and exciting ways you come to see me, Elen-ai," he said, barely looking up as he placed a page onto the pile to his right.

"Halen is putting up announcements that he's demanded you recognise Serenah's legal claim to the throne." The words all but tumbled over each other as they left Elen-ai's lips. She held out the crumpled notice for him to see.

Gidyon stared at her for a second, his blue eyes flat. "Of course he is."

"He really is a right bastard," Elen-ai said.

"Well, we cannot send out people to try to tear them down. It will simply look as though I am afraid the claim is valid. I will have to respond."

"Try to get some sleep tonight," Elen-ai suggested, knowing that he almost certainly wouldn't.

"I will try. Thank you, Elen-ai. We are lucky you happened upon this now." Already, his mind was working on what he would do. Elen-ai could see it in the way his eyes no longer were quite focusing on her. There was no point in staying. She had no suggestion on how he should respond other than poisoning the entire Katan family. Despite how desperately she would have loved to undertake such a task, she knew her suggestion would not be taken up.

Figuring that her exit from Gidyon's rooms would perturb the guards outside given they hadn't seen her go in, Elen-ai went back out the window, easily moving around the outside of the Palace. She was halfway to her own rooms when she changed her mind.

The light still burned in Kaine's room, too. He looked up from the book he was reading in bed as she came through his window. Despite his surprise at her entrance, he remained reasonably composed. "What are you doing here?"

"I went to inform the Family of Halen's letter," she said.

"Thank you for telling me?" His confusion was dulled by the slight smile that touched his lips.

"Well, my bed will be cold. But you're already in yours." She closed the window and stepped toward the bed. She probably should have told him about the proclamations that Halen had put around Herran, but she selfishly wanted just a few more hours where she could forget about the actions of such a greedy, callous man.

The hint of a smile broadened into an outright grin as he put the book aside.

TEN

"Well, one thing I have to say for him, Halen has played this masterfully," Gidyon admitted a few days later, striding into the council chamber whose walls were papered with more maps, charts, and notes than ever. The room had been transformed into a space of political war council, inhabited almost constantly by some combination of Gidyon, Elen-ai, Silius, Nikalus, and Kaine. From within the room, they had coordinated the sending and receiving of messages across the Second Country, mapping out the political terrain as news from spies in the seven households and across the Second Country reached them. So far, the Veertaks had unequivocally declared their support for Gidyon, while the Bertaks had declared their support for Serenah. The remaining five families had failed to declare, although the Tak and Aardan were almost certainly going to release a declaration of neutrality within the coming days. That left the Rasatan and Harete families as the deciding factors. That was not a prospect with which Elen-ai felt comfortable, especially as Gidyon's exchange with Rania had led him to believe that her family would renege on their promise to support him.

"I think things are almost certainly going to come to a battle," Gidyon continued.

"Of the wits?" Elen-ai asked hopefully.

"If that is what eventuates, obviously we should send you in, Elen-ai."

The levity of the exchange poorly concealed the deep dismay they both felt over the fact that all of Gidyon's efforts to delegitimise Halen's actions had failed.

"What has happened now?" Kaine asked.

Gidyon strode over to the table where food and drinks had been placed hours before and picked up a small bread loaf. While Elen-ai thought to herself that he probably could be eating something slightly less stale, she was nevertheless glad that he was eating anything at all. Besides, the fine flour with which Palace bread was made was probably better stale than the coarse stuff used to make breads in the lowborn areas. He chewed as he composed his response, looking with slight disdain at the roll in his hand as he registered that it was far from fresh. With a shrug, he swallowed and took another bite. "It seems that, even though I did not enact the full reforms I wanted to thanks to the Council's objection, the minor change I made to how Herran's judges operate has been raised as evidence of tampering with the legal system."

"But that's nonsense," Silius exclaimed. He stood up, stepping around a precarious stack of books that Kaine had placed there the day before and ordered nobody touch, and looked at one of the pages Gidyon obligingly pulled from a pile with his free hand. So much communication had flooded in and out of the palace that Elen-ai couldn't understand how Gidyon kept track of one particular page.

"How many lowborn know enough about the legal system to know that what Halen's saying is nonsense, though?" Nikalus pointed out to his older brother. "Consider all they will take from such a claim: the King has tampered with the law to serve his own ends."

"Anyway," Gidyon said, cutting across his uncles' exchange. "Apparently the legal response that we spent so many sleepless nights crafting is invalid because of the tampering with the legal system that I have apparently conducted." He did a magnificent job of concealing his frustration with the futile effort that had been expended, but Elen-ai could see it in the clench of his jaw, nevertheless.

"I could have done so many better things with those nights," Kaine grumbled. He threw a glance at Elen-ai who quickly looked down to hide her smile. Regardless of how little sleep either of them had got, she had managed to make her way to Kaine's bed every night. She had only ever slept beside someone for several consecutive nights once before, and that had been so that she could get close to a contract. The woman had been an acceptable bedmate, but she had snored, which irritated Elen-ai. Fortunately, Kaine did not snore.

"All of us could have," Gidyon said, either ignoring or missing the implication behind Kaine's comment.

"Anyway, with this new accusation, he has an excuse to march against Herran and take it by force."

"The people of Herran will never stand to have the city taken by one of the Seven Families – especially not one that seizes it with an army," Elen-ai's response was a kneejerk comment. The idea that one of the Families might try to claim Herran as their own was repulsive to anyone who had been born in the city. The importance of the families being kept at a safe distance from the crown was taught to all children of Herran. It was vital to the security and stability of the country.

"If the streets are overrun, they may have no choice but to yield to him," Gidyon replied grimly.

"And Halen has the knowledge of warfare and combat to take Herran?" Kaine asked.

"At this stage, I honestly would not be surprised if he had been studying warfare for years." Gidyon sounded tired. "But superior numbers alone may make up for any lack of finesse on his part in any case."

"You know, I really don't like him," Nikalus said conversationally.

The unexpected sarcasm caused everybody in the room to chuckle, even Silius. It was a welcome relief from the imminent prospect of war tearing the Second Country apart. Almost immediately, however, sobriety returned to the room.

"We need to ask the Veertaks if they are willing to send troops to our aid," Gidyon said as he went over to stand in front of the map of Herran pinned to a wall.

"Even if they do agree, they don't have a large number of trained fighters who they could send to us," Silius replied. It seemed his information network rivalled even the Family; they hadn't been able to give Elen-ai any idea of how many trained fighters the Veertak family actually had in their employ. She tucked both the knowledge of Silius' spies and the number of Veertak fighters away in her mind to report back to the Family.

"And the Royal Guard is how many people?" Gidyon asked.

"A few hundred strong," Nikalus answered.

Gidyon turned to Elen-ai. "Do you think we could ask the people of Herran for help?"

She considered the question, standing and pouring herself a drink to give herself time to think. "I think some people would be willing to fight for the city. The Katan are not well loved by the lowborn of Herran. Some – those for whom the prospect of a man on the throne is still too much to bear – may actually march themselves over to Halen, although I think most will simply stay in their homes and hope that whatever strife occurs does not touch them."

"Some is better than none, though," Gidyon said.

"Yes, but how do you propose we use them? Give them a sword and point them at Halen and his forces?" Silius asked, his nose wrinkling in disdain at the idea.

"I'd put them in drills with the Royal Guard as soon as possible," Elen-ai suggested, unsure if Silius' question was even directed at her. "And I wouldn't give them swords. Spears, perhaps, may be easier for them to use." The image of a group of people who had never held a sword before swinging them wildly was a horrifying prospect.

"The Royal Guard exists to protect the Palace, not to train people off the street," Nikalus protested.

"The Royal Guard won't be able to protect the Palace if Herran is overtaken by Katan fighters. Besides, who else would you have train the city's lowborn to fight for us?" Kaine said.

"I think Nik has a point, Kaine," Silius said. "You can't disrupt the daily routine of the Royal Guard. It is important that it doesn't look as though we are panicking. Perception of Gidyon's control may be just as important as our ability to defeat Katan forces on a battlefield, if not more so. There is more than one battle going on here."

"Let those who are willing to fight for us train with the Palace Guard." Gidyon's decision halted the disagreement between his uncles and Elen-ai. "And maybe see if any of Herran's duelling competitors would be willing to join our people, as well. They at least will be able to use a sword. Nik, would you make the arrangements?"

Nikalus shot a glare at Kaine before stalking from the room, punctuating his irritation with a toss of his blond hair.

"Should I have worded my decision more nicely?" Gidyon wondered aloud once Nikalus had left. Concern flitted across his features.

"He'll be fine," Silius reassured him. "We're family. You don't have to worry about politics or diplomacy with us. Even if we disagree privately, we will all always support you in public. And we will do everything possible to make sure you win this."

Even though Elen-ai did not always find Silius to be the most palatable company – he was a bit too pompous and too severe – in moments when he spoke with such quiet effusiveness and loyalty, she could not find someone she respected more. She had seen Silius' unwavering loyalty to Gidyon in enormous amounts over the days since Halen's ultimatum had arrived. And she had seen how Gidyon in turn drew strength from the support of not simply Silius, but all his uncles. If the bonds of family alone were sufficient to guarantee victory, the Royal Family would win any challenge.

"Sil is right, Gid," Kaine said. "We're in this together."

Gidyon sighed, his shoulders slumping as he let go of his rigid self-control for a moment. He ran a hand through the spun gold of his hair and sat down for the first time since he had entered the room.

The door slammed open and Nikalus re-entered, a letter in his hand. "I'm sorry, Gid," he said, his face grave. Any trace of his frustration at his nephew's disagreement with him had vanished.

Gidyon's face fell even further. He took the linen page from Nikalus. He read it twice then hurled it to the floor. He stood, completely rigid, then quietly said, "I need a moment," before striding from the room.

"The Harete family has declared for the Katan claim," Nikalus explained to the perplexed Elen-ai, Silius, and Kaine.

"Janyce is Halen's niece, it's not entirely surprising," Kaine pointed out as he gave a worried glance toward the door through which Gidyon had left.

"But she and the rest of the Harete family despise one another," Silius said.

"Perhaps being situated between the Katan and Bertak lands might have been a compelling reason to throw their lot in with them," Nikalus suggested.

Elen-ai walked over to the map, looking at the way the Harete forest was bordered by the clay-rich soil of the Katan lands and the mountainous Bertak estate. The dense forest would likely make assaulting the Harete family with outright force difficult, if not impossible. But there were many threats that could be levelled against them other than direct attack. If the Bertak and Katan forces blockaded the forest, then the Harete family would be cut off from the outside world, unable to export the timber from which they made their fortune, and unable to bring in any supplies. The threat alone of such action might be enough to foster the allegiance of the Haretes. That certainly was what Elen-ai would do in Halen's position. She shook her head. She was starting to think like a warmonger, not an assassin.

"Are we certain that they will all march on Herran?" she asked.

"I would be surprised if they didn't," Nikalus answered. He sounded so worn down.

"He always knew it would come to this, didn't he?" Elen-ai said.

The war maps, the correspondence with the military expert, the plans within plans. Gidyon had known all along that this was going to be the outcome of his power struggle with Halen, and he had been preparing for it even as he tried to avert it. The weight of trying to prevent a war on the shoulders of a seventeen-year-old boy seemed criminally unfair. Elen-ai hated Halen not only because of his greed for power and delusions of grandeur, but also for what he was doing to her friend. She could go without sleep, she could use any weapon put in her hands and improvise several more, she could taste the most subtle of poisons, she could weave the shadows about her so that nobody could see her. But she was as hopeless and helpless as she had ever been in that moment. There was nothing that she could do to help ease the burden that had been placed on Gidyon.

Gidyon's uncles were silent, perhaps having arrived at that conclusion before her. She turned from the map to look at the three men, varying expressions of dismay and concern drawn across their faces. She felt tears prick her eyes at the unfairness of the situation. "I'm going to check on Gid," she said, and left the room before anything else could be said.

The King was simply standing just a few paces down the cold corridor, staring out a window. The two guards outside the war room's door regarded him with uncertainty, but he did not appear to notice the scrutiny.

Elen-ai stood beside him. The guards shuffled back, giving them a measure of privacy. Gidyon said nothing, his attention focused on the garden below. An unpleasant wind buffeted the winter-blooming flowers, their ice-blue petals bringing no sense of warmth to the scene. That same wind forced its way through the cracks in the walls and windows. At least, Elen-ai reflected as she waited for Gidyon to speak, shutters – what most buildings had, given the expense of glass – kept wind out completely, even if it also kept out light, too.

"Why won't they support me?" he asked in a low voice. The confused heartbreak on his face was devastating.

She delivered that brutal truth as gently as she could. "They don't believe in you, Gid."

"They don't believe in me?" he repeated, his incomprehension mingling with hurt.

"I know you, and I know you're a wonderful ruler. But most people haven't had the opportunity to see that. So all they see on the throne is the sort of person they've always been taught needs to be kept away from it – a man."

"I know all this." Gidyon waved his hand in a tired motion. "I just ... what do I need to do to change their minds?" He sounded so defeated. That terrified Elen-ai.

"Most people do want to believe in you, Gid," she said.

"So how do I give them something to believe in?"

"Defeat Halen, prove that this is your throne and you can – and will – hold it."

"Ah yes, I'll just do that, then." His mouth curved in an acerbic half-smile.

"I know." She chuckled.

"Sometimes this all seems so impossible, that there is no way for me to beat Halen," he admitted.

"If it helps," Elen-ai paused and put her hand on top of his where it rested on the sill. His skin was already cold. "I believe in you, Gidyon."

He tore his gaze from the garden and looked at her. The defeated look was gone from his face, replaced with his usual composed determination. "It does."

Gidyon strode back into the council room with renewed resolve, Elen-ai following him, his customary shadow.

"All right, what must we do to ensure we defeat Halen Katan?" he asked.

"I think we need to ask the Aadran and Tak families to support us," Nikalus suggested, as though Gidyon had never left.

The proposal was met with a sceptical look from the King, who had gone once more to regard the map on the wall.

"They have very little need to throw their lot in with anyone," Silius pointed out. "Their wealth is so significant and the alliance between their families so strong, that their position within the Second Country is quite secure, regardless of the outcome."

Gidyon turned, the beginnings of an idea written across his face. He pushed back the strands of hair that had fallen across his eyes and stared off into the distance. After he had turned the thought over in his mind sufficiently, he said, "I might have a way to push the Aadran family into feeling that supporting me is in their best interests." He looked at Elen-ai. She immediately understood his line of thought.

Even though almost nobody had known for certain about the relationship between Zekken Aadran and Queen Latana, Zekken had admitted to Elen-ai that his mother, the formidable Aadran matriarch, was aware that something illicit had existed between her son and her queen. When she had first learned this, Elen-ai had even entertained the suspicion that Arlena had been behind the first attack on Gidyon and Latana to ensure that her family would be protected. If anyone had uncovered the breach of the sacred neutrality between the throne and the Seven Families, both Latana and the Aadran family would have been utterly ruined. While it was a compelling motive to seek murder – indeed, the Family had been engaged for far more trivial reasons – Elenai had ultimately decided that Arlena was not the kind of woman to order an assassination that failed. She was, however, the kind of woman to go to great lengths to protect her family's reputation and position of power. Even the Taks, whose business and family were entwined with the Aadrans, would desert them if the truth came out. Perhaps Gidyon did in fact have something that might be used to prevail upon Arlena to persuade the Tak family that it was in the best interests of both clans to support him.

"What do you mean?" Silius did not hide either his confusion or the desperate hope in his voice.

"I think I may be able to convince Arlena to support us, and to persuade the Taks to support us, too," Gidyon said, refusing to elaborate, to his uncles' visible consternation. They did not know what his mother had done, and he would keep it that way.

"You'd need to get there quickly," Elen-ai said.

"And discreetly," he replied, an excited smile dawning on his face. It was the first time she had seen true hope in his face since Halen's letter had arrived.

"I assume we're thinking the same thing?" she confirmed, unable to hide a smile of her own. The idea of travelling once more with Gidyon across the Second Country, just the two of them, was lovely, despite the circumstances.

He nodded.

"Would we be riding kittanae?" Elen-ai asked, unable to keep the excitement from her voice. She often visited the wonderful beasts, but had never ridden on one. She was most keen to, although she would never have admitted that aloud.

"I am certain that we could arrange that."

She had to restrain herself from clapping in childish delight.

"Are you honestly suggesting just the two of you travel across the country to try to convince two families to lend their forces to ours? You can't be serious," Silius objected.

"It is the only way we will get there and back in time," Gidyon told his uncle. The expression on his face made it clear that the King had made up his mind.

Silius opened his mouth to object, then threw his hands up in resignation. "If this is what you want to do, you know I am unable to stop you. But this carries with it an incredible risk."

"If this is what Gid thinks is best, Sil, maybe it is what's best," Kaine said, his own reservations obvious in his expression, despite the support he voiced.

Silius relented with a nod, although the tight press of his lips spoke loudly of his disapproval.

They farewelled the Councillors from the Third Country later that day. The bitter wind had abated, leaving the chill to hang in the air. The air outside was like a knife, so still and so cold that it felt like it cut into Elen-ai's skin. Freya was almost lost to sight under the mountain of scarves and throws that engulfed her. Councilman Hart did not seem to struggle as much with the cold, but he too looked as though he would be happier when they reached the warmer climate of the Third Country.

>From underneath the fur-lined hood that almost completely covered her face, Freya smiled at Elen-ai. She engulfed Elen-ai's hands in her own gloved ones. "I have greatly enjoyed getting to know you."

"And I you," Elen-ai told her. "Although, it's good you're leaving now, before things get worse."

"I will be praying that the Goddess watches over you and Gidyon," Freya replied. "He is a good king to your people. I wish we could stay and help."

"This is not your fight." Elen-ai smiled at the earnestness in Freya's voice. She really would miss her.

"When – not if – you prevail, will you come to the Third Country?" The Councilwoman looked hopeful.

"I've never been," Elen-ai admitted.

"Then you must come. As my guest," the other woman insisted.

Elen-ai relented with a laugh. "I promise I will visit you."

As she watched the two Councillors confer quietly with Gidyon, Elen-ai realised how sad she was that Freya was leaving. Freya had saved Gidyon's life, and she and Ashtyn were the only people outside the Family who actually understood the gifts of faith. But, as saddened as she was by their departure, Elen-ai knew that the foreigners should not be caught in the oncoming conflict. As she had said, this was not their fight.

"You should reach the border without much trouble, although I still worry," Gidyon said. "Are you sure that you do not wish to be escorted by Royal Guards?"

Elen-ai did not need to see Freya's face to know that the woman was smiling.

"I'm sure we'll be safe," Ashtyn said, amusement in his voice.

Elen-ai had seen Freya kill several attackers without laying a hand on them. Her formidable gift did not just heal but could also be used to kill. She was all the protection they might need.

"Be safe, King Gidyon. We will wait to hear news of your victory." Ashtyn's voice was formal and strong, carrying clearly across the still air of the courtyard. "Your hospitality and friendship will not be forgotten."

As the foreigners' carriage left the Palace courtyard, Nikalus murmured something in Gidyon's ear. The King strode over to Elen-ai.

"I am sorry that they are leaving," he told her softly.

"Me too," she replied.

He placed his hand on her shoulder. "If you are ready, we will set out for the Aadran estate tomorrow. The preparations have been made."

"Provided it doesn't rain, we should be able to make it in just over three days' hard riding."

"Thank you for coming with me, Elen-ai," he said.

"I'll always come with you, my King," she told him.

They stayed side by side in the knife-cold air, watching as the Councillors' carriage made its way down the hill until it turned a corner and was lost from sight.

ELEVEN

Light and heat from the fire blossomed across the ground. As was so often the case, the King was lost in his own thoughts, staring into the fire as its light flickered across his face. He drew the fur-lined cloak more tightly about him as a penetrating breeze whispered across the night. The heat of the combat training they had undertaken earlier had long since faded from her muscles, replaced by the slight ache caused be three days of hard riding. Elen-ai had been instructing Gidyon in the craft of fighting almost every day since the first time they had travelled across the Second Country. Gidyon had always stubbornly found time in his days to be given instruction by Elen-ai, even if it was late at night or early in the morning. Even out on the road, he refused to cease training, despite the weariness the hard travel visibly imposed upon him. Elen-ai had not protested when he insisted. He may be required to put those skills to use quite soon, and while her punishing instruction, building on top of his life of sword lessons, had made him a better than average fighter, she wanted to ensure he had every chance to win in a fight. That meant practice.

This was their third and final night of travel. The kittanae had been as magnificent as Elen-ai hoped they would be. Despite the trepidation which had engulfed her when she first approached them in the palace yard on the morning of their departure, the beast on which she rode – Hlevan – had purred when she stroked its coat, and docilely allowed her to mount it. The ground had flown by underneath the powerful gait of the animals over the days of travel. The curious motion of the animal's movements underneath her had at first been disorienting, but Elen-ai eventually accustomed herself to it. She could understand why the animals were so highly sought.

Fish slowly cooked in the coals of the fire. Occasionally, the flames danced with particular intensity, and the water in Lake Aadran would flash with the light. Mostly though, the lake made itself known in the gentle sound of the water lapping against the shore. Were it not for the pressing need to reach the Aadran house, and the deep chill of winter, the serenity of the night would have been quite absorbing.

Elen-ai broke the silence. "I think Kaine may know about Zekken."

Gidyon spared her only the most fleeting of glances. "What did he say to you?"

She thought back to the conversation that had occurred in his bedchamber the evening before their departure.

It had been deliciously warm in his room. As they lay together, limbs heavy with sated drowsiness, Kaine had said, "Do you really think that Gidyon will be able to threaten Arlena into supporting him? She may consider the threat more easily resolved by joining forces with Halen."

The pleasant afterglow had sloughed off her at Kaine's inference he knew about Zekken and Latana's relationship.

Kaine must have seen the shock on her face. "So you do know. You really are blindly loyal to Gid, you know."

"I am not."

"What of his secrets don't you know?" Elen-ai couldn't tell if he was angry or simply curious.

"Does it bother you that I'm this close to him?"

"Do you want me to be jealous?"

Infuriated to have him question her relationship with Gidyon, she rolled out of the bed near-impossible speed. She did not want to play these games, especially not with Kaine. The hide-and-seek of discovering someone else's feelings or thoughts was tiring enough in every other part of the Court. Kaine's questions about her loyalty to Gidyon went too far. Her friendship with the King was not to be subject to the same scrutiny as everything else in the world of the Palace. She should have known better than to be indirect with someone who had grown up playing the games of the Court.

He reached after her. "Don't worry. I'll never speak of it. I only bring it up because I do wonder if Gid is taking the best course of action here."

After a second's hesitation, she had allowed him to pull her back onto the bed and close to him. He kissed her, his mouth was warm and sweet. He broke their kiss long enough to whisper in her ear. "Just come back in one piece."

"Elen-ai?"

Gidyon's voice, and the chill of the night air. brought her back to the present. The tingle the cold breeze left on her bare skin was not dissimilar to the way her skin felt underneath Kaine's fingertips. Gidyon was looking at her expectantly.

"He didn't say much. I just think he might know about Latana and Zekken."

Gidyon gave a long sigh. "I don't suppose it really matters. He would never speak of it. What unsettles me is the scope of the carelessness my mother seems to have demonstrated."

Elen-ai idly weaved shadows around her, flicking her outstretched forearms in and out of sight. "I think very few people were in a position to ever guess. Kaine was one of them. He is also quite perceptive about certain things – things like this. More so than Silius or Nikalus."

Gidyon's gaze fell to her arms. "You like him."

She pulled the shadows up to her shoulders. "I suppose I do," she admitted.

"Am I correct in remembering that anyone in the Family who wants to marry and have children must leave the Family?"

"I don't want to marry and bear children." Her response was a reflexive one. "And I don't really think Kaine does either," she added thoughtfully.

"That was not what I meant," Gidyon said.

Elen-ai slipped the shadows over her completely so that she vanished from sight.

"Sorry, I do not mean to make things awkward," Gidyon said, perhaps worrying that he had pried too far and her disappearance from sight was her way of saying as much. "I am glad that you and Kaine have each other – for as long or as little as that may last. You are both very dear to me."

"And we would both do anything for you," Elen-ai reappeared into view to tell him, before flickering back out of sight.

The King shook his head as though trying to clear it as he looked at Elen-ai, or rather, the blank space where she sat. "I beg that you stop that. I am getting a spectacular headache watching you. Just decide if I can see you or not."

Elen-ai tightened the weave of the shadows around her. When she spoke, her voice would have seemed disembodied to Gidyon. "Better?"

"Oh, much." The dry sarcasm in his voice made Elen-ai chuckle.

"How do you do that, anyway?" he asked.

Elen-ai slipped the shadows down to her neck. Her head floated seemingly out of nowhere. "I just find the shadows and give them, well, a bit of a tug."

"A bit of a tug?" Gidyon made no effort to hide his incredulous amusement.

"I don't know how to describe it," Elen-ai said. "I just find the shadows near me and pull them over me."

"Do you have to think about your god when you do it?" The light of the fire turned Gidyon's blue eyes orange-yellow.

"I never have to think about the Shadow God," Elen-ai replied. "My faith is always just there." She made a gesture with her hand to emphasise the comment, but realised that she was still shielding it from view.

"But do you draw on that faith?" Gidyon asked.

"I've never really thought about it. My belief in the Shadow God has always been there. I've always been certain. I don't know what it would feel like to not have faith."

Gidyon held his hands out in front of him. A slight frown crossed his face, then the darkness around his splayed fingers receded as his hands began to glow ever so slightly. It was similar to what Elen-ai had seen around the priestess of the Divine One's hands when she had inadvertently intruded into Gidyon's religious instruction. But something about seeing the light at the King's fingertips scared her. No ruler had commanded the light of the sun. To summon light was the stuff of legends, from a time when gods and humans had walked hand in hand. For Gidyon to have true faith and be able to harness the power of the Divine One's light was as unprecedented in the Second Country as a man on the throne.

Elen-ai told herself to stop being foolish. If she was going to think that way, she was just as much a figure of legend as Gidyon. Her playing with shadows would have terrified any casual observer. If anyone were ever to witness that, she would be just as quickly relegated to a figure from legend as Gidyon would – just like Freya from the Second Country, who could heal and kill with a thought. It was simply disconcerting to see Gidyon's faith manifest so clearly. He had kept his piety hidden, and as such, his ability to command light was unexpected. Shadows were different. They were everywhere, easily found and easily moulded. To manipulate shadows seemed to her far less awe inspiring than summoning light in the middle of the night.

"How long have you been able to do that?" she asked. She loosened her grip on the shadows as she looked intently at the light in Gidyon's hands. They fell away and the rest of her reappeared to sight.

He shrugged, his eyes still on the yellow-bright light surrounding his fingertips. "Always, I think. But for a long time I never paid it much attention. When I was little, I thought everyone could do it, and then I thought that it was just my imagination."

"So when you realised that Freya had healed you—"

"I knew that I had not been imagining things," Gidyon said.

"How do you make the light appear?"

He made a little motion with his head that could have meant anything. "I do not really know how to explain it. Maybe I just find the light and give it a little tug." He turned to look at her, a cheeky smile on his face.

"Just because you're the king and able to summon light, doesn't mean you can be smug about it. Can you do anything else with the light?"

In reply he turned his hand to face up. The light slipped down from his fingertips to form a glowing sphere that rested in his palm. The shadows it cast clashed with those from the fire. Then Gidyon closed his hand and the light went out.

"It is not as though I could ever do anything with it," Gidyon said, the faintest suggestion of disappointment in his voice. "It would scare people far too much."

Elen-ai agreed with him, but did not say as much. She thought it might hurt him to hear that opinion corroborated.

They remained silent for a while, each preoccupied with their own thoughts.

"What are you thinking?" he asked, eventually.

"How do you plan to deal with Zekken?" She finally asked the question had been with her since they left Herran.

She glanced at him.

He was pressing his lips together in thought. "I do not know," he admitted finally.

"He might be able to persuade Arlena to support you if she refuses," Elen-ai said.

"I know," he replied. "I have been wondering whether or not I should appeal to her through him. I do not know that I want to owe him a favour, though."

"Do you really think he'd call that favour in?" she asked.

"Not really. But I do not want to owe him anything."

"And if that's what it takes to secure your crown?"

Gidyon sighed. The sound carried the weight of his anger at his mother and Zekken. "Then I will do it."

Elen-ai reached across the space between them and placed a hand on his shoulder. It was all the comfort she could offer him.

"You know, I have never actually spoken with him about it. Any of it," Gidyon said.

Of course Elen-ai knew, but she also knew that it was his way of telling her that he wanted to discuss this matter. "Do you want to?"

"Not really. It would be too dangerous. Besides, he might not even be my father." Gidyon reached to examine the progress of the fish.

Elen-ai didn't point out that having Zekken as a father was probably preferable to being Erek's son. While Zekken had conducted a dangerous illicit love affair with Latana for years, at least he hadn't stabbed her before Gidyon's eyes.

"I think the fish is ready," Gidyon said before Elen-ai could say anything else. Deftly, he flicked the fish from the coals.

"I still can't believe you know how to fish," Elen-ai muttered as she watched him.

Gidyon declined to respond to her comment, skewering the fish and handing one to her. The flesh practically fell off the bones. Steam from the fish rose into the cold night air. The meal was plain but satisfying, and the fact that the fish was so hot it all but burned her mouth was a welcome warmth.

"Seriously, where did you learn to catch and cook fish?" Elen-ai asked as she waited for a piece to cool. She threw the tail across to the kittanae who were curled together nearby. They raised their heads with intelligent interest and fought gently over the scrap.

Gidyon gave a smug smile. "The Herran market," he told her. Until his mother's death, Gidyon had gone to the markets in Herran every week. Elen-ai had accompanied him once. She had seen for herself that he had friends there. It wasn't unsurprising to think that one of them might have taught him to fish.

"Surely there wouldn't be that many fish in Herran's harbour," Elen-ai said between bites. "Too many boats, and too many people fishing."

"There weren't," Gidyon replied. "That is what made it tricky."

"Did you even ever catch any fish?" Elen-ai asked.

"Of course I did." She could hear the smugness in his voice.

"Outrageous," she muttered. "Do you miss going there?"

It was a silly question. Gidyon had passionately argued with his mother that he should be allowed to continue visiting the market, even when Latana feared there was a threat against his life. Of course he was going to miss that weekly outing, along with many other parts of his old life.

"Often."

"Why don't you go there, then?"

Gidyon scratched the bridge of his nose. "I am their king. Not their prince, not the son of the queen. I rule them. I cannot walk among them like I am one of them." The sadness in his voice was unmissable, as was the certainty that signalled the decision was a final one.

Despite the fact that she knew he was the king, that he ruled the Second Country, Elen-ai had never truly felt what exactly that meant until that moment. She looked out beyond the fire. Here, as with the Tak lands, the Aadran estate was flat plains.

The lake was a smooth sheet of water that had settled itself into a dip in the endless fields of grain. Mist had risen from the land and was now brushing the lake's surface. The ephemeral conglomeration which could have been mistaken for smoke, were it not so far away from the fire, moved across the surface of the water with an imperceptible slowness. It seemed so preposterous that she was sitting here in the biting chill of winter, looking at this sight beside her king. Gidyon was her friend. She had seen him cry, rage, struggle with who he was, and other people's perceptions of who he was. But he was not simply that friend, but also her ruler, and the ruler of everybody within the Second Country. Try as she might, Elen-ai couldn't quite touch that reality even as she comprehended it.

They lapsed back into silence as they ate the fish, the crackle of the fire and the almost inaudible lapping of the lake's waves enough sound for them. The quietude of the open land was so distant from the palace and the constant noise of some activity being undertaken.

After Gidyon had finished his fish and thrown the bones across to the kittanae, he spoke. "Elen-ai?"

"Yes?"

"When will you go back to the Family?" Asking the question, he certainly didn't sound like a self-assured king who knew too well the need to separate himself from his people. He sounded like an uncertain young man.

"I don't know," she admitted.

"But you miss your home."

"I do," she said cautiously. "But I also like being by your side."

"If – when – you go back to the Family, will we still be friends?" There was a childish quality to the question that tugged at Elen-ai's heart.

"Of course we will, Gid." But even as she reassured him, she wondered if that would be true. Assassins and kings did not inhabit each other's worlds, and there were many good reasons for that.

He scrutinised her face for a moment. "I gave you up once. I do not want to do it again." He didn't say it with a great flourish or any significant emotion. It was simply the quiet, emphatic statement of a truth that had curled itself around his heart.

"Gid, I promise that I will do everything I can to ensure that we are still friends."

The ground rustled as Gidyon lifted himself up to kneel, turning to face Elen-ai properly. "I swear before the Divine One that you, Elen-ai of the Family and Shadow God, are my friend, and that friendship is something I will never deny or turn away from."

Profoundly touched, Elen-ai reached across to take his hands. "I swear before the Shadow God, that you Gidyon, my King, are my friend and always will be. I swear that I will never forsake you, nor will I leave you." She offered the vow without even thinking.

His hands tightened around hers, the flickering fire casting light and shadow across their linked forms before he let go.

"It might be silly, but that made me feel better," he admitted.

"Don't think that, Gid," Elen-ai said. She too felt a slight relief. Breaking a vow to a god was not something one could do lightly, especially not when the two people making their oaths had genuine faith. The fact that she and Gidyon had vowed their friendship before their gods somehow made her feel that she and he were now bonded inextricably, that nothing could keep them separate, even if the worlds of an assassin and king were not supposed to meet.

When they were ready to sleep, practically smothered in the furs and blankets that barely kept the cold of the night at bay, the concern that Kaine had managed to instil in her returned. Gidyon was taking the first watch, still seated and facing the fire. Elen-ai had, as she always did, offered to take the watch for the whole evening, but he had refused, as he always had. From her cocoon of tentative warmth, Elen-ai looked at the dark mound that was Gidyon and worried what would happen if Arlena turned on them or failed to support them, despite any promise of ruin with which Gidyon might threaten her.

"Gidyon, how do you know that this plan to get Aadran support will work?" she asked so softly that her voice might have been lost amid the fire's crackle.

He didn't turn around but stayed looking into the fire, but in his reply she could hear his smile. "I have faith," he told her.

TWELVE

The Aadran family home was as imposing as its matriarch. It rose up from the flatlands as they approached. Here was wealth cultivated over generations. The simple elegance of the house's design, visible even from far away, spoke to the absence of need to add any unnecessary flourishes to prove how much power or status the Aadrans had. Despite the suggestion of rain hinted in the smudge of clouds that hovered on the horizon, crisp winter sun had shone on Elen-ai and Gidyon's morning. That sun now shone on the Aadran home, glinting off the building's many windows.

The current inhabitants of the Aadran residence in Herran, servants and one or two minor family members, had been notified of Gidyon and Elen-ai's impending arrival. They had in turn sent this information on to the Aadran estate by messenger birds. Messages that were trivial – or so time-sensitive that the threat of interception was secondary – were sent among the powerful families of the Second Country by birds. It had been a concern that Zekken may learn of Elen-ai and Gidyon's travel to the Aadran estate and attempt to apprehend the king, but it was a risk they had decided was worth taking. Consequently, a line of people was waiting for the royal visitors in the neatly maintained yard. Elen-ai wondered whether they had been standing there all morning or if someone had spied their approach across the flat land. For her own amusement, she hoped that it was the former.

Arlena headed the line of welcomers. Unusually, Zekken was not by her side. It would not be surprising to learn that she had banished her son and right hand from this particular welcome. As ever, she stood perfectly straight, dressed immaculately in a blood-red tunic and white trousers, hands clasped loosely in front of her.

Gidyon dismounted and handed the reins of the kittanae to a servant who had come forward expectantly. "Lady Aadran." His voice was clear and carried across the manicured yard. "There was no need to go to all this trouble for us."

In reply, Arlena bowed before her king, her servants following suit. Elen-ai stood awkwardly next to Gidyon. She was not required to bow in such circumstances, Gidyon had made that clear. But she still felt silly standing next to Gidyon as everybody bowed to him.

"It is a great honour to be visited by our ruler. No effort is too small," Arlena said once she had straightened. "You must have ridden hard to get here in only three days, even on kittanae. Can we offer you refreshment, or the opportunity to bathe?"

"A bath would be most welcome, Lady Aadran," Gidyon said, allowing her to lead them into the house. As they passed through the grand arch of the doorway, Elen-ai suppressed a gasp. The entrance hall was drenched in quiet opulence. While it didn't quite match the beauty or impressive scale of the Palace's entranceway, the polished stone, rich carpets, and the friezes on the wall painted by the hand of an undisputed master, created a light-filled, spectacular space that had done to Elen-ai exactly what it was designed to impress.

"Welcome to our home," Arlena said, the sweep of her hand drawing the eye to the two staircases that curved away from each other. Between those staircases was the centrepiece of the magnificent entrance: a beautiful shrine to the Divine One. Elen-ai suspected the shrine was a relatively new installation in response to the religious fervour sweeping across the Second Country.

However, it fitted the space perfectly. The gold that coated the sun symbol caught the morning rays shining through the tall windows. The carved iconography that surrounded the sun depicted to the most exquisite detail the faces of the figures who were looking in rapture at the glory of the sun.

"I've never had the good fortune to visit your home, Lady Aadran, but I must confess, it is truly magnificent." Gidyon craned his head to look at the high ceiling – painted with an image of a softly clouded blue sky, like the entrance hall of the Palace.

Arlena gave the barest suggestion of a smile. "You are too kind, my lord. Although this is but a small part of the building."

He returned his gaze to their host. "I look forward to seeing the rest of it, given what I have seen so far."

"And you, lady Elen-ai, what do you think of our home?" An almost imperceptible challenge edged Arlena's voice. Clearly, the Aadran matriarch was well aware what Gidyon had come to ask of her and was going to make them work for everything she might give them.

Elen-ai had in fact been in the Aadran family home on a few occasions, each time under a contract for the Family. Once she had hidden herself in an airing closet on the second storey for two days. From her hiding place, she had listened to the comings and goings of the household, sneaking out only in the middle of the night when the household was asleep to steal food and relieve herself. But despite the time that she had spent here – unnoticed even by her victims as she ended their lives – she had never even glanced at the entrance hall.

"I could not have anticipated how truly beautiful your home is, lady Aadran," she said honestly. "Why, some may say that it even comes close to rivalling the Palace."

Pleased with her own slight jibe, Elen-ai noticed the stern woman's eyes flash ever so slightly. "Gal-an will show you to the rooms we have prepared for you."

They were led up one of the staircases and along several corridors by the servant, who had leapt forward at his mistress' command. The door at which they stopped was an ornate piece of work, painted with an idyllic scene of a field in summer. Before Elen-ai could look too closely at it, Gal-an opened it to reveal one of the most sumptuous rooms Elen-ai had ever seen outside the Palace.

If Elen-ai hadn't known that the Aadran household had only been given three days' notice to prepare the rooms, she never would have thought it. The painted scenes adorning the walls gleamed with a lustre that made them look new. Even the furniture looked as though it had only just been finished, so immaculate was each piece. A fire burned merrily in the fireplace, and from the look of it, had been doing so since at least the early hours of the morning. Katan-made vases nestled in various corners, filled with an assortment of fresh and dried flowers. Normally, that many flowers in winter would have been spectacular on their own, but the fact that the Aadran household had so many Katan vases to simply spread about a room entirely overshadowed the display of wealth and resources that the flowers represented. Katan vases were singularly rare, as most of the clay workers in the Katan pottery houses specialised in bowls or plates. The clay of the Katan estate, despite producing spectacular pieces of crockery, was incredibly difficult to work. Years of training was required to produce a plate of good quality, let alone the delicate and wafer-thin plates that Elen-ai had seen at only the wealthiest of tables. The depth of skill required to craft a vase with the temperamental material was almost virtuosic.

"You have done a magnificent job. I already feel at home." Gidyon's voice was warm as he addressed the servant.

The man regarded Gidyon with a wary amazement. Clearly, he was uncertain about this boy-king, but that uncertainty warred with the astonishment at being given a compliment by his ruler. "We drew baths for you both," he eventually settled on, showing Gidyon and Elen-ai into a bathing chamber that held two huge stone tubs of steaming water. Unseen servants must have scurried only just ahead of them to fill the baths. The two small packs Elen-ai and Gidyon had brought with them had been placed at the foot of a massive bed. They looked utterly out of place in the magnificent room due to its modest size and lack of adornment.

"Thank you," Gidyon said, dismissing the man with the simple inflection of his tone even as he thanked him. It was a trick Elen-ai had seen his mother use when she had first been brought before Queen Latana. It was no less authoritative now than it had been then.

The servant bowed and left the room, enough control instilled in him not to scurry away from the male ruler and his inscrutable companion.

"The Royal suite," Gidyon murmured, perhaps more to himself than to Elen-ai. He turned in a slow circle to observe the fastidiously beautiful surroundings.

"Did they really get all of this ready in only three days?" Elen-ai asked.

"Queens do not often visit the Families, but just in case they do, all of the Families have a room specially prepared for the possibility. The rooms are reserved only for the use of the ruler – it is why we did not stay in any of them last year. Most of the furniture in here has only been used a few times and stays covered when the room is unoccupied. I would assume that they brought in an extra tub for us, though," Gidyon explained as he took off his outermost coat.

Elen-ai thought it was supremely wasteful to have an opulent room that cost more money than she could possibly comprehend almost always empty, but she had long since learned that the lives of those born into wealth and power were by their nature wasteful. She waited in the achingly beautiful room while Gidyon bathed first.

He was quickly out of the bath and Elen-ai slipped into the water of her own tub, grateful that she was out of the clothes coated with mud from the hard, long ride. The water was warm and scented lightly with something that smelled, impossibly, of berries.

"You know they would have given us servants to help us bathe if we had requested it," Gidyon called to her from one of the other rooms. He sounded amused.

Elen-ai dutifully soaped her hair, scraping her fingernails across her scalp to dislodge the grit and grease that had settled there. "That would have been off-putting," she called back.

"What, you mean you do not want people to scrub you down?"

"Normally I wouldn't want to do anything without the assistance of at least one servant," she said sarcastically as she heaved herself out of the tub. Even despite the warmth of the fire, after the heat of the water, her skin prickled once exposed to the cooler air.

"Ah yes, Elen-ai, your hidden preference for luxury and attendance." Gidyon threw her an amused look as she retrieved some clothes from her pack, a towel wrapped firmly around herself.

She dressed quickly, ensuring that her blades were all properly secured underneath her clothes, and turned her attention to her hair. It had grown longer than the short crop she favoured. Water had gathered on the bottoms of the strands, making the back of her neck unpleasantly cold. As she furiously towelled her hair dry, Gidyon shoved a brush in her face.

"What's that?" she asked suspiciously.

"Yet again, your brilliant and honed skills of observation make themselves known," he told her. "A hairbrush."

"Yes, obviously. What's that doing here?" She recoiled from him and it.

"Well, I thought you might like to brush your hair," he said patiently.

She glared at him for a moment, then snatched the brush from his hand.

"You do know how to use it, don't you?" Gidyon asked.

Her response was to turn away from him, struggling with a tangled snarl that had somehow managed to wind itself into her hair.

"Do you really think that Arlena believes we're lovers?" Elen-ai asked, knowing that Gidyon found the assumption many had made about them awkward. Sure enough, when she turned back to look at him, he had an expression of painful discomfort on his face. It was a delightfully petty revenge for making her brush her hair.

"I would imagine there is some doubt, given you are now being called my – what are we calling you now?"

"I think adviser. I must say, I'm surprised people haven't taken more issue with the idea that I'm your lover," she said, taking delicious glee in placing emphasis on the last word.

"You are not from one of the Seven Families; that is all that concerns people right now." He shrugged, trying to look as though he wasn't bothered at all by the word 'lover'.

She completed her coiffure and threw the brush down on the bed, relieved that she was finished with the pointless preening. "All right, I'm ready. Let's go and blackmail Arlena."

The room in which Arlena received them was as spectacular as the other areas of the house they had seen. Arlena was standing by an enormous window, looking out at the sea of yellow-green winter grain that began at the end of the house's boundary and stretched as far as the eye could see. It was a magnificent sight. Once more, the fact she was alone rather than accompanied by Zekken, or indeed any member of her family, was striking. Despite her solitude, her presence more than filled the room.

Arlena bowed low at their arrival. Even if she had declined to support Gidyon's claim to the throne, she still recognised him as her ruler. That was something, at least.

"The Royal suite is truly beautiful, Arlena," Gidyon said by way of greeting.

"It humbles me to hear you say that, your Majesty," she said, perhaps a sardonic note to her voice.

"May we speak privately?" Gidyon asked. Making the request was a courtesy he did not have to extend to Arlena. Gidyon could simply have ordered that they speak without the presence of the servants standing discreetly at the room's entrances.

Yet offering her that politeness was also a reminder of his authority. Arlena pursed her lips ever so slightly and nodded. At her gesture, the servants withdrew immediately, closing the doors behind them. No doubt, at least one or two ears were pressed against the doors – the Family knew well that servants were often the best sources of information.

"Would privately not also mean the exclusion of lady Elen-ai?" Arlena asked, one eyebrow arching as her gaze rested on Elen-ai's still-damp hair.

"No." Gidyon made no other offer or explanation, the single syllable firm and unmistakably final.

Arlena's other eyebrow joined its raised companion before both settled back in their normal place. Elen-ai knew these looks of surprise were deliberate. No member of the Seven Families allowed such obvious expressions to cross their faces unless they desired it. That Arlena had so openly displayed such an expression was her insubordination in response to Gidyon's assertion of his authority. Elen-ai supposed she couldn't blame her. If she had been an authoritative dowager, she too would have been rankled at being ordered about by a young man who seemed not to realise that his place in the world was not to take the throne or indeed to command those who were his elders, and most likely wiser than him, too.

"Very well then. May I be so blunt as to ask what brings you to our corner of the Queendom? I can only assume it is some purpose other than hearing the songs that our new resident minstrel has written." The understated sarcasm, in the world of the court, might as well have been an obscene gesture. Elen-ai made no attempt to stop her own eyebrows from ascending.

"Lady Aadran, I do not seek to create any pretence. You are well aware that the Katan family has challenged my claim to the throne. You and I both know that my cousin, Serenah, is not suited to rule, nor is her grandfather. Despite what he may think of his own capabilities." Gidyon took a step toward Arlena, who remained by the window, her face impassive.

"Even if I did believe that about your cousin, if Halen's ploy is successful and you are deposed, that still leaves his granddaughter on the throne," she pointed out coolly.

"And the way of the Second Country would be utterly disrupted. How would Serenah rule impartially? Surely she would be inclined to favour those who marched for her. The Bertak and Harete families would almost certainly be given whatever they asked. How might that erode the Aadran family fortunes?"

"Certainly, you make a compelling argument for throwing the weight of the Aadran family behind Halen and his quest to take the throne from you." Arlena smiled tightly.

Gidyon's face closed, an unsettling stillness falling across his features that a moment before had been quite imploring. "I know you find him and his methods distasteful."

"That is ultimately irrelevant when I am forced to consider what is best for my family. Sometimes we must do unpleasant things to protect those we love." Arlena's hand turned briefly upward in a gesture to emphasise the comment.

"Or for those who bear your blood?" Gidyon asked softly.

The stiffening in Arlena's already perfectly straight posture was only noticeable to one who was watching with intense scrutiny. Elen-ai found herself holding her breath, worried that Gidyon had shown his hand too early. It was only possible that Arlena might have been Gidyon's grandmother, but it was such a direct reference to the utter social ruin she faced if her son's relationship with Gidyon's mother ever became publicly known, that the threat was a brutal one indeed.

Arlena inhaled, the sound loud in the absolute quiet of the room. "So you want me to support you? Send my people to die for someone who should not be our ruler? The way I see things, neither you nor Serenah deserve to sit on the throne. Perhaps the best thing would be to let you both fight it out and then deal with whatever undesirable outcome arises." She made no attempt to hide the derision or tight anger in her voice. This was not a woman who liked to be threatened. "The Aadran family will always survive. We have wealth, we have power, we have our own people trained to defend our lands. What obligation is actually incumbent upon us if your mother decided that instead of bearing a girl, she would simply put a man on the throne and in so doing threaten the stability of the Queendom?"

Instead of answering her question, Gidyon walked slowly across the room to examine one of the paintings. Following him with her gaze, Elen-ai noticed that the figures in it were members of the Aadran family. Arlena too watched Gidyon, anger making her features pinched.

"Where is Zekken?" Gidyon asked quietly. "Normally in such a meeting, he would be by your side, as Elen-ai is by mine."

"I am the head of the Aadran family," Arlena snapped, her reserve gone. "It is ultimately my decision whether or not we support you, my King."

From where she stood, Elen-ai could see Gidyon's slight smile. Getting Arlena to lose her composure was no mean feat and it had now given Gidyon the upper hand he had been worried he would not attain.

Arlena's anger at herself for losing her control was obvious in the slight flare to her nostrils and clench of her hands. She too knew that she had just given Gidyon the leverage he had been seeking. Now was the time for Gidyon to go in for the kill, to turn that lack of restraint against her. Elen-ai felt herself tense in anticipation. Verbal exchanges such as this one had a curious and beautiful similarity to a physical fight. However, like any good fighter, Gidyon did exactly what Elen-ai would never have expected.

"Arlena. I am asking for your help. Please." His voice was so gentle, so imploring. Where Elen-ai would have gone in for the kill, he threw away his advantage to place himself once more at the matriarch's mercy.

Elen-ai looked to the woman. Arlena made no effort to hide her surprise. Or perhaps her surprise was so powerful that she could not conceal it. "Why should I risk the lives of Aadran women and men to keep you on the throne? You are a man, and your very existence brings with it," she hesitated so that she could find the correct word, "complications."

Gidyon turned to face her. "I might not be the right sex but I do want to do the best by my people. All my people."

Elen-ai sensed an unspoken understanding flash between the two powerful people. At that exact moment, they certainly looked as though they could be related, although she could not say if that similarity came from the fact that both of them understood the burdens of power and leadership in a way that loaned them a certain likeness, or because of shared blood.

"There is the faintest possibility that I might have been wrong about you," Arlena admitted. "Maybe we should talk at greater length." She motioned to the chairs. Gidyon took one of them. Elen-ai remained standing, her presence almost forgotten. Exactly the way she preferred.

Gidyon and Arlena had been talking quietly for almost ten minutes when a knock sounded at the door.

"My apologies. They should know we are not to be disturbed," Arlena said, vexation crossing her face. She raised her voice. "Yes?"

The door was opened by a cautious-looking servant, evidently aware that she was breaching her employer's strict instructions. "I'm terribly sorry to interrupt, my lady," she began, the slight tremor in her voice betraying her fear at the prospect of invoking Arlena's displeasure. "A bird has come with a message for you marked urgent."

Arlena sighed and held out her hand. The servant scurried across the room and placed the paper in the matriarch's outstretched hand. Arlena excused herself to the king, who made a gesture that indicated she should not worry, and she quickly scanned the paper. Her lips pursed as she read its contents, and she looked as though someone had whispered a series of particularly vulgar profanities in her ear.

Halen Katan was marching on Herran.

THIRTEEN

The debate between Gidyon and Elen-ai was furious. Arlena had graciously offered them a few moments to privately discuss the news of Halen's decision to try to take the capital by force.

"I'm not leaving you," Elen-ai insisted for perhaps the fourth time.

"You must. What if for some reason word does not reach my uncles of what is coming toward them?" Gidyon asked. In the face of her stubbornness, he was infuriatingly rational. Although, she could see the tension at this news underneath the calm logic that he was pushing onto her.

"Of course they'll know. How could they fail to have word passed to them of a Shadow-cursed army marching across the countryside?" She swung her arms wildly as if to emphasise how difficult it would be to overlook an army.

"I need you to go and help them, and I need to stay here and secure the assistance of the Aadran and Tak families," Gidyon said. The calmness with which he spoke seemed to belie the fact that now at least, the threat against him was real, and very much imminent. She had no idea how he was so calm.

"I can't leave you here on your own," Elen-ai said stubbornly. She crossed her arms in front of her chest and tried to stare down her friend and king.

"Elen-ai, I have already lost if I fail to secure Aadran and Tak help. Without them, my life is forfeit." Gidyon stood before the window, in almost the same position that Arlena had been when they had first entered. The clouds Elen-ai had earlier thought would cross the skies and pour rain down upon them had remained on the horizon. With his features cast into shadow by the brightness of the day outside, it was hard to see the nuances of Gidyon's expression. She wondered if Gidyon had moved to the window for that exact reason.

"I won't leave you," Elen-ai said.

"I can order you to go." His voice was low but he may as well have shouted at her.

"I'll ignore it," she said defiantly.

"And you will then be disobeying the direct order of your king." Suddenly, the authority that Elen-ai had seen Gidyon use on others to bend them to his will had been turned on her.

She held his gaze for a moment, only able to properly see the intense blue of his eyes. Unable to stare him down, she dropped her eyes, looking instead at the beautiful red threads of the carpet. "As you wish, my King."

Even though Gidyon had been right to point it out, Elen-ai still couldn't help but feel wounded that he had, as her king, ordered her to go. As far as she was concerned, for most of the time he was her friend first and king second. Except when things like this happened. She wasn't even angry, just filled with a vague sense of sadness that he had chosen to remind her of that now. Only half a room separated them, but it may as well have been half a world.

"Elen-ai, please. You will be faster on your own, and perhaps I will be faster on my own here, too," Gidyon said. He was pleading with her now, begging her not to hate him.

That horrified Elen-ai more than the fact that he had given her an order. Kings did not beg. The fact that he now humbled himself before her in such a fashion was terrifying. Something about that felt more wrong than anything she could have imagined, and she realised her error. She relented immediately. "Gidyon, I'm sorry. You're right, I'll go."

He stayed by the window for a moment longer, his features still washed out by the light as he looked at her. Then he nodded. He strode across the room to the door through which Arlena had exited several minutes previously. He opened it and came face to face with Zekken in a quiet but heated conference with Arlena.

Zekken had put on weight since Elen-ai had last seen him at Latana's funeral. He did not possess the strikingly good looks of Erek Rasatan, but the way he had carried himself had given him a certain charm that was quite disarming and endearing. Yet the grief-rounded face, and, more strikingly, the way his features seemed to have settled more naturally into an expression of dismay, had robbed him of that appeal. It was quite a shock to see such a dramatic change in his appearance.

Whatever conversation mother and son were having was cut short by Gidyon opening the door. The King and the man who believed himself to be Gidyon's father stared at one another in shocked silence.

Zekken spoke first. "Are you all right?" The words practically tumbled from his lips, desperate eagerness making him reach his arms out toward the King as if by touching him, he could assure himself of Gidyon's relative wellbeing.

Gidyon took an involuntary step back to evade Zekken's hands. Hurt at the rejection showed clearly on the man's face. Elen-ai almost shook her head. If he behaved like that in front of anybody else, talk was bound to occur.

Arlena all but pushed her son into the room and followed him, closing the door firmly behind her. "Really," she scolded Zekken.

Gidyon came to stand beside Elen-ai. He folded his arms across his chest in the same stance Elen-ai had taken only moments before and waited for either Arlena or Zekken to speak.

Zekken broke the silence, to his mother's obvious disapproval. "Are you going back to Herran?"

Gidyon took his time before answering, rocking back slightly onto his heels. "If I were, would I be accompanied by Aadran fighters?"

Zekken opened his mouth, then apparently reconsidered answering on his mother's behalf. It was the first sign of sense he had demonstrated. He looked to Arlena. If the woman had possessed skills of the Divine One, Elen-ai was certain she would have incinerated her own son in that moment. Fortunately for Zekken, it seemed Arlena was not as devout a believer as Gidyon.

"We have yet to arrive at any agreement," Arlena said. "But I must confess, Halen being so bold as to actually march on Herran has certainly changed things."

Elen-ai could sense Gidyon's relief. It mirrored her own. "I would greatly appreciate the opportunity to continue to speak with you on this matter. Elen-ai is heading back to the capital as soon as possible, given what we have just learned about the Katan movements. I assume we can continue our discussion about such matters after her departure?"

"Of course. If there is anything we can do to assist, just ask," Arlena said, the offer seemingly quite sincere.

Gidyon gave her a nod of thanks, then he and Elen-ai returned to the Royal suite to prepare for Elen-ai's departure.

As soon as they entered the rooms, Gidyon went to the desk by the window and began writing. Elen-ai exchanged her light formal tunic and soft trousers for a more durable and warmer outfit. She made sure all of her blades were securely transferred to the garments, double checking with a lifetime's training that they were sharp and ready for use.

A brisk rap on the door preceded Zekken's entrance. He did not wait for a response before coming into the room.

Gidyon immediately stood up, making no effort to temper the obvious fact that he did not want Zekken to be there. "What do you want?"

"I wanted to talk with you." Zekken sounded doggedly desperate. It was pitiful.

"We are busy." Gidyon turned toward the desk.

"I know, but I just—"

Gidyon whirled back toward the man. "What can you possibly say to me, Zekken?" His eyes were cold and hard.

"We used to be so close, Gid."

"That was before I found out why you wanted to be close to me," Gidyon snapped.

"That shouldn't remove all that came before," Zekken begged.

"It most certainly should," Gidyon said, unmoving, unreachable.

His harshness left Zekken silent for a moment, staring at the King with uncertain balefulness. "You know, I miss your mother every day. I loved her so much." His voice was a hoarse croak.

Gidyon's roar filled the room. "She was my mother, and you took that from me. Your stupid, reckless affair with her took that from me because now I have to live every day with the legacy of that, knowing that I cannot do one single thing wrong. And even then, if what you and she did ever comes to light, all of the Second Country will rise up against me. I can't miss her, I can't mourn for her, I have to live with the mistake she committed with you." The grief that he had carried with him, nursing quietly for months sat openly on his face. In the silence that followed his explosion, he continued. "I have nothing to say to you. Erek might have killed her, but you took my mother from me. I can't think of her now without thinking of why she died. And I can't think of her the same way because of that."

"I'm sorry." Zekken's eyes gleamed with tears.

"Get out," Gidyon told him. Elen-ai could see tiny tremors all along Gidyon's body.

"Gid, please let me know what I can do." Zekken stepped toward the boy he believed to be his son.

Elen-ai could stay silent for no longer. "Your king gave you an order." Her voice snapped across the room like a whip.

Zekken slowly turned his head to look at her. "I forgot you were here," he admitted, sounding dazed.

"Are you going to disobey an order from your king?" Elen-ai asked, clenching her hands into fists by her side, wanting to hit him for the distress he was causing Gidyon. She almost did, but she knew that was not what Gidyon would have wanted, so she bit down on her natural impulse.

Zekken blinked once, twice, then his head bowed. He cast one last look at Gidyon, then he left. With Zekken's departure, Gidyon sank down into his chair. He stared blankly ahead for a long, long moment, then the King of the Second Country put his head into his hands and wept.

"Would you like to talk about it?" Elen-ai asked him.

He did not raise his head. Perhaps he did not want her to see his tears. Instead, his voice was muffled through his fingers, the words coming between sobs. "There's nothing to say."

"Are you certain?" Elen-ai hovered near him uncertainly. Comforting people who were mired in the depths of grief was not her forte. She had normally departed long before it came time for grief. Eventually, she moved close to Gidyon and put a gentle hand on his shoulder. He leaned slightly into her touch, continuing to sob.

"I can kill him, if you'd like," she said, receiving a watery chuckle in reply.

He raised his head, offering Elen-ai a glimpse of his pale, tear-blotched face. "If that were how I dealt with all my problems, I think there would be very few people left in the Second Country," he said. He swallowed in an obvious effort to push back a fresh bout of tears.

"But those who'd be left would be very loyal to you," Elen-ai pointed out.

She was rewarded with a tenuous smile. The King took a breath, fighting valiantly to compose himself. "I am all right, Elen-ai," he tried in vain to reassure her.

Elen-ai raised her eyebrows, her most sceptical expression on her face.

"He took me by surprise more than anything. I honestly was not expecting him to be so," Gidyon paused and his eyes – reddened from crying – brightened afresh with tears, "so like that."

Her grip on his shoulder tightened. She understood what he meant. Something about Zekken's total prostration before Gidyon was deeply unsettling. It was as though Latana's death had seen the gentle warmth of Zekken's demeanour disappear, to be replaced with a man totally adrift from any composure. It had certainly been a shock to see the change in his appearance and demeanour, too.

"I can't even hate him. He is far too piteous for that," Gidyon said miserably.

"It's a lot easier to hate someone than see them as flawed," Elen-ai told him.

He nodded, his eyes fixed straight ahead, almost certainly not seeing any of the suite in front of him. Then he let out a shuddering breath, and while tears still threatened to breach his eyes, they did not fall any longer.

After his exchange with Zekken, Elen-ai wanted to leave Gidyon less than ever. It was not that she thought he was unable to cope on his own. Gidyon had more than proved his capabilities on a great many occasions. It was that she did not want him to be alone in the household of the man his mother had loved, surrounded with the reminder of his grief and anger. But before he had ordered her to go, he had asked her to go. Returning to Herran was the only thing that she could actually do for him, so she would do it.

"Should we send word to the kitchens and ask for supplies?" Elen-ai asked. She could offer him no more words of comfort. As he himself had said, there wasn't really anything further either of them could say that the other did not already know.

The blue of his eyes was made even more brilliant by the red that had been brought to them by his tears. "It's a good idea." His voice was hoarse. He said nothing further, seeming to lapse back into simply staring in front of him.

Elen-ai continued her preparations, summoning a servant and requesting that provisions be ready within the hour for her departure. There was more that she should have discussed with Gidyon – plans, contingencies, messages – but the King was silent, staring reflectively into his hands, and she did not wish to trouble him.

Elen-ai moved around the room silently, gathering the few things she needed. When she was six, the Mothers and Fathers had taught her how to have the lightest of touches, making her fingers sure, swift, and delicate. Clumsy hands were traitors, giving away those who could tread without even stirring the air. While stealing was something that was not encouraged unless absolutely necessary, the children of the Family were granted this one exception for the year while they perfected the skill of possessing nimble and deft fingers in the streets of Herran. After that time, anybody who was caught liberating anything that was not duly paid for in some way or another was punished by the Mothers and Fathers, often creatively. Elen-ai was especially glad for the skill now. She did not want to disturb Gidyon with any rude or unnecessary noise as she selected the items she would need for her journey back to Herran and packed them into her bag.

Finally, she was ready to leave. "Ah, Gid?" she said, reluctant to disrupt him.

He looked at her as though she had woken him from sleep.

"Time for me to go. Is there anything I need to take with me?"

"Yes, one moment." Obvious effort to focus creased his forehead. He finished the note he had been writing when Zekken had intruded, leaving splashes of ink on the page in his haste. "Give this to Sil."

Elen-ai stowed it away in her small pack. "Anything else?"

Gidyon gave a small laugh. She couldn't blame him. There was much they should have discussed, but they were out of time. She offered him a sardonic smile. "I know."

"Well, do try and be safe," Gidyon said.

"I'll always be the last person standing in a fight," Elen-ai reassured him. It was true. She was never concerned about her own safety in any confrontation that may arise. But not every threat was a knife that she could deflect, and not every battle was hers to fight. "Are you certain that you'll be fine here?"

Gidyon placed a hand on her arm. "What I am staying to do here is the sort of task, the sort of place, where I will always be fine," he promised. Of that, she had no doubt. Elen-ai had never met anybody who was as adept at navigating the nuances and trickeries of politics as Gidyon.

"When I secure the allegiance and support of the Tak and Aadran families, I will come to Herran as soon as I can with their people. We need to delay the Katan forces for as long as possible to give me the chance to arrive with reinforcements," Gidyon said. His voice grew stronger as he spoke, and the devastated young man who she had tried to comfort a few minutes ago had retreated in deference to the king.

Elen-ai nodded. "I'll make sure it happens," she promised.

"You do not seem particularly worried about the fact that I might fail here," Gidyon noted. He even managed to pull a real smile to his face. His humour reassured her.

Elen-ai pulled him into a hug, holding him as though she could lift all his troubles for just the briefest of moments. Then she released him and looked him straight in the eye. "I have faith" she told him. "In you."

FOURTEEN

Elen-ai pushed herself and her kittanae as far as they both would and could go. The only time of rest that she allowed herself was a little over an hour just before dawn to sleep, more for the giant feline than for herself. Alone, she focused completely on the experience of riding the kittanae. It was magnificent, striding across the land in easy loping bounds. Aside from Hlevan, her mount, who she found herself becoming more and more attached to with each hour that passed, the cold was Elen-ai's constant companion, pricking at her exposed face until the skin felt as smooth as polished stone.

Evening had well and truly fallen when she reached Herran, only two days after leaving Gidyon. She had seen no sign of Halen's army as she made her way across the Second Country, but that did not mean that he and his people were not advancing on the capital. The Aadran family had no reason to lie, and their network of informants was as good as any. The cheer that Elen-ai witnessed in the streets of Herran as she made her way to the Palace, the kittanae drawing stares from those she passed, seemed utterly incongruous with the urgency and worry that had settled in her stomach. A few optimistic stores were still open, the lights blazing invitingly inside, offering a refuge from the cold and dark. Chatter and laughter seeped from the taverns. Even the exclamations of wonder at the sight of the kittanae being ridden through the streets seemed utterly devoid of care. Under less worrying circumstances, she would have wanted to be within one of the taverns, not riding a beast of the highborn. Indeed, a part of her wished that someone else could worry about the advancing army, the safety of the throne and Herran, and the politics of those who cared nothing for others, and she could instead slip inside, hidden by the raucous sound of the lowborn relaxing at the end of the day. She pressed on, though, guiding the kittanae up the hill to the Palace, entering streets that were reserved for the wealthy. They did not gather in taverns like the city's lowborn but instead dined within their own walls. At the doorway of the Katan city residence, Elen-ai pulled the kittanae to a pause. Royal guards stood outside the front door. She had almost forgotten Gidyon's order that the household of the Katan city residence be placed under house arrest. The guards were totally impassive, and even with their presence, the house looked unchanged. The shrine still stood outside, the gold glinting in the light strewn by the lanterns and peeking through not-quite-covered windows. The urge to spit on the door was overwhelming, but Elen-ai did not wish to debase herself by sinking to the level of pettiness that Halen himself had exhibited. There was no way that she would ever give him the satisfaction of such an act.

Her face at the Palace gates was all that was required for her admittance. The guards – a double guard, she couldn't help but notice – lowered the weapons that had been raised at her approach.

The grand foyer was as cold as ever, illuminated by braziers in the walls that had been lit, even though nobody else would have been moving through the grand space that evening. The beauty of the entranceway was once again lost on Elen-ai as she ascertained from a servant that the King's advisers were to be found in the council room.

She made her way through the Palace at a swift walk. Even at such a pace, her footsteps made no sound on the corridors that normally echoed even the slightest sound. The few guards and servants she passed nodded greetings to her, worry stealing into their expressions as they saw the grim fretfulness on her own face.

The door to the council room was opened by the guards as she approached, and she strode into the warmth of the room with no fanfare other than the surprise at her unannounced arrival. The three brothers looked at her, the drawn and haggard lines on their faces confirming before she even asked that they too had heard of Halen's march upon Herran.

"Where's Gidyon?" Silius asked.

Elen-ai did not begrudge his lack of formalities. In his position she would have been just as blunt.

"In the Aadran lands," Elen-ai said. She held up a hand to forestall the objections that she knew would come. "He ordered me to come back. Here." She unslung her pack and drew from it the message Gidyon had written.

Silius took it wordlessly, his lips pursed in anger and worry at his nephew's decision to send away the protection that Elen-ai's presence by his side assured.

He turned away from Elen-ai as he read Gidyon's message. His head bowed slightly and his shoulders hunched as he paced past his brothers. Kaine mouthed a hello at Elen-ai, accompanying it with a tired smile. Within a minute, Silius finished reading, the linen page coming down to his side with a snap. "Well, it seems my nephew has some preparations for us to make in addition to the ones we have already implemented."

"Do you need me?" Elen-ai asked.

Silius shook his head. "Your particular set of skills cannot be put to use yet."

Elen-ai did not take the comment as a personal jibe. Once she might have, but she had been around Silius long enough to know that he was this way with everybody, especially when other, more pressing matters, like the imminent arrival of an army, were holding most of his attention.

"I'm going to go back into the city. I have something to attend to," Elen-ai told the brothers.

Nikalus' eyebrows rose at Elen-ai's announcement. "Will you return to the Palace?"

She nodded, but the three men were already turning back to confer with one another, trusting that whatever her business, it would be in service to Gidyon's cause. Kaine threw her a parting look and she gifted him with a smile before she left. It seemed a lifetime ago that once, all three men had distrusted her and objected to her presence in the Court.

Walking back through the Palace, Elen-ai could sense the agitation of the guards and servants. As she had rushed through to deliver Gidyon's message, she had simply thought her own nerves and worry were making her see what she was feeling in the faces of others. Now, she could feel the tension that was tightly bound around the Palace. Clues that spoke to the preparations underway were everywhere. More servants moved through the Palace than was normal for that time of night, and the distant clang of weapons suggested training was being conducted by the Royal Guard, again, not a usual occurrence at this hour. But what really unsettled Elen-ai was the atmosphere of uncertain anticipation in the great building.

Outside, the cold of the night had intensified during the short time she had been with the brothers. Or perhaps now that she had been given a small reprieve from the cold, she felt it even more keenly. Elen-ai drew her cloak more tightly about her and went back down the Palace hill and into the city. This time, she avoided the Katan house, despite the detour adding a few minutes to her journey. She did not want to be reminded of Halen or faced with the temptation of defacing his beautiful, expensive shrine.

The Family's home was as reassuring as ever: warm, dark, and with a slightly spicy scent that Elen-ai had never been able to identify as anything other than the familiar smell of her childhood. The Father who greeted her showed no surprise at her entrance. Elen-ai wondered yet again how her approach could possibly have been noticed, and how the Mothers and Fathers had chosen who to send to greet her. Those questions, however, were set aside in the face of the enormous request she was about to make.

"My Daughter." He greeted her with the impassive calm that she had always known in her Mothers and Fathers.

"Father." Elen-ai weathered his scrutiny.

"What purpose brings you to us, Elen-ai?"

"Halen Katan is marching on Herran," she said.

"We are aware. The youngest of our children have already been moved to where their safety is assured."

She did not spare the time to ask where that was. Instead, she pushed forward to what she had come to ask of the Family. "I believe the Family should fight for the King."

The serenity of the house cracked. Ears that were aware of the conversation with her Father were no longer passive listeners, but suddenly keenly interested in what was being said. Suddenly there was a tension in the house similar to the one that wound its way through the Palace.

Her Father's expression did not change, although perhaps his eyes became a little colder, his words a little more carefully chosen. "This is not something that I would ever presume to speak to, my Daughter."

She nearly crumbled then, feeling the horror and hostility of the very house at the blasphemy that she had proposed, but she held herself tall. "Then who can speak on the matter?"

For a moment she thought he might strike her for her insolence. After nearly a week of travel in the cold, with little opportunity for her to practise or train properly, Elen-ai had significant doubts about her ability to hold her own in a fight against any member of the Family. However, the moment passed and he wordlessly turned on his heel. She followed him through the house to its uppermost level with no small amount of relief.

The rooms to which she was being led were rarely frequented by the children of the Family. Here resided the Family's Grandparents, those who no longer wished to take on the day-to-day responsibilities of life within the Family. Elen-ai had only ever seen her Grandparents a few times in her life. Mostly, she had been offered glimpses of them watching as the children trained in weaponcraft or lessons. Only once had Elen-ai directly spoken with one of them, when she had been brought before them immediately prior to her first contract. She had been so full of youthful certainty in her capabilities, of the fact that her body, nubile with youth and years of training, was the Shadow God's most superior weapon. The Grandfather who had spoken for the circle of elders had looked her over once, then knocked her from her feet. Even now, she had no idea how he had managed it. She had never seen him move, but she had certainly felt the blow of his arm against her and the sting of humiliation that spread throughout her as she lay sprawled on the floor.

"You always know less than you think you do," he had told her kindly, heaving her to her feet with a gnarled hand that held strength not only from years of practice, but years of lessons learned and taught.

The fact that she was being brought before her Grandparents now did nothing to alleviate her sense that she was being brought before some tribunal to face a terrible judgment. Her Father knocked on the door, the slightest hesitation obvious before he raised his hand.

"Come in, my Son." The imperious voice held an authority that could not be missed. Its tone reminded Elen-ai of Gidyon, or Arlena Aadran.

Elen-ai and her Father entered the room, which was lit by the soft glow of candles rather than torches on the walls. Seven people sat in cross-legged conference. None of them gave any appearance of being particularly troubled by the intrusion into their space or the impending battle for control of the city and the Second Country. Their wizened frames would fool the casual observer into thinking they were harmless, but Elen-ai knew they were all deadly. Most Grandparents still took occasional contracts.

The quiet discussion across the semicircle of seemingly ancient people ceased as Elen-ai stepped into the room. She felt their gazes bore into her. Nobody stood, nor did anybody seem to be preparing themselves to act as spokesperson. Instead, she was forced to stand in front of them as they sat comfortably and appraised her.

The sound of the candles was louder than the breath of the nine people in the room, the warm flickering sound of the burning wicks was almost deafening in the space which was otherwise silent. Then a Grandmother spoke. Hair the colour of pure, pure snow hung about her face. It was uncharacteristically impractical for a member of the Family to have hair hang free like that.

"You would ask the Family to take a side in the forthcoming battle." There was no anger in her voice, no judgment, nothing at all.

"I would," Elen-ai replied.

A Grandfather said, "The Family does not involve itself in the affairs of those foolish enough to believe that power is best measured with weapons and riches." His head was completely hairless and his face was richly wrinkled.

"This is not a question of weapons and riches. It is a question of the Second Country – our country. If the Katan family takes the throne—"

159

The Grandmother who had first spoken cut her off. "Then the Family will still accept contracts, still train our children, still continue to exist. Those old families are not like us. They are not our concern." She dismissively waved a hand that resembled a gnarled tree root. Elen-ai had no doubt that the hand in question would still be able to extinguish life with frightening ease.

"With respect, Grandmothers, Grandfathers, the Family is as old as any of the powerful families of the Second Country," Elen-ai countered.

Another Grandmother leaned forward. Her hair was the colour of an angry sky, her eyes were a more vibrant blue than even Gidyon's. "It may be that we, like the old families, fought in the battles of the Godskissed Continent long ago, but those who formed the Family came together precisely because they did not wish to inhabit that world where such fighting continued. They wanted the certainty that their skills could earn them enough to survive and protect their own. Nothing more."

"And that is a fine reason, but perhaps it is time for that tradition to be broken," Elen-ai said.

Another Grandfather said, "How do you, Elen-ai, come to us and suggest this when your own impartiality is so compromised? You call this boy-king a friend, you bed his uncle. You come asking the Family to risk itself and its children for your own cause."

Shame burned Elen-ai's cheeks. There was too much truth in the accusation for her to even try to deny it.

The Grandmother who spoke retained dark colour in her hair, perhaps could even have been mistaken for a younger woman but for the way her eyes gave away her years. "What have you to say for yourself, child?"

Elen-ai marshalled herself. She would not cry, or whisper out her excuses to these people. She was their Granddaughter, a child of the Family, and she was stronger than simply dissolving in the face of this barrage. She had every right to stand in front of them and speak her piece. "It is not wrong for a child of the

Family to hold their own opinions and thoughts. I am a loyal Daughter. This is my home, and it always will be. But I have been inside the Palace, inside the world of the wealthy, and I think that the right thing to do is to support Gidyon against Halen and his allies." Her voice was clear and strong in the room. It seemed to carry through the entire home, heard by all who were straining to listen to what was being said in that uppermost part of the house.

"The right thing?" The Grandmother with the white hair who had first spoken sounded distinctly amused. "We are not so arrogant as to claim we know right from wrong. Those judgments are best left to the gods, my Granddaughter."

"That's a convenient excuse." The insolent words were out of her mouth before she could stop herself.

It sounded as though a hundred tiny breaths were suddenly drawn in. Elen-ai almost brought her hands up to cover her mouth as though to push her words back inside, but she stood resolute, her hands locked against her sides.

"Elen-ai. Not the most clever, most adept, or most deadly of our children. Who are you to tell us, your elders, your grandparents, how we should behave?" The bald Grandfather made no effort to disguise the threat or ire in his voice.

"I am just a child of the Family." Elen-ai met his gaze. She was afraid that she might crumble under the fire and iron she saw there.

"Isn't it time you run back to the Palace? Surely some errand needs to be run," he said. His voice was cold.

"I am a child of the Family. Not a servant of the Palace. I come to you as your Granddaughter, telling you that I think this is not the time for the Family's neutrality." Elen-ai clenched her jaw so tightly that she knew it would ache for days afterwards. Her gaze roved to each of the Grandparents. On their faces she saw no encouragement, no warmth, no expression at all. "Perhaps if that will not convince you, then consider this: the Katan family is not the Royal Family. Will our unwillingness to take a contract on the Royal Family extend to them? Even if it does, will Halen ever feel truly secure? How long until he seeks to hunt us down, to remove us as he is seeking to do to the Royal Family?

"Or if not that, how stable do you truly think the Second Country will be under his rule? He may be able to procure fighters to steal the throne, but he can't buy the hearts of the people. A man on the throne may be unpleasant, but a member of the Seven Families on the throne can only lead to more warfare. We believe in the balance that currently exists because it is safe for us. There is no guarantee of that under the rule of this foolish, bloodthirsty man." More than anything, Elen-ai wanted to turn on her heel and run from the gaze of the seven ancient assassins. The weight of their judgment was almost more than she could bear.

"We promise you nothing, Granddaughter. It is time you leave us," said the Grandmother with the snow broth hair in answer to her diatribe.

Elen-ai did not need to be told a second time. She left, only noticing then that the Father who had brought her in had at some point disappeared. Nobody guided her out, a fact for which she was immensely grateful. She did not think that she could survive the judgment of yet another member of the Family for her request that they fight on behalf of Gidyon.

Elen-ai slipped into Kaine's unoccupied room. The fire slumbering in the hearth warmed the space. Elen-ai gratefully discarded her cloak, content to simply be in the room even if he was not – even if he did not come back to his room that night at all. Taking the first moment of stillness that had been offered to her in days, she sat cross-legged on the bed and breathed deeply.

She prayed. Prayer had always brought her comfort. It had always been an opportunity for her to still her thoughts when they raced, to calm her heart when nothing else would settle it. The chant of worship to the Shadow God were the first words children of the Family were taught to speak. It was as familiar to her as breathing. When all else was uncertain, she had found certainty in her belief.

Yet now her prayer only sufficed to remove the edge from her raging emotions. She could sense the presence of the Shadow God across the veil separating immortals and humans, but today she could not lose herself in the awe of something larger and infinitely more complex than herself. Her preoccupation, her fear, her anger, were too great for her to clear her mind and truly pray.

Her eyes flew open at Kaine's entrance. He did not appear to be surprised to see her there. "It's Divine-cursed cold outside," he said by way of greeting.

"It'll likely be snowing in the Katan highlands. Maybe that's why he's so desperate to control the throne, to get away from the snows in winter," she replied.

To his credit, Kaine did smile, but the joke fell flat in the face of the Katan army's impending arrival.

The children of the Family had no need for fear. They lived with the certainty of their own survival. But she did not feel like a child of the Family at that moment. She felt like she was out of time, out of place, and out of home, buffeted by forces with which she had never held any interest in consorting.

She couldn't say exactly what she sought from Kaine, but she knew that she wanted him. He crossed the room and came to stand in front of her. The gold of his eyes blazed in the firelight as he looked at her. She could see his own fear meeting hers in the space between them.

"Are you all right?" he asked softly, reaching out to caress her cheek. The tenderness was unexpected. With the intrigue, and violence, and fear, Elen-ai had felt that there was no place in the world for any gentleness at that moment. It melted her.

Instead of answering the question she pulled him to her, crushing her lips against his. He tasted like spices and sweetness mixed together, a taste that was now exquisite in its familiarity. She had never considered how the thrill of discovering someone could be surpassed by the delight of knowing them. He sighed, his hands coming to delicately rest on her back. She wasn't all right – how could she be? But she would take whatever respite she could from the fear, uncertainty, and loneliness that had descended upon her as she had ridden away from Gidyon two days previously.

FIFTEEN

She was exercising in one of the courtyards when Kaine found
her the next morning. A fine drizzle had set in just after dawn,
and the clouds that covered the sky were the dirty grey that
promised snow in higher areas of the country. He watched her
cartwheeling her body end over end.

"What are you doing?" he asked after a while.

She halted her tumbling and sprang nimbly to her feet in
front of him. The week of riding had not put her as out of shape
as she had feared, a fact for which she was grateful. "Preparing
to fight," she answered.

"Why?"

"Because I'm going to be fighting." She breathed deeply,
not liking the slight catch to her breath. Despite her worst fears
being unfounded, she was nevertheless less fit than she wanted
to be.

"You should be in the back tents, calling orders with the
rest of us," he said. Three tents were going to be placed on a
slight hill near Herran that overlooked what would become the
battlefield. From that vantage point, messages would be sent to
the forces to adjust strategy as the battle unfolded.

Elen-ai sank into a deep stretch. She looked up at Kaine as
she spoke. "I'll be more use to you if I'm fighting."

He opened his mouth to disagree, but Elen-ai drew the
shadows around her so that she shimmered out of sight and circled around him faster than he could draw breath to put into

165

speech. Her blade came to rest against his throat. She released him just as suddenly. A hand constricted around her heart when she saw the wary fear in his eyes. She hadn't meant to leave him afraid of her, but her worry and preoccupation had made her temper short, and she had chosen to make her point with blunt brutality.

"As you wish." He shrugged and left her to continue her training.

She glanced at his retreating back, but she found no room in her heart to nurture any worry over what she may have just done. This was how she kept the fear that was bubbling in her stomach at bay, by focusing on the ache of her body as she honed herself into the most sublime weapon she could possibly be. She glanced up at the sky, wondering if the rain would develop into a heavier storm. It didn't really matter. She would continue her practice even in a torrential downpour. Being able to negotiate slippery ground, or see through a sheet of water that seemed to hang from the sky, were things for which she had been trained. Fate did not always grant clear skies and perfect conditions and it was the responsibility of any member of the Family to turn such things to their advantage. This was what she knew. This was what she could do. Gentle words and sweet embraces were not of her world, and she could not use them to offer comfort to those around her. She could only offer the certainty of her blades and deadly skills.

When she went to Kaine's bed that night, neither of them spoke of what had transpired between them in the courtyard. She fleetingly wondered as his deft hands removed the strap on her arm that held some of her blades whether she was simply there to seek desperate, mindless comfort, and he to find that in her. But then he pulled her to him and scraped his teeth along her skin, and the delicious thrill danced its way along her skin. Her musings flew from her mind, chased away by need and desire and the desperation to forget even for a fleeting second, the worry that had descended upon her and refused to leave.

Two days after Elen-ai arrived back from the Aadran lands, the Veertak forces arrived. Even high in the palace, the charge of fear and anticipation that ran through Herran at the sight of the fighters marching toward the capital, could be felt. Those from Herran who had agreed to fight for Gidyon had dutifully trained every morning in the flatlands outside the city – the only possible place a battle could take place – but there was something final and confronting about the mass of fighters from another family arriving. It meant that war had truly nestled itself in the heart of the Second Country.

Still no word had been heard from Gidyon. Elen-ai had never felt so united with the three royal advisers as she did in their shared concern for the King. The four stood just outside the grand entrance of the palace as the Veertak carriage drew up. Elen-ai's place within the Royal Family, while still a mystery, had been a constant for so long that nobody bothered to question it anymore. Those who might have found consternation in her presence were by now, mostly too preoccupied with the prospect of war to wonder about the origin of the King's ever-present, ever-silent adviser.

The Veertak army was camped on the outskirts of the city, its presence causing no small amount of consternation among the residents of Herran, by all reports. Even though the men and women in allegiance to the Veertak family were here to fight for Gidyon, there was an undeniable wrongness to their presence that gave the air an oily taste which lingered on the tongue.

The faces of the two ancient Veertak family leaders were grave. That solemnity made them look even older. They unabashedly held hands as they walked across the yard to the steps of the Palace, a curious note of tenderness amid of the horror of the bloodshed and nastiness that swirled around the Second Country.

"Silius, Nikalus, Kaine, Elen-ai. It is a shame that we meet again under these circumstances," Valena said. Her stoicism didn't quite succeed in concealing her uncertainty and anger.

"Valena, Varl. We truly cannot tell you how grateful the Royal Family is for your support." Silius' deep voice was unusually melodic in the cold stillness of the morning.

Varl offered them a tight smile. There was no need for him to say anything else. His disgust with the Katan actions had been sufficiently expressed on other occasions.

"Please, it's too cold out here, especially after your long journey. Let us continue our discussion inside," Silius suggested.

"That's most considerate of you," Valena told him. "We have also, at the King's request, brought with us one of our scholars, Kar-am." She gestured toward their carriage. At her motion, a woman who looked as though she was of an age with the two Veertaks came forward with a ponderous slowness. A lowborn as evidenced by her broken name, the woman wore clothes that were nowhere near as fine as the garments of the Veertak leaders. However, her back was just as straight as Valena's, and while she showed appropriate deference to the Veertaks in waiting until she was summoned, there was a clear degree of respect that the Veertaks felt for her.

"Welcome, Kar-am," Silius said.

The old scholar bowed low to them. "It is an honour." Her voice sounded like a tree branch being twisted in the wind. It set Elen-ai's teeth on edge.

The ensemble moved through the Palace in silence, the shuffle of feet echoing in the halls.

Once everyone was seated in the golden sitting room – the room in which Elen-ai had first met Latana – refreshments were brought and the real discussion began. Kar-am's tiny form reminded Elen-ai of the Family's Grandparents. While this woman did not seem as though she would be able to deal deadly blows with her fists, Elen-ai felt that the sparkling intelligence in her eyes would be just as deadly as any knife.

Kar-am had a habit of waving her hands around as she spoke, punctuating her comments with gestures from her curled fingers, as though she could almost push the point she was making into the mind of her audience.

"We will need to assemble a camp immediately," she said, her arm darting forward and a crooked finger extending in Silius' direction.

"Where?" Nikalus asked.

"In front of the city, of course. The Katan forces will come from either Harete or Bertak way. We have the opportunity to claim the favourable ground in front of the city. Gives our people some space to lose ground if they need to." Her arm waved back and forth, as though she were swatting away an insect flying around her head.

"Lose ground?" Kaine's expression was one of equal parts confusion and concern.

"Yes. Not all victories are earned on the front foot. We may not need the space, but I want to have it and not need it rather than not have it and need it." She did not spare the time to linger on further explanation, but moved on to the matter of the loyalist army's composition. She did not need to point out that the time until the Katan army arrived was short, and they would need all of it to give themselves the best chance to win. They all were far too keenly aware of that already.

The next day, Elen-ai accompanied the inspection of the Veertak forces as they were amalgamated into Herran's defenders, and a camp for the loyalist forces was properly established. For such a peace-loving family, the Veertaks had managed to muster a surprisingly large force. Under the guidance of Kar-am, the two forces were maneuvered around the land so that the camp was more strategically positioned. Elen-ai had never seen so many people in an open space. It was almost overwhelming. For the most part, she stayed next to Varl and Valena, conversing quietly with them as the woman who had enjoyed their family's patronage now put a lifetime of study into effect. She directed where tents should go, how the various forces should be grouped, the exact placement of spear racks. At one point, she rushed forward and seized an enormous sword from a member of the Royal Guard – she had made members of the Royal Guard commanders due to their training – and began gesturing with it as she directed the arrangement of some fighters.

"She certainly seems to know what she's doing," Elen-ai said as the three of them watched Kar-am's exuberant gesturing.

"When she was a little more mobile, she used to be a truly phenomenal swordswoman," Varl said.

Elen-ai thought back to the duel that had been staged during the Council. The memory of Halen's sickly sweet breath and the menace he had exuded still evoked the profound sense of unease and discomfort she had felt at the time. She could have so easily ended his life in that moment. If she had acted then, would she still have been walking on what would soon be a battlefield now?

"Did she win any competitions?" she asked, realising that Varl and Valena were waiting for her to say something.

"Oh, several. She fought before Gidyon's grandmother," Valena said. The cold brushed pink along her cheekbones, emphasising the hauteur of her face. She would have been a truly striking woman in her youth. She was still a striking woman now.

"It makes sense that she would be interested in warfare," Elen-ai said.

"When she retired from competing, she became interested in the theory behind fighting on larger and larger scales," Varl said, his eyes on the people who were moving obediently at the instruction of the tiny old woman.

"She travelled into the Fourth Country by herself to conduct research," his wife added, respect for Kar-am's dedication to her field in her voice.

"Does she think that we will win?" Elen-ai readjusted her scarf against the wind that swept across the wide, open space. The fact that Valena and Varl seemed not particularly concerned by the icy wind left Elen-ai amazed.

Varl's loud exhale did not inspire confidence. "She does love a challenge," he said. "And she does seem positive. Although she has suggested that our chances might be improved with the addition of the Aadran and Tak forces."

It was obvious that he did not say she believed they would win.

Dinner that evening was sombre. There was still no word from Gidyon, and the concern elicited by this silence weighed on everybody. The worry made the food, despite it being as superb as ever, impossible to enjoy. The meal was finished quickly, and the little party moved into one of the sitting rooms to play a game of fa'thong. Up to eight competitors could play at a time, vying to remove each other's pieces from the board. The winner was the last person with any pieces remaining. It was a game of strategy, with the pieces restricted in how they could move across the squares, and it required consideration and the ability to correctly judge how opponents would behave. The more people who played, the more complex the elements to consider became. Some called fa'thong a game of war strategy. Elen-ai found it somewhere between appropriate and profane that it was the game that had been selected for that evening. It was, however, also one of the few games that was suitable for so many people.

Elen-ai had seen Gidyon play fa'thong at the Tak house in the previous spring. The game, against Arlena Aadran, and Karan and Serek Tak, had been outrageously intense. All were competitive people. Elen-ai had left the room to confront Zekken about her suspicions that he and Latana were lovers, but she had later found out from Gidyon that Arlena had won. He claimed his loss had been deliberate. To win would have been precocious he explained, but he had been certain that he could have.

This game was far less competitive – nobody really wanted to play, but they also wanted to fill the evening with something other than dwelling on the imminent arrival of the Katan forces. Elen-ai played a good game, but she was the second to be eliminated after Nikalus. Perhaps unsurprisingly, eventually Kar-am won, defeating Valena with a brilliant series of moves. It was a small comfort that the military strategian was victorious, but Elen-ai wondered if the woman's ability to win a game of logic and tactics meant she could successfully direct an army of people, rather than pieces that conformed to very specific rules in how they could move, and what they could do.

Silius half-heartedly suggested that one of the Palace minstrels play for them, but the Veertaks declined, citing lingering fatigue from the journey to Herran. The relief was palpable.

Nikalus offered to escort the Veertaks to their rooms – they were being housed in the Palace rather than their Herran residence. Silius regarded Elen-ai and Kaine across the table after Nikalus and the Veertaks had departed. The pompous figure Elen-ai had first met seemed to have vanished since her return from the Aadran estate without Gidyon. He looked old, and like he had not slept in several days. It seemed he was going to say something, but instead he simply gave a sigh and bade them both goodnight. He strode from the room with a purpose that Elen-ai suspected he did not feel.

Wordless accordance saw Elen-ai and Kaine walk back to his rooms in a companionable silence. The worries of the days and the coming battle hung over them both, but both were content to leave them unvoiced. There would be time enough for those fears to be said, to be lived.

Piles of books still littered Kaine's chambers, despite the fact that legal arguments against Halen were no longer any way to stop him. Elen-ai liked that his rooms were disordered. It felt like a home.

He drew her to him, and she let him hold her like they were sweethearts with no greater concern than the blossom of their love. She rested her head against the curve of his neck, enjoying the warmth of his skin. The pulse in his neck beat deafeningly against her temple. With each pulse, it reminded her how delicate people were, how easily they could be felled. It was both a comforting and unsettling thought.

At length, he drew away. "I understand if you still want to fight against Halen. I wish I could persuade you to stay back where it's safe, though."

She shrugged, not wanting to be drawn into conversations about war and death.

"I just want you to know that if I could, I would be beside you. But the only thing I'll do is get myself killed, or have you looking after me the whole time. If Halen wants to argue about the nuance of laws, I'll be the best person to—"

She interrupted him. She wanted to hang onto the moment in which they weren't inhabiting a world of worried anticipation just a little longer. "What was Gidyon like as a child?"

Memory clouded his golden eyes as he thought, acquiescing to the request which she had not put into words. "He was always more serious than other children. You know, we have some children here in the Palace – the servants who live here, some of them have children. Gidyon took his first lessons with them, even played with them, but he was always different from them, and not because he was a member of the Royal Family. He was so diligent with his lessons, so grave."

"It sounds as though he always knew he was going to rule," Elen-ai said.

Kaine bit his lip as he considered her observation. "He took the idea of being adviser to a sister who would be born after him very seriously. I suppose we always did tell him, from the moment he was born, that it would be his job to look after her."

Elen-ai felt a pang for a little boy with hair the colour of sunlight gravely nodding as someone told him that his whole life would be looking after someone who didn't even exist yet.

Kaine chuckled. "Once, Gid arranged the other children in a classroom and tried to teach them the principles of advanced mathematics. He couldn't have been more than eight or nine. None of them had any idea what he was saying – he'd surpassed the standard lessons by at least two years at that point. Those poor children, they were so polite. None of them said anything the whole time he was talking."

"He must have been so lonely," she murmured.

"He had us," Kaine protested. Faint hurt edged his words.

She had never been more grateful for the Brothers and Sisters beside whom she had grown up than she was in that moment.

"I know, we weren't enough." Kaine's voice was filled with regret. "I think that until he met you, he didn't really have a friend."

Elen-ai, daughter of the Family, was nearly brought to tears by the simple statement. "I can't..." She did not know how to put into words how inadequate she felt as Gidyon's friend. She could not imagine what it was like to be Gidyon, so solitary, and so strong. She had never admired anyone more.

"Do you think that we can win this?" Kaine's question came abruptly, concern giving him the illusion of looking much older than he was.

Elen-ai thought about Gidyon negotiating, wheedling, charming the Aadran and Tak families. She considered a little golden-haired boy with bright blue eyes trying to teach a room full of lowborn children about mathematics, and she found herself smiling, despite the fear and uncertainty that had descended over what seemed like the entire Second Country. "I have faith," she told Kaine.

SIXTEEN

Halen's army arrived three days after the Veertaks and their forces. Elen-ai stood alone on the walls of the Palace and watched the figures march onto the plain beyond the city. From such a distance, they looked more like smudges on the far-away field than people who could, and would, kill those who stood between them and the city. She shivered. The dark tide crept onward, seemingly without any end. Suddenly, the combined forces of Herran and the Veertaks encamped outside the city walls looked far less numerous. She wondered how they could possibly hold the city against the number of people that Halen had amassed. The ominous blue-black rainclouds overhead seemed a fitting backdrop as the Katan army set up camp.

She heard Silius approaching. She did not move, knowing he would use every moment of the journey to compose whatever thoughts were in his head. Eventually he came to stand beside her, his breath heavy from the walk, making tiny clouds in the cold air. Elen-ai did not think that he would appreciate the suggestion that he incorporate some light exercise into his daily routine.

"For a long time, I did not trust you," he said in the typically blunt manner to which she'd grown accustomed. She said nothing, letting him finish whatever he had come to say. She had learned to coexist with him well.

"You are a member of the Family. You are paid to kill. I thought my sister insane when she hired you to protect Gidyon.

But you have ensured his safety. Kaine seems to trust you completely, although his judgment might be compromised given the nature of your relationship with him. Yet you have been a loyal subject to Gidyon, and a loyal friend to this family."

Elen-ai remained looking straight ahead, watching as Halen's army arrayed themselves opposite the loyalist forces. Somewhere among them was the man himself in all his vile glory. Her fingers curled into fists at the thought of him.

"We have received word from Gidyon," Silius said quietly.

Elen-ai's head snapped around to look at him. "And?" Desperate worry curled its way around the single word.

"He is returning to Herran as fast as possible. With Aadran and Tak forces."

Elen-ai's exhalation was a long plume of steam. The relief was almost overwhelming. She could see that relief reflected in Silius' face, too.

"Thank you for coming to tell me," she said.

"I wanted to thank you, also." He did not smile. His face remained as impassive as ever. "It is good that you have been with us."

At that moment, the rain promised by the clouds came down in a heavy sheet. Together, Elen-ai and Silius left the Palace wall and went back inside.

Kar-am had ensconced herself in Gidyon's favourite council chamber. The old scholar had liberally drawn over the maps pinned to the walls. The many coloured lines and squiggles made sense only to her, but she seemed content with her work, which Elen-ai supposed was the important thing.

"So, the other side has arrived," she said with what could only be described as restrained glee, the moment Elen-ai and Silius entered the room, shaking off the rain that had settled on them.

"Yes, and quite a lot of them, too," Silius said.

"So I saw. Our reports were reasonably accurate about their numbers." Kar-am sounded more impressed by the efforts of the scouts and informants than worried by the size of the Katan army. She turned to a map of Herran and its surrounds on a table and bent so far over it that her nose practically brushed the map's surface.

The rest of the room's inhabitants – Kaine, Nikalus, Varl and Varlena, watched her with silent anticipation. Kar-am did not seem to be particularly aware of her audience. Her mouth moved silently as she thought, her fingers tapping some kind of rhythm on the map. Eventually she straightened.

"Nobody can fight while it's raining," she declared.

Her audience was a good one. No one said anything. Some consensus had led to the recognition that it was best for Kar-am simply to talk until she was finished.

"If they attack, we can stand firm and cut them down in the mud as they slip their way over to us. Same thing if we attack. Even after the rain, attacking on soaked ground creates the same problem, but with better visibility, so whoever's being attacked has time to prepare. We can't do anything. The good news, though, is that they can't either. Unless they're very stupid, in which case, that's good for us." She interlinked her hands and massaged her fingers, a slightly triumphant look on her face.

"So we need to wait until the rain stops and the ground dries?" Silius asked.

She nodded, the wispy white hair on her head flapping with the movement.

"Is there anything that we can or should be doing in the meantime?" Nikalus asked.

Kar-am tilted her head to one side, half closing her eyes as she thought. "Without knowing more about what sort of troops they have, not particularly. It looks as though they're building catapults."

"Catapults? But I thought they have only been used in the Fourth Country," Kaine said with alarm.

"That doesn't mean that Halen doesn't have them. I've instructed some of our people to try to build a few, but they're quite tricky to actually construct," Kar-am said. Her enthusiasm for the destructive devices was a little unsettling. No such things were necessary in the Second Country thanks to the peace maintained by the political structure. Knowledge of catapults came from reports and sketches brought to the ears of the powerful and the knowledge-hungry by people who had passed through the violent factional Fourth Country. There, the machines had been used in the power struggles between the various warmongers, destroying opponents' fortifications, or even simply destroying the towns that fell under opposing lands in order to force surrender. To think that they had come to the Second Country made the world feel as though it had tipped on its side.

"So what will give us an edge?" Nikalus asked.

Kar-am thought for a moment. "Knowing more about what he has. How many people are there, exactly? How many archers does he have? What sort of weapons are his hand-to-hand fighters using? Spears, swords? Do they have shields and, if so, what kind? If we know these things, we can adjust where and how we place our own people."

"How can we know any of this?" Silius asked.

The old woman shrugged, returning her attention to the map laid out in front of her. "We can't, unless someone is there in person. But that would be too dangerous."

"Unless you could get in unseen," Elen-ai said.

"Well, yes, then one could find out all of those things." Evidently assuming that getting into the enemy camp undetected was a hypothetical impossibility, Kar-am didn't even look up.

"I'll do it," Elen-ai said.

Kar-am lifted her head. She looked as though she was on the verge of objecting, but then she scrutinised Elen-ai properly.

"I didn't see it at first," she muttered more to herself than any-one else. "Your people have a way of eluding notice."

For a moment, Elen-ai had overlooked that Kar-am didn't know she was a member of the Family. It seemed that her place within the Palace had become so familiar, so comfortable, that she had forgotten the need for secrecy about her identity – for a second, she had simply thought of herself as a part of the Palace apparatus. The moment of discomfort was alleviated by the fact that everybody else in the room was aware of who she was and did not seem to care that Kar-am now knew. Kar-am herself cer-tainly seemed to have put no further thought into Elen-ai's iden-tity as a member of the Family.

Elen-ai's eyes flicked to Kaine, wondering if he would object to her sneaking into the Katan fighters' camp, in the same way he had been against the idea of her fighting in any battle. But he simply looked preoccupied.

"I'll go there once it's dark," she said.

The rain stopped just as darkness fell. Elen-ai skipped over the peaks and troughs of slippery mud on the field of the would-be battleground, her steps so light that she barely collected any mud on her feet. Wearing dark clothes and with the shadows gathered around her, she was invisible to everyone.

The troops who Halen had convinced to join him, as well as though he had simply bought, were arrayed over a large space. Even from a distance, the sight of so many people amid the myriad of tents and campfires was incredible. Elen-ai's skin crawled at the prospect of that many bodies charging into battle. Until that moment, she had never truly appreciated how wonder-ful the absence of war within the Second Country had been.

Elen-ai circled around the unlucky souls squelching through the mud on patrol. Even had she not been wreathed in shadows, they were unable to see more than a little way in front of them.

She was an invasion of one into the camp, and had she wished, she could have killed everybody in her path.

The sound of several thousand conversations was surprisingly soft as Elen-ai slipped into the camp and wove through the network of people, fires, and tents. Amid the songs, chuckles, and clatter of dice, gentle moans suggested some members of Halen's army were passing the time in a more private manner. Every noise that reached her ears was at once familiar yet strange. All of these activities were to be found in most establishments across the Second Country, yet it was as though she were hearing it all for the first time as they clashed together in the open air.

The people in the camp appeared so disconcertingly ordinary. Yet they were here because they were fighting for a man who was so despicable. It did not make sense, and left Elen-ai unsettled in a way she had not before felt.

Despite the fact that she had been trained in the use of every weapon imaginable, the composition of the army was a foreign music to Elen-ai. Yet she had undertaken to report on the army, so she persisted, trying to make sense of what she saw. Amid the hum of voices she could hear the elongated vowels of the Fourth Country's speech. The foreign fighters stayed together, declining to mingle with the inhabitants of the Second Country. Swords either strapped to their waists or placed within easy reached marked them as different to the Second Country fighters. Elen-ai's countrymen paid little heed to the spears neatly stacked far away from them, seeming more intent with the task of swapping stories. A disconcerting number of the campfires were surrounded by these foreign fighters. It took only a glance for her to know that all of them were hardened to fighting. These were the people who would carve through any battle, who would be the true threat. Near a particularly dense gathering of Fourth Country fighters she spied the huge shapes that could only be catapults. Counting four, she moved on.

She walked around a man relieving himself on the side of a tent – why he thought that was an appropriate place, she had no idea – and continued deeper into the camp. In the middle was Halen's tent, larger than any of the others and with the sun symbol of the Divine One stitched ostentatiously into the side . A minstrel played nearby, presumably for Halen's amusement. Elen-ai truly despised the Katan leader – who brought a minstrel to play for them on a campaign to usurp their rightful ruler?

Only one guard stood outside Halen's tent. It confirmed Elen-ai's suspicion the man was elsewhere. Lighter than breath, Elen-ai slipped past her. The opening flap to Halen's tent stirred as though by a passing breeze, but that was all that marked Elen-ai's entrance into the tent, and it certainly wasn't enough to arouse the suspicions of the guard. Elen-ai felt sorry for whoever had been tasked with erecting and dismantling the tent each day during the army's march toward Herran. It was enormous. She was certain she would find something more useful here than simply counting the soldiers in the camp. Kar-am had given her one other instruction: find out if there was a particular time when Halen was planning to send his people across the field to fight.

Despite the size of the tent, there was a surprising absence of any ornate furnishing. A small brazier smouldered near the entrance, offering the most meagre of light through a haze of smoke. It was more than enough illumination for Elen-ai. She crossed to a writing chest and rifled through its contents. This sort of reconnaissance she had done more times than she could remember. It was almost soothing to slip into that comfortable, known rhythm as she scanned each paper, trying to discern any information about what Halen was planning.

The Shadow God was evidently smiling upon her, for she found references to archer numbers, swords, and spears, amid the pages of correspondence and notes, all of which she memorised. Halen was obviously a man who organised himself with a painstaking attention to detail. That much was evident in the way he had gone about demanding the throne for his granddaughter. The timing, the execution, it all spoke of months, perhaps even years, of planning. There was no other way that he could have mustered this many people to fight for him so quickly. Perhaps he had anticipated Queen Latana's failure to produce a female heir years before anybody else, and recognised it as something of which he could take advantage.

There was, however, no information on when Halen was planning to send the people who he had managed to convince to risk their lives for him to try and take the capital. All she could find were messages about "being ready to muster when the word is given", or "ensuring weapons can be rapidly accessed". As she flicked through the communiqués, she breathed out a curse. A sense of desperation filled her. She wanted to find out everything she possibly could to help the people who were willing to die defending Herran and Gidyon's claim to the throne. She felt keenly the strain of knowing how many lives were going to be thrown so carelessly at one another. She spent another moment rereading every scrap of paper, but there was nothing that gave any indication of when exactly Halen was planning to attack. With nothing more she could glean, it was time to go. She replaced everything where she had found it with practised efficiency. But as she was about to close the final drawer, the tent flap was flung open and Halen strode in. Elen-ai silently cursed. She had been so absorbed in her task, shed missed the sound of his footsteps approaching the tent. She was caught. She prayed nobody in the Family would ever hear about this unforgivable lapse. She would almost certainly never be allowed to return to them if the fact she had allowed her emotion to blind her senses to her surroundings became known to them.

For a moment, Halen simply stared at the black-clothed figure on the other side of his tent. She bit down on her burning hatred and ensured her expression was settled into one of hard neutrality. Then she straightened, kicking the drawer closed with an effortless movement. Her eyes never left his, the hardness in her expression a thousandfold reflected in her eyes. The eyes of someone for whom taking life was a business. In the dim, hazy light given by the brazier, he would barely be able to make out her face, but her eyes would be shining like his, and she hoped he could discern her resolve in them.

Halen's mouth had opened in surprise, but he closed it, evidently deciding against calling for the guards who Elen-ai could sense – now that she was focusing – outside the tent.

"I assume that if I call for my people, I'll be dead before they can come in?" he asked. It would have been impossible for him not to know she was a member of the Family.

She lifted her shoulders in the most imperceptible shrug. It seemed he had not yet recognised her, but she was sure that he would quickly arrive at the correct conclusion. She could simply leave, but he would use the fact that a member of the Family had been in his tent to gather yet more support among the people of the Second Country. For all his faults, he was a clever man. She had little choice but to stay and try the best way out of this.

"I did not think that the Family interfered with matters related to the Royal Family," Halen said, slowly stepping farther into the tent. Elen-ai stayed where she was, waiting for him to identify her. She didn't know what he would do with the fact that one of Gidyon's advisers was a member of the Family, but she knew he would twist it to his advantage.

"If you're a member of the Family, why am I still alive?" Halen asked, taking another step toward her. While he could not see her face clearly, she could see his perfectly thanks to the skills of the Family. His forehead furrowed as he worked through the question. Then he arrived at the conclusion: "Lady Elen-ai."

She almost struck. It would have been so easy to close the distance between them. She could have done it in the space between heartbeats. But to leave Halen dead in the middle of his own camp would only point to some form of foul play. Questions would forever be asked about Gidyon as a ruler, and the Second Country had already been rended in two. The only way for something close to peace to return to the Second Country was if Halen was properly defeated. So the moment passed, and Halen's death at Elen-ai's hands slipped ignominiously away.

"So, the boy who would be king has a kept assassin. Or the Family has a kept king. I did wonder how he has remained so safe." A smirk worked its way across Halen's face. "It has been a question I could not answer: what compelled Gidyon to retain you, and why you seemed so loyal to him. Perhaps the rumours are true and you are his lover."

Elen-ai crossed the remaining distance between them in a move too quick for him to see. "Are you certain that you want to irritate me?"

Halen chuckled, apparently unfazed by the demonstration of her capabilities. He had been sucking on a candied lolly, and the sickly sweetness of his breath invaded her nose. Another flash of rage accompanied the realisation that he had been goading her.

"If I am found dead, then nobody in the Second Country will think that your king is legitimate in anything he does. I know you wouldn't harm a hair on my head." His confidence was foul.

Elen-ai seriously considered shearing off a lock of his hair to spitefully prove him wrong. "Don't worry, Halen, I won't hurt you. I'll leave that to Gidyon, and the people who fight for him. Tell me, how many of the people here did you have to pay to get them to march on Herran?" She moved away from him, gliding to the only chair and seating herself.

His face tightened at her insubordination, but a pleasant lightness remained in his voice. "You would not be surprised to learn that there are a great many people who do not feel it is appropriate that a man should have the throne. Once they knew that my granddaughter had a claim ... well." He spread his hands in lieu of finishing the sentence.

"And of course you will have no hand whatsoever in her rule."

Halen laughed. They both knew that he would be king in all but name. Just like they both knew that he was practically drooling at the mere thought of such an eventuality. In her mind, Elen-ai flowed across the room and wrapped her hands around Halen's neck, and he died knowing that she had been the one to kill him.

"If so many people support your claim, why did you have to hire swords from the Fourth Country?" she asked instead of killing him in one the hundred ways she so desperately wanted to.

"There is no harm in being cautious, my lovely assassin," he said, not seeming to be even slightly embarrassed that she knew he had hired foreign mercenaries. "After all, once my beautiful granddaughter ascends to the throne, money will be the least of my concerns." The way he inclined his head meant that the meagre light from the brazier shone on his bald pate. It should have made him look ridiculous, but instead it gave his face an unexpectedly sinister cast.

"You do realise that you're insane?"

"If I were insane, would your pointing it out make me less so?"

The fact that Halen's logic had a point snapped the final slender thread of Elen-ai's self-control. If she couldn't kill him, she could at least scare him. Halen couldn't have seen Elen-ai draw or throw the knife, but he certainly felt its impact between his feet. He glanced down at it, surprise on his face. Before he could react, two more knives were on either side of his boots, so close that one had even nipped the leather.

"You'll be nothing more than a footnote in the pages of history," Elen-ai snarled. Despite the three knives at Halen's feet, it looked as though she hadn't moved in the chair at all.

He slowly lifted his gaze from the blades to her. "Even if that's true, at least I'll be remembered. Will the same be said of you?"

Elen-ai slithered across the room, collecting her knives with a movement that was too fast to be seen. Halen had to turn to find her at the entrance to his tent where she paused so that she could deliver one parting comment. "I don't need to be remembered. It's enough for me to know that I'm on the right side of history – the side against you."

Rendering herself invisible, she ran across the campsite so quickly that her feet barely touched the ground. No one noticed her passing. She was simply a part of the night breeze.

SEVENTEEN

Kar-am received Elen-ai's information on the Katan forces with much enthusiasm. The old scholar's eyes brightened, and she scribbled on a map, all the while muttering excitedly to herself. After several moments had passed, it appeared as though Kar-am had entirely forgotten that Elen-ai still stood there. Finally, it became apparent that Elen-ai would have to interrupt the woman's conversation with herself. "I can't be sure, but I think Halen will order his people to attack as soon as possible."

The prediction had caught Kar-am's attention. She looked up, hand poised above the page, her eyes refocusing on Elen-ai as though surprised to find her standing there. "Why do you say that?"

"He found me in his tent. He wouldn't know what I discovered, but I wouldn't be surprised if he attacks as soon as he can to forestall any advantage we might have. But," Elen-ai paused for a breath, trying to work out the best way to explain what she had seen in the man. "Even if he hadn't caught me, I think he would attack without caring about the lives he might lose. He already thinks that people are disposable. He won't care about how many lives are lost if mounting an attack sooner gives him some advantage – even just a small one. The fact that he's paying many of them to fight for him would only contribute to that decision." Elen-ai fought the urge to twist her hands together as she waited for Kar-am to consider the statement. She was certain of her conclusion, but that didn't mean others would readily accept her assessment. She had observed enough people from the shadows to know the kind of person Halen really was, though. And her encounter with Halen in his tent had merely confirmed what she had long thought of him.

After many moments of contemplation, the old woman nodded. "We'll muster an hour before dawn to be ready for such an attack from the Katan side. You should get some rest before then. I believe you will be fighting tomorrow, and you'll want to be alert."

Elen-ai went to Kaine's chamber, unsurprised to find him still awake and reading. This time, it was not some arcane legal text but a volume on warfare tactics.

"Not your normal bedtime reading," she said.

He jumped. She had entered his rooms and moved through them with her customary silence, not paying any thought to alerting him to her presence. But he did not seem upset by the surprise. She liked that. He placed the book aside and offered her a weary smile. "Kar-am was kind enough to lend it to me."

"Anything interesting?"

He shook his head. "I've no taste for in this sort of thing."

Elen-ai crossed the distance between them with deliberate steps, pulling him to her. "Kar-am believes that Halen will order his people to attack at the first chance that arises. I'll be on the field in a few hours with the rest of the soldiers."

She had kissed his mouth so many times that it was now wonderfully familiar against her own. His hands on her offered a certainty that she was still there, still alive, that things were still as they should be, for at least a little while longer.

That promise of normalcy had only been an illusion. While dawn was still some way from arriving, Elen-ai headed down to encampment of loyalist forces and took her place in the unit of sword fighters to which Kar-am had assigned her. Elen-ai had no idea what exactly a unit was supposed to be, but neither did any of the people around her. Kar-am's explanation had been simple enough, though. Move when the enemy moved, and try and stay close to one another in battle. The people around Elen-ai stamped their feet to keep warm, rubbing together hands that would soon clutch weapons. Kaine's chamber seemed a world away in the chill pre-dawn light. The cold seeped into Elen-ai. She stamped her feet to try and stay warm. The waiting made the anticipation and dread settle in her alongside the cold. She longed for a cloak, but when the fighting did commence, she could not afford to be encumbered by such a billowing garment. She had lost count of how many times she had checked to ensure all of her blades were in place, but she performed the action again, as much for her own comfort as the meagre warmth the movement offered.

The city had practically been stripped so that any cloth royal colours – purple and gold - could be given to the Herran fighters. They needed to be able to identify one another so that they did not mistakenly attack the wrong people. Kar-am had been most insistent about it. People wore purple or gold – yellow, really – cloth in a variety of manners. Some were fortunate enough to have shirts or jackets in the colours. Elen-ai herself wore a shirt of deep purple, pilfered from somewhere in the Palace. Most of the people around her simply had strips of yellow or purple securely tied around their arms or waists. Yet the colours gave the army a ragtag sort of unison.

Elen-ai glanced skyward. Clouds still covered the sky. Drizzle so fine that it could be mistaken for mist quickly set in. Elen-ai wondered if Halen would attack after all. If not, the entire loyalist army would have been waiting for the last half hour for nothing. Somewhere behind her, close to the safety of the city's walls and separate from any fighting, Kar-am and the rest of the Royal Family stood. They would be watching the progress of the battle, sending down orders to particular groups of fighters in response to whatever Halen's army was doing, but they were too far away to chart the progress of any individual fighter. The thought that Kaine would be looking at the fighting but unable to see her made Elen-ai double check that every blade, every buckle, every lace, was exactly where it should be. She wanted to see him again.

Finally, the sky began to lighten until it was possible to see further and further and some modicum of colour seeped into the landscape. The white-green of the frosted grass stood out starkly against the brown of the earth. Elen-ai's breath was a cloud in front of her.

She glanced up to the walls of the city – if you could call them that. The cities and towns of the Fourth Country were truly walled in preparation for an attack, but the peace that had gifted the Second Country for so long had made such protection unnecessary. The walls that denoted the beginning of Herran were more a collection of houses. Even the field in which they stood could have been called a part of Herran, filled as it was in summer with the makeshift camps of the poorest residents, those who came to scratch out a meagre living by performing the lowliest jobs that could be found, such as cleaning the refuse from the streets. In wintertime, those poor souls crammed into dwellings that should only have housed a third as many. Many a tragedy had gone unnoticed when such structures caught fire, and everybody inside perished. Some of those people stood beside Elen-ai now, their skeletal forms obvious even under the clothes that had been given to them by the Palace. The offer of food, clothing, and coin had brought a surprising number of people to fight for Gidyon. It was impossible to tell if their allegiance was to the king or the comforts they were offered. Elen-ai wondered uneasily if paying those desperate for sustenance to defend Herran was akin to Halen hiring mercenaries to fight for him. She wanted to say the actions were worlds apart, but she was no naïve child. The Palace's offer was using the lowborn of the Second

Country just as Halen did. Such was the way of the world when the rich and powerful fought. At least these men and women beside her were fighting for their city.

Katan forces mounted their attack three long and tedious hours after dawn, once the drizzle had cleared. The unit leaders of Gidyon's army shouted for the defenders to hold their positions. Kar-am had ordered with a terrifying fierceness that no offensive action be taken. Where the ground wasn't frozen, it was wet and slippery. Any charge would result in people falling over, becoming stuck, losing their momentum. From there, it would be easy for the Katan fighters to cut them down as they struggled for purchase in the unforgiving earth. Halen must have felt he had fighters to waste on a charge across the treacherous ground.

The first wave of Katan fighters appeared as a dark line that became thicker as they approached. Horns blared as the Katan troops came closer and closer. Elen-ai hefted the sword she had been given, taking a small measure of comfort from its weight. The people around her – her unit – mirrored her action. Most of the other fighters in the loyalist army were equipped with spears, which were easier to use, especially with little training. Elen-ai did not allow herself to be distracted by worry about the undertrained army in which she stood. She pushed her mind instead to think of her own skill, to ready herself for the coming fight, for it would be the hardest fight of her life.

Alarmed shouts from the rear attracted Elen-ai's attention. One of the two catapults the Herran forces had managed to build had collapsed. Women and men scrambled around the debris. One or two unfortunates had been struck by beams or ropes. It was a gruesome sight. The other catapult appeared to still be intact, its cup filled with large rocks. Then its ropes snapped. The deadly projectiles flew across the battlefield and crashed into the line of Katan fighters, but because the ropes had snapped rather than been released, a few fell short, landing amid the Herran soldiers, too. Screams of pain and terror split the air. Fortunately, Elen-ai had not been in the path of the catapult, but she couldn't help but worry that this was some kind of sign as to how the battle would fall. The Katan catapults returned fire. They appeared to be slightly more successful. Deadly debris rained destruction onto the loyalist ranks. Some held shields, baskets, pieces of wood, anything they could find, above their heads in a desperate bid for some protection. But the Katans too were struggling with their own hastily erected catapults. Even as she watched, Elen-ai saw one of the shadowy mountains topple sideways. She glanced back one more time at the disasters that had been the loyalists' catapults. Such was the outcome when scholars tried to put into practice dangerous ideas without first testing them. Elen-ai wondered what else of Kar-am's theories would be proved wrong in practice before the day was out.

As the Katan forces drew closer, a wave of arrows from behind them came speeding from behind them. Once again, the loyalist forces held anything they could use to protect themselves above their heads. The thick thud of arrows raining down was almost deafening, but it was over quickly. The loyalist army held its position as its archers replied with their own volley of arrows onto the Katan forces which grew ever closer.

The archers of both sides sent over waves of arrows in a desperate bid to thin their enemies' ranks, and then the Katan army was too close, and the real battle began. The forces met in a cacophony of sound and blood and violence. Elen-ai threw herself into the battle with a vigour she had not realised she possessed. The sword was an extension of her arm, biting into flesh with hungry metal teeth. She gave herself to the blood song. This was everything that she had been made to do, fighting in the most pure of forms. She was not forged for the world of the court, or the subtleties of games played by those who did not truly have to bear their consequences. The only toys that she had ever been given were weapons, made to fit her tiny hands. She had been trained and broken, and trained again. She had been forged to be the victor in any fight. The months of constraint and intrigue in the court had almost made Elen-ai forget what and who she was, but that self came roaring out in the clash and crash of battle.

Elen-ai was vaguely aware that the light had become brighter as the morning wore on, and that people around her were falling with a distinct absence of any grace or poeticism. The Royal Guard, who only occasionally put their training into practice where they fended off robbers when escorting something for the Royal Family, were barely more efficient than the low-born. If anything, many of the lowborn fought better thanks to the fact that in the less refined world of the Second Country, brawls were commonplace. As she hacked and slashed her way through any enemy who crossed her path, Elen-ai wondered if this battle bore any resemblance to the tomes and recollections that Kar-am had collected over her lifetime. Somehow, she doubted that this bloody, messy, disaster was the sort of thing documented in the records of tactics and battle outcomes. There was a difference between a tale recounted to an interested audience or words on a page, and the slick feel of blood, the ache of muscles, or the jagged cries of pain from those left wounded and dying on the ground.

A momentary lull hours later saw Elen-ai rouse herself from the bloodlust which had saturated her very being. The exertion of hours of fighting had covered her with a sheen of sweat. The chill of the morning had long since fled her. She looked at the battle surrounding her, and despair threatened to choke her when she saw how many Katan fighters still stood. They far outnumbered the people alongside whom Elen-ai fought. Despite the hope to which she had desperately clung, she could see no way that Halen would not win this battle. Indeed, it seemed a miracle that the loyalists had held out for so long. Once he had overpowered the defenders of Herran, Halen's troops would simply march through the city streets until he battered down the Palace doors and claimed the throne. Elen-ai forced down the sense of hopelessness and threw every last part of herself back into the fray. If Halen was victorious today, she would take down as many of his people as she possibly could. It was the only thought that gave her comfort and she drew on it to keep fighting with every last drop of her strength and speed.

The feel of wind whispering past her drew her out of her violent reverie. She knew what that sensation meant, even as she struggled to believe it. members of the Family amid the fighting. The grace with which they danced from person to person was quite beautiful. The bloody carnage they left behind was breathtakingly spectacular. The deadly skills of the Family were all too often used in secret. However, here on the battlefield, there was no need to hide themselves. They were fighting for their lives, for their city. The death they swiftly brought to any opponent they encountered made those loyalists around them fight even harder.

A tap on her shoulder had Elen-ai whipping around, blade in hand – she had lost the sword perhaps half an hour previously, leaving it in the belly of a man as she had swung to block a blow from a woman foolishly trying to surprise her. Instead of an attacker though, she came face to face with the grinning mountain that was one of her Brothers, Al-et.

"Are you really that surprised to see us, Sister?" he asked. A man charged at him before she could reply. He fended the attacker off with no obvious effort.

"I can't say I expected you," she gasped, her breath stolen by the surprise of her family's appearance rather than the exertion of the fighting.

"Why ever not?" He grinned. The gold tooth he had inserted after his fiftieth kill winked at her.

"I didn't think that the Family would fight." Elen-ai took a moment to parry a blow aimed at her head. The woman who held the offending blade was from the Fourth Country by the look of her. There was a silken manner to her movements that suggested she was very practised in the art of killing. It meant that Elen-ai had to concentrate a little and momentarily, her conversation with Al-et was ceased. She parried another blow, then whispered around the woman to stab her in the back of her neck.

Al-et shouted, "Good to see you haven't lost your touch."

She made an obscene gesture at him. "Why is the Family fighting for Gidyon?" she yelled back once he had finished dispatching two women. Unfortunately for them, they had decided that the fact he was conversing with Elen-ai would mean he would be an easy kill.

He twirled his axe. He was showing off, now. "You apparently made a good case to our Grandparents."

A smile broke Elen-ai's face in two. Despite the gore, the sweat, and the sweet ache that told her that her muscles were beginning to strain, she felt once more that victory might be possible. She threw herself back into the fight with renewed energy.

The members of the Family had woven themselves across the battlefield. They were phenomenal. Everyone they touched fell and stayed down. They were harmed by only the luckiest of blows. But even the influx of the Family and their deadly efficiency was not enough to truly turn the tide of battle. Members of the Family might have brought down anyone who came near them, but the battlefield was large, and the number of Katan fighters so very enormous.

"Keep them from entering the city." The cry boomed across the battlefield, taken up by those defending Herran from those seeking to take it for themselves. Soon it was a deafening roar, but the desperation within it could not be missed. There were too many Katan fighters for the defenders to keep at bay. Even the Family could only thin their numbers, perhaps provide a slight delay. But it would only be a matter of time until the attackers made their way into Herran.

Despair once again weighed down Elen-ai's heart. Despite all that she had done, despite the Family defying the impossible and coming to fight, it seemed that Herran would still be lost. A sob made its way up her throat as she slashed and danced. She could fight until there was nothing left of her but a blade and the will to hold it, but there was no way that it could be enough.

The sky seemed to mirror her anguish, having turned an ominous black. It was only the early afternoon, but darkness was seeping over the land. Rain, thunder and lightning looked as though they were ready to engulf the frenetic and bloody battle-field, throwing the entire scene into even further chaos.

And then the cries around her took on a different tenor. Wondering what Halen could possibly do now, what terrible and bloody force he could introduce to rip through the tired, bloodied defenders, and break into the streets of Herran where he would destroy anybody or anything that stood in the way between him and the Palace, Elen-ai hardly dared to raise her eyes beyond the immediate melee to see. There she saw the new fighters ap-proaching the battlefield. Elen-ai's heart painfully tightened at the thought that Halen had somehow managed to hide a force of reserve fighters so that they could sweep in and destroy the tired and bloody loyalists who had been ensconced in battle all day. In that second, Halen seemed to her not a man, but a figure with godlike powers. She almost fell to her knees, giving up and let-ting the battle simple wash over her. But then she saw a flash of golden hair and her heart squeezed painfully with a wild joy she could barely contain as it pounded through her. Gidyon had fi-nally arrived with fighters from the Tak and Aadran families.

EIGHTEEN

The arrival of the reinforcements was a magnificent sight. In the dark that had swept across the sky the land, Gidyon's hair glowed, drawing the eye to him amid the reinforcements. He rode his kittanae at a reckless pace, leading his forces.

The fighting stopped almost entirely as every single person in the fray turned to watch the King approach. The King of the Second Country was spectacular, almost like a vision. Even from far away, Elen-ai could see in the set of his face the determination that he would not lose this fight, that he would never see his throne lost. He was leading several mounted riders. Behind them was a mass of unmounted fighters. Gidyon drew his sword and held it aloft. On the graceful feline whose stride seemed more akin to flight, Gidyon looked like a figure straight out of legend.

The air was so still that from the other side of the battle-field, Halen's furious scream to his archers was clear. "What are you waiting for? Fire on him."

The cold of the day washed over Elen-ai for the first time since the fighting had begun. Gidyon wore leather armour, but his head was unprotected. If a lucky arrow struck him, then he would almost certainly die. She could only watch as the volley flew in an arc across the rapidly closing distance between Gidyon and the battlefield. The pale wood of the arrows stood out against the blue-blackness of the sky, almost beautiful in their flight. They hailed down around the King. A few struck people near him, but Gidyon was mercifully untouched.

The call to release came again, and another barrage of arrows arced across the air, seemingly suspended in flight. Once more, everybody – not just Elen-ai – appeared to hold their breath as they waited to see whether the battle would be ended by one lucky arrow. One arrow did find a mark of sorts, lodging in the neck of Gidyon's mount. The beautiful beast stumbled, then came crashing to the ground, the King falling with it. Elen-ai heard a strangled cry, then realised it was hers. A fall like that, especially with an animal as large as a kittanae, could be just as fatal as an arrow hitting home. Time seemed to stop as beast and boy tumbled. Elen-ai could hear her own heartbeat, thrumming through her body, feel the rasp of air against her throat.

Then Gidyon rolled clear of the falling animal and pushed himself to his feet. He barely seemed to worry about the other riders thundering past him who might trample him. Gidyon now stood alone, a solitary figure in the space between the two armies, the near-profane sight of the wounded kittanae beside him somehow serving to make him look even more startling. He had miraculously defied death three times in a row.

A cheer rose up from the loyalist fighters. Astonishment, pride, and relief made the women and men fighting in Gidyon's name scream in wordless rapture at what they had witnessed. The cry broke the spell of stillness that Gidyon's appearance had caused and the fighting resumed. Caught between three different assailants, Elen-ai was no longer able to watch Gidyon's progress. She was vaguely aware that another volley of arrows was released and sailed toward the King, but she could not look to make sure that he was not hit. She could only pray that he had once more managed to defy death.

The fighting took on a new intensity as the defenders found themselves reinvigorated by the sight of the reinforcements, their king, and his escape from harm. Elen-ai could feel the change across the battlefield as the line of mounted Tak and

Aadran fighters swept through it. She too was caught up in that sensation; she didn't even realise that she was uttering a guttural cry until she felt the rawness of her throat when she paused to draw breath. She hacked, slashed, twisted, turned without thought. She didn't even notice whether she was running down men or women, all she could feel was the ache of her muscles and the resistance when blades met flesh. Elen-ai all but flew between her victims. Sometimes she would pause to properly engage an assailant who found themselves directly in her path, sometimes she would simply reach out an arm or leg, and whoever she had chosen as her unlucky target went down. Her legs covered in mud, her arms and face smeared with blood, she should have looked terrifying, and to anyone who she was about to strike, she did in fact look like a sending from their worst night terrors. People from both sides were falling, exhausted from the unrelenting hours of fighting. Some were even unharmed, simply lying in the mud, uncaring if death did in fact claim them, uncaring even if the end of the world came. But she still moved as though she could evade exhaustion itself, every turn, pivot, thrust, a graceful piece of poetry in action.

Elen-ai eventually came to the end of her dance and she paused to regather herself. She stood surrounded by people doing their utmost to remain alive, and in that moment of stillness, the reverie of bloodshed in which she had been caught up was broken. The salty smell of blood mingled with that of earth, opened bowel and bile. Even the four months she had spent working in a slaughterhouse at age nine, which she had thought had made her utterly indifferent to the unpleasant smell and sight of death, had failed to prepare her for this. The reek was overpowering. It seemed to rise from the earth and assail the senses with the same ferocity as any of the fighters on the field. It was almost overwhelming to see the number of fallen bodies that surrounded her. So many forms covered the ground that it seemed impossible enough people were still able to continue fighting. Yet even as she stood, some optimistic fool rushed at her. She simply dropped low and pushed up with her blade, goring her enemy with a brutal efficiency. As she rose to stand fully upright once more, the sound of another feral battle cry reached her ears. The Tak and Aadran foot soldiers had finally reached the battle. The sound of weapons clashing mixed with cries of pain, deafeningly loud as both loyalists and usurpers were invigorated by the arrival of these new fighters.

Nearby, a wounded Herran fighter dragged herself through the muck of battle towards the tents where the wounded were being treated. Something about the woman's desperate determination to try to save herself pulled Elen-ai away from the call of fighting. In swift strides, Elen-ai went to the woman's side, pulled her up, and slung one arm around her shoulder.

"Can you walk?" Elen-ai asked.

The woman gave a feeble nod.

"Come on."

They half-crawled, half-ran back toward Herran, weaving through what had once been ranks of men and women and was now simply chaos.

The woman collapsed completely as they neared the edge of the battleground, and Elen-ai carried her the rest of the way. She laid the woman down among the unending lines of bodies inside the first tent she reached. As soon as the woman was out of her arms, Elen-ai would have struggled to find her amid the pain, mud, and blood that left everybody in the tent looking exactly like one another.

She took the moment to stretch and ease the ache that had taken root deep within her muscles. The sound of battle was muffled by the walls of the sheets of canvas slung over an array of poles to keep the bloodied wounded under cover that a generous soul might call a tent. Somewhere further along, there were actual tents, but as the battle had continued and more people had dragged themselves away to seek help, the structures that had been erected to offer them even the most meagre of shelter had become increasingly crude.

Elen-ai called for help and one of the few attendants yelled at her to wait. There were all too few people in the tent with the training to help those who needed it. Many of the wounded would die as relatively minor wounds went untended and became fatal. The smell of the injured was almost worse than it had been on the battlefield. It was a certainty that, on the other side of the battlefield, there were Katan fighters arrayed in an almost identical way. Elen-ai was struck by the pointlessness of the battle that raged on even as she stood surrounded by the wounded and dying. The thought brought to life the anger at Halen that Elen-ai nursed within her. Here was a man willing to knowingly end so many lives simply for the sake of his own greed, his own ego. In that moment, she vowed to the Shadow God that even if he won this battle, even if he claimed the throne for his inept grand-daughter, she would still bring death to Halen Katan. If it came to Halen residing in the Palace, all but sitting on the throne himself, it would almost certainly mean that Gidyon and his uncles were dead, that the country she knew and loved was irrevocably changed. If that eventuated, the only thing that Elen-ai could do would be to end the miserable life of Halen Katan, no matter if it meant that she would be never allowed back to the Family, even it meant her own death. As she stood in the tent, surrounded by the stench of blood and gore, she prayed to the Shadow God and promised that if the worst came to pass, she would take Halen's life with her own hands.

Elen-ai left the area devoted to the wounded. The tents had been placed on a rise so that if rain did come, the casualties wouldn't be lying in pools of water. Of course, the ground was already cold and damp from the preceding days of rain, and lines of bodies almost completely filled the tent. If the battle continued for much longer, there was no more room even for makeshift tents on the slight hill; the wounded would be forced to lie outside.

Elen-ai turned to the battle raging below, the crash of weapons and the guttural cries of pain and rage filled the air. Gidyon was somewhere in the melee, but amid the sea of people, it was impossible to pick him out. The terrible thought occurred to Elen-ai that he might be wounded or dead, rendered anonymous by mud and blood. If that were the case, then this terrible fight was continuing for no reason. The prospect that Gidyon might be dead filled Elen-ai with dread that left a sour taste in her mouth. That taste became more bitter as she looked out across the battlefield and realised that despite the reinforcements from Tak and Aadran, the Katan fighters still had superior numbers. Moreover, after battling rain and mud during their march across the Second Country to arrive at Herran in time, the Tak and Aadran fighters were tired. Elen-ai could see it in the sluggishness of their movements. They were being slaughtered.

The vantage point laid the battle out before her like a map. The members of the Family were not visible, but where they went could not be missed for the trails of dead they left in their wakes. The hired fighters from the Fourth Country were brutal, giving no ground. Their movements were efficient, practised. They were unshaken by the chaos of the battleground or the extent of the carnage through which they waded. And then there was everybody else, the citizens of the Second Country who had been conscripted through the promise of a meal, money, or some ideology. Some had broken and were fleeing toward Herran, or the dubious safety of the plains. A surprising number held their ground, though fatigue shone through their sluggish movements. It was safe to assume that all were desperately praying that their waking nightmare would soon be over.

The light was bleeding quickly from the land as Elen-ai made her way toward the fray. With the clouds pregnant with rain, it would soon be too dark to tell friend from foe. Elen-ai grabbed a sword from a fallen body and cut her way through the crush of exhausted bodies to the heart of the battle. Three times, she came across her Brothers and Sisters, and she exchanged a tired, knowing nod with them. She wondered how many of them would fall before the battle was over. Their deaths would be on her conscience. Fighting anybody who was stupid enough to engage her, she searched in the fading light for Gidyon. Finally, she saw a flash of gold. Of course, he was in the thick of battle, despite the danger. It was just one more reason she would follow him to the ends of the earth if he asked. Or even if he didn't.

She hacked her way through to Gidyon's side. Six soldiers fought alongside him: two members of the Royal Guard and two each from the household guards of Tak and Aadran, ensuring his sides and rear were protected. A fighter from the Fourth Country towered in front of Gidyon. Elen-ai didn't hesitate. She ran the woman through, pushing her body aside as it fell. The corpse fell to the earth with a thud, leaving Elen-ai and Gidyon staring at one another across it.

"Your Highness." Elen-ai looked Gidyon over to ensure he was uninjured. Other than a thorough coating of mud, he seemed miraculously unharmed.

"It's good to see you." Gidyon gave her a smile that managed to reach his eyes. "Your lessons have been very helpful today." His words ignited comfort in her at knowing that even though she hadn't been by his side, she had still been able to protect him.

Before Elen-ai had the opportunity to reply, she was forced to parry a swing from an attacker who had managed to sneak between two members of Gidyon's guard. While their blades were locked, Elen-ai stomped on his foot, then stabbed him in the eye with one of her blades.

Once, Gidyon would have been horrified by the demonstration of her brutal skills, but all he said was "Thank you," once it was clear that the man was not going to get up again.

"We won't be able to keep this up." Elen-ai had to shout across the roar of battle which had suddenly crescendoed around them.

The expression on his face told her that he had already arrived at that conclusion. Any reply was curtailed as a group of Katan fighters charged them, intent on ending the battle by killing the king. Precious light fled even further as for several moments, Elen-ai and Gidyon became preoccupied with dispatching their attackers. Two of Gidyon's guards fell and Elen-ai was forced to fight three people at once before loyalists came to their aid and they were momentarily clear of enemies.

A flash of lightning from the harbour side of Herran was proceeded by a growl of thunder that temporarily drowned out the cacophony of battle.

"Gid, if it starts to rain, we'll be in trouble. Most people will barely be able to see if it gets dark. With the rain, they won't know who they're fighting," Elen-ai yelled.

Gidyon didn't respond; his blade remained at a 'guard' position, but his thoughts were clearly not on defending himself.

"Gidyon," Elen-ai yelled. "I don't know how we're supposed to win this." At last she voiced what she had tried so hard to not admit. No matter how she considered it, the battle did not seem as though it could be won. Elen-ai had not realised until that moment how much she had hoped that Gidyon had some brilliant plan to defy the odds. She had not realised the extent of her faith in Gidyon until she felt that faith beginning to be shaken.

Gidyon closed his eyes. It seemed a foolish thing to do in the middle of a battle. His lips moved, but she could not hear what he said. She moved close to him, looking around for potential attackers.

"What?" She placed her ear so close to his lips that she could feel the warmth of his breath against her face. It was a poor position for her to be in if they were attacked.

"Don't you believe in me, Elen-ai?" She could hear a sad smile in his voice. "Step back."

She didn't hesitate, didn't question; she simply obeyed the order of her king.

Gidyon let his sword fall to the ground and raised his hands high above his head. Elen-ai wondered what he was doing, but she did not interrupt him. Her task now was to ensure he was undisturbed. She raised her blade, watching with keen eyes for anyone who might come toward her king. The land was almost completely dark now, that blackness only punctuated only by distant lightning strikes. It was possible that the storm would pass them by, but Elen-ai had her doubts. She parried one attacker, lost a blade as she threw it into the eye of a second would-be assailant, then thrust her sword into the face of her first attacker.

The man fell. His blood seemed impossibly red in the dark, even with her Family-gifted sight. Then Elen-ai realised she wasn't seeing with the skills of the Family. Gidyon's hands were glowing, possible to almost be mistaken for a ray of light which had managed to break through the thick, dark clouds. , the light unwavering like a sunbeam breaking through cloud. Then it became stronger. Then it was so bright that Elen-ai's eyes watered. The fighting around them had stopped as people looked for the source of this sudden light.

The light became so bright that Elen-ai couldn't look directly at it. Instead, she dropped her gaze to Gidyon's face. His eyes were closed, the expression on his face was serene. The glow grew even brighter, piercing the darkness of the battleground to touch everybody, and Elen-ai could not even look at Gidyon's face any longer. Now no one fought. Silence reigned. Everybody was looking to Gidyon – the king who was summoning the sun amid the darkness.

It was impossible to know who knelt first, but from wherever it started, the action spread like a ripple until every person on the battlefield, including Elen-ai, was kneeling in the mud and blood, beside the bodies of those who had fallen, beside the person who until a moment ago they had been fighting alongside or against, bowing their heads in reverence to the king – their king, who held the sun in his hands.

NINETEEN

Three days after the battle for Herran and still Elen-ai's muscles ached from the hours of fighting. She spared a thought for the others who had not been trained from birth by the Family. They must be in agony.

The bustle of the Palace reached her ears as she lay on the bed in her rooms. The sounds were familiar to her by now; servants moving discreetly through the building, the Royal Guard performing a drill – they must have been in immense discomfort returning to such work so soon – the snip of shears as the gardens were tended. It was different to the near meditative quiet of the Family's house, interspersed with the occasional hum of conversation, the thuds and whisper-soft grunts of training. Even the creak of the old house moving in the weather was a far more unobtrusive noise than the sounds of the Palace. Yet the everyday noises of the Palace had resolved themselves into a familiar tune that no longer struck her anew each time she heard it.

At some point during the fighting, she had sustained a shallow but long slash across her shoulder blades. Only once it had been pointed out to her amid the disarray of the battlefield's dismantling had it begun hurting. Since then it had stung with an intrusive constancy. Never more had Elen-ai wished for Freya's presence and her healing skills.

The knock on the door which rang through her chambers was followed immediately by Gidyon. Since the battle she had spent very little time by his side. So many things had demanded his attention that it had been impossible for Elen-ai to keep up with what he was doing. Or at least, that was what she had told herself.

He closed the door behind him. "Am I interrupting?"

"No." Elen-ai sat up. She winced as the movement pulled scabs across her shoulders.

The King approached her, his uncertainty obvious in the sound of his steps as he crossed the small sitting room to enter her bedchamber. Rather than come and sit beside her, he remained standing in the doorway. After a hesitant moment, Elen-ai patted the space next to her on the bed. He sat.

"Everything all right?" she asked.

He gave a little shrug, looking down at the embroidery on the bed's coverlet rather than at her. "I suppose. Judging and sentencing people is not exactly my favourite thing to do."

"I'm sorry I haven't been—" she began, but he cut her off with a wave of his hand.

"You have done more than enough. You deserve a rest."

"And you? You came all the way across the country, threw yourself into the fighting, and now you're still going."

"A ruler does not live for themselves but in service to their people." Gidyon was obviously reciting something he had been told often, yet that made it no less moving to be reminded of how seriously Gidyon took his duty.

"Halen never would have understood that," Elen-ai said with quiet firmness.

Gidyon gave another little shrug. "I do not know. He might have. Sometimes I think that deep underneath it all, he honestly did believe he was doing the right thing. But then he became so caught up with his ego and greed that it was impossible to separate the two."

"He never wanted to do right by the people of the Second Country. Not in the way that you do." The fierceness in Elen-ai's

tone caught her by surprise. Gidyon was long past needing protection or reassurance. He had proved that time and time again.

"Do you know what they are calling me?" He didn't look at
her, instead gazing at the painting of Herran's harbour on the
wall.

Elen-ai had, but she chose to let him tell her.

"The Sun King."

"Better than the Pretender King or Boy-King," she said.

"They think that my reign is blessed by the Divine One. That
I am some form of Divine incarnation."

"Don't you believe that?"

Gidyon was silent, giving due consideration to the question.
"I do not know what I believe."

"Well, with the support that you have, you could do anything you like," she pointed out.

"That scares me, though," he said. "I do not want to be able
to do anything. The reason we have justices, the reason we have
the power of the Seven Families, is so that whoever sits on the
throne cannot simply do what they want."

Elen-ai slung an arm across the King's shoulders, giving
him a quick hug. "If you want, I can always tell you when you're
being stupid."

A smile tugged at his lips. "Ah yes. 'I am terribly sorry, but
my friend thinks I am being stupid, so I will not be proceeding
with this particular idea, after all'. I am sure that will be well received."

She laughed, resting her head against his shoulder. In reply,
he tilted his head to gently brush against hers. For a moment,
she forgot what had transpired on the battlefield. Rather than
being the Sun King who had brought two armies to their knees,
he was once more simply her friend.

"Have you spoken with Kaine?" Gidyon asked.

"A little."

Gidyon opened his mouth to say something further, then hesitated. She knew why. Like her, like everyone, Gidyon's uncles had been unsure how they should approach their nephew. Unlike Elen-ai, though, whose struggle lay in the uncertainty of how to treat as a friend someone who had inspired awe across an entire country, and as a result, someone whose every command would be obeyed without any question, Gidyon's uncles were still struggling to understand what magic Gidyon had within him that allowed him to summon light. For them, Gidyon had gone from being their king to being a figure who walked hand-in-hand with their god. It was one of the other reasons that Elen-ai had secluded herself over the past three days. She did not want to have any discussion of Gidyon's acts with Kaine. She did not want to have those sorts of discussions with anyone.

"I feel very alone," Gidyon said, so softly that it was almost as though had hadn't even meant to actually voice the feeling aloud.

Elen-ai pulled her friend more closely to her. "Don't say that."

He shook his head ever so slightly. The catch in his breath spoke of a battle to contain tears.

"You're never alone," she promised him. "You'll always have me."

They left her rooms and walked together through the Palace corridors. Almost certainly Gidyon had somewhere to be, but there was no sense of urgency in his demeanour. Elen-ai looked at the walls as they passed. It was as though she was seeing them again for the first time. The careful arrangement of the coloured tiles formed beautiful patterns that gave the corridor a sense of light and beauty. Elen-ai couldn't begin to imagine how painstaking it must have been to envisage such a design, let alone place the tiles so that every small square fit together as part of a larger whole.

"It's a shame that the tiles will be destroyed if you knock down this wing," she commented.

Gidyon looked at her in confusion before casting a glance at the walls. "They are terribly outdated."

"But they're so beautiful."

"Elen-ai, nobody tiles their walls anymore. It has not been done for at least thirty years." Gidyon sounded amused.

"So? Don't you think this is beautiful?" Elen-ai stopped in front of a section that had been tiled only in blue and white. The blue tiles were arranged in a growing spiral radiating out from a small centre. Against the starkness of the white, it was quite arresting. The windowsills of that section had been painted alternately white and blue, too.

"It is very visually impressive," Gidyon admitted.

"So you're the Sun King. If you like it, just have them put in tiles. Who's going to dare to say you have old-fashioned taste?"

It was good to hear him laugh.

They continued on to the council chamber. The maps had been removed from the walls and the stacks of papers and books that had transformed the space into a veritable maze had been returned to their appropriate places. Elen-ai thought she should cease to call it the war room in her mind. Yet she could not think of it as anything else. Gidyon's uncles were waiting for him. Elen-ai's eyes met Kaine's. He looked as though he had a world of questions to ask her, but she immediately dropped her gaze.

"We have a problem," Silius said the moment the door closed behind them.

"Another attempt to take my throne?" The wry amusement in Gidyon's tone suggested he did not think that was very likely.

"No. But we need to decide what we are to do with Halen and the rest of the Katan family."

"Execution is a possibility," Nikalus suggested.

Gidyon shook his head. "If he had won, he would have executed all of us. I do not want to be like him in any way."

"Well, he can't remain in the Second Country. Even if he's imprisoned, he may still have enough influence and intelligence to cause trouble," Silius said.

Gidyon turned to Kaine. "What legal options do we have?"

Gidyon's uncles were all noticeably wary of him. They hesitated before speaking, and didn't allow their gaze to meet the King's for an overly long time. Elen-ai could see the faintest edge of hurt in Gidyon's eyes at the treatment he was receiving. In summoning light, he had elevated himself to something that separated him from others beyond the mere fact that he was their King.

Kaine looked at the wall in an almost convincing pretence of consideration. "We could definitely throw them all in the jail."

"Remember, we have to deal with the Rasatan and Bertak families as well."

Nikaus' reminder was either directed at his nephew or his brother. It meant that he conveniently did not need to look at Gidyon as he spoke but could instead turn to Kaine.

"They placed their support behind Halen and the Katan claim. And, of course, the Bertak family has been breaching the law with the illegal workers." When the Royal Guard had arrived at the Bertak estate to place the family under house arrest until Gidyon decided what to do with them, they had discovered that supporting the Katan army was not the only morally questionable thing the Bertaks had been doing. Citizens from the Fourth Country who had fled the violence there were working in the Bertak mines. Not only was such a proliferation of undocumented workers illegal, but after a brief preliminary investigation, it had been determined that the Bertaks were woefully underpaying the refugees – another crime within the Second Country.

"I think we imprison the heads of the Bertak and Rasatan families," Gidyon said. "And impose several sanctions and taxes onto those who adopt the leadership."

Kaine nodded. "That would all fall within some form of law or legal precedent."

"But the Katan family?" Silius prompted. "I do think we should consider execution, like Nik said."

"I will not kill them. Not even Halen. Serenah is my cousin and your niece. And Serenah's mother is your sister. I do not understand how you can suggest this." The sharpness to Gidyon's voice when addressing his uncles was not new. What Elen-ai had never seen, though, was his uncles practically cower in reply to his firmness.

"My apologies." Silius looked somewhere over Gidyon's shoulder rather than meeting the King's eyes. Nikalus immediately dropped his gaze to his feet like a chastened child, and Kaine remained staring at the wall in a magnificent pretence of contemplation.

A hand squeezed Elen-ai's heart when she thought of Gidyon's earlier quiet confession, that he felt isolated from everyone around him. His uncles' responses to him would do nothing other than reinforce this. With time, hopefully, they would drop this posturing and return to the relationship they once had with their nephew.

"What about exile?" Kaine suggested.

Gidyon nodded thoughtfully. "If we do this, do I have the right to take their land from them?"

His question earned him a surprised look from even Elen-ai.

"There is no law permitting it," Kaine said. "But then again, there is no law to prevent it."

"All right then. That is what I want to do. Strip them of their land and wealth, leaving them enough coin to survive, and exile them until Serenah dies."

There was a certain brutality to the decision that Elen-ai quite liked.

"What if they try to garner support while in exile?" Nikalus asked.

"What, try to overthrow the Sun King?" Silius smirked.

Elen-ai felt Gidyon tense. It was one thing for him to refer to himself as the Sun King, or for her to do it in jest. It was another thing entirely to hear his own family use this title.

"I will not let Halen make me into his executioner. Jail is too good for him. Let him live with his shame," Gidyon said finally, carefully emphasising each word so that there could be no mistaking his intent.

"I'm sure I could draft a list of laws that set out your right to take their land," Kaine offered awkwardly.

"I would like to have the warrants and precedents ready within the next two days," Gidyon said. "I want them locked up or about to leave by the time we hold some kind of memorial for the fallen. Now, if you will excuse me, I believe there is a builder waiting to discuss the new wing. I have told him that I particularly like the curly bits in his design." Gidyon caught Elen-ai's eye. The tension with which he had addressed his uncles had vanished, replaced by a mischievous smile playing about the corners of his mouth. She bit her lip to keep from laughing. The shift from severe king to playful friend was disconcerting, but she was reassured to see that the Gidyon with whom she could share a joke, or playfully deride, was not overshadowed by the Sun King.

"It's a good idea to make an alteration to the Palace, especially after this victory," Silius said, approval on his face even though he still did not quite meet his nephew's eyes.

"I was thinking that we would put a room in there called the assassin's room," Gidyon said, still looking at Elen-ai. The cautious smile that he offered her warmed her heart. Even though he might now be known as the Sun King, a figure more steeped in legend and reverence than truth, he was still her friend and always would be.

"We can discuss where exactly we can send our friends from the Katan family later. I would assume the Fourth Country would be a fitting place for him, though, given his obvious affinity with their hired fighters. Elen-ai, did you want to come along to the meeting?"

Elen-ai responded with an expression that perfectly conveyed what she thought about the prospect of discussing building styles and techniques at length.

Gidyon laughed. "All right then. I will find you later," he said, and with that promise, he left.

Elen-ai made to leave once Gidyon had departed, but was arrested by Silius clearing his throat in a manner that left no doubt he wished to say something to her. "Do you have a moment?"

The way he spoke made it clear that he wasn't asking her at all.

Elen-ai obliged by staying where she was, even though being given a command rankled somewhat. By some unspoken accord, the three brothers stepped closer to her. She chose to wait until one of them spoke. She had a growing sense that she was not going to like what followed.

Silius spoke with his characteristic bluntness. "You have to choose. Stay here, or go back to the Family."

"I'm a daughter of the Family. I can't just leave them. And I can't leave Gidyon, either." She recalled her promise to Gidyon only an hour or so earlier, and the way his three uncles had been so distant from him, so wary of him. Perhaps she was the only person who was not waylaid by such sentiments and could treat him normally. She simply could not leave him alone.

"Think about it, Elen-ai," Kaine urged her, his golden eyes earnest. "He will have to marry soon. You won't be able to just stroll in and out of his rooms then. How will that seem to his wife? What about his children? How will your inconsistent presence be explained to them, a lowborn aunt who happens to kill people for a living? And what if his friendship with you – who you truly are – is discovered? People may now think that ... whatever power he may possess has been bestowed upon him from the Divine One, but if there is enough substance to the rumour that he consorts with assassins, how long until people begin to whisper that he has made some pact with a malevolent demon, courtesy of the Family?"

Elen-ai began to disagree, but he cut her off.

"I know that the Family does not harness the power of demons. But consider it from the perspective of the other lowborn, of the other inhabitants of the Second Country." His golden eyes implored her to understand the logic behind his words.

"I—" Elen-ai felt as though he had just pushed a knife between her ribs. The knife sat there, making each breath a sharp jab in her side.

"Don't mistake what we are saying," Nikalus said. "What you have done for Gidyon and the Second Country can never be overstated. But you cannot endanger everything that you have helped build."

Elen-ai curled her hands into fists. "So I'm a liability to Gidyon, now."

"You always were." For someone normally so brusque, when he spoke, Silius' voice was surprisingly gentle. "But there were larger risks to his position than you."

"So if I choose to stay here, what would you do with me?" She scanned the three faces before her. The earnest expressions they all wore made it so much worse. They, like her, were only looking to protect their king's best interests.

"You would officially take on the mantle of King's adviser, like us," Kaine said.

"The Veertak would confer upon you some form of qualification that would make such a title legitimate," Nikalus added.

"Adviser?" Elen-ai crossed her arms. She hoped they would not see that her hands were trembling. "And you would give me duties to perform under this title?" She restrained herself from adding 'like a trained animal'.

Silius nodded. "You would be ideal for travelling, as well. Your unique set of skills means that you would be safe, and able to spot what others might not. You could ensure that the Seven," he caught himself, "Six families are all behaving, not seeking to undermine Gidyon in any way."

Tears of anger now threatened to force their way into her eyes, but Elen-ai blinked slowly, refusing to let them be seen. "You want me to spy for you. So I'd barely be here, and I'd be spying for you."

"If that's how things work. But you wouldn't be spying for us. You'd be doing it for Gidyon," Silius said.

Elen-ai stared straight ahead. She dared not look at Kaine. She didn't know what she would see in his face, and she was afraid of what she may see there if she did turn her eyes to him.

She fought past the desire to scream, run, fight. She truly had been in the Court for too long. Instead of doing what came naturally to her, she raised her chin, allowing her arms to fall down to her sides, her hands open. "I will consider your proposal," she said, her voice even. It was the kind of response that would have made Gidyon proud.

With that, she left the room, her back as perfectly straight as ever. The air in the corridor was particularly chilling after the stuffiness of the war room. She told herself that it was the shock of the cold that was making her eyes water. She almost believed it.

She did not turn at the sound of running footsteps. She didn't need to. She knew the sound of Kaine's footfalls. She sped up but he drew level with her nevertheless. She did not look back.

"Elen-ai, please wait." Kaine gasped for breath, pausing for a moment, then jogging to catch up with her again. "Could you please stop for a moment?"

When she did not acknowledge his request, he grabbed her hand.

Faster than thought, Elen-ai put him on the ground, one of her blades drawn and a whisper away from his eye.

To his credit, Kaine kept his nerve, staying perfectly still on the cold floor. "I know this is a difficult thing to ask of you."

Elen-ai straightened up in a movement too fast to see. "Get away from me," she snarled.

Kaine clambered awkwardly back to his feet. "Please."

She remained completely inert while he laboured to stand. She stared at him, her face a mask.

"Please," he repeated. "You know we're correct."

She took a step toward him. He looked very much as though he wanted to take a step back, but restrained himself.

"How would you feel if I asked you to choose between your family and someone you loved?" Despite her desire to shout, she asked the question in a voice that was so soft that the anger and anguish behind it could almost be missed. Almost.

"I know. I know it's not fair. I'm sorry." His handsome features were distorted with emotion, and she saw how hard it was for him to ask this of her.

It was the apology that broke her. Anger, violence, even betrayal, she could deal with and still come through. But that heartfelt apology twisted the knife that he had lodged in her, and she felt the tears slide down her cheeks.

He pulled her to him and she had nothing left in her to resist any longer. She cried softly into his shoulder, letting him put his arm around her and whisper "I'm sorry" into her ear over and over.

TWENTY

After the chill of the outside air, the warmth in the Family's home was almost overwhelming. The tip of Elen-ai's numbed nose bloomed into sensation. She had never been able to tell what discrete scents comprised the smell of the Family's home. All she had ever known for certain was that it was the comforting smell of home.

The sound of muted activity within the depth of the house made its way to Elen-ai's ears. The efficient clang of cooking noises and light-hearted chatter came from the kitchen where lunch was being prepared. The home felt alive, exactly as Elen-ai had known it for her entire life. Unlike her most recent visits, there was nobody to greet her. Something about it made her feel less like a visitor and more like she was merely stepping back home after a day on the streets.

Elen-ai followed her nose to the kitchen, craving the camaraderie of her family. Her stomach gave an angry growl at the familiar scent of a family recipe, learned by observation and refined by years of practice.

A brief silence descended when Elen-ai entered the kitchen. She stared back at the four Family members who seemed shocked to see her. Their expressions made her pause, uncertain of what to do or say. Two of her Brothers and one of her Sisters were holding knives. It occurred to Elen-ai that those kitchen knives were lethal enough on their own, let alone in the hands of those trained to use anything and everything as a weapon. Once, she wouldn't have given that truth a second thought.

"Good. We could use the help," the Father who was standing near a bubbling pot said. With his comment, activity resumed as though it had never stopped.

Elen-ai took a proffered knife and began to slice vegetables. The dish they were cooking was one she knew well, a vegetable-based stew that nourished the soul. Unlike at the Palace, meat was a rarity that the Family consumed only once or twice a week. It was so with most of the Second Country's lowborn.

It had been so long since she had done this sort of work that it felt almost like a dream to be once more in the kitchen surrounded by her family, performing a task as menial as chopping vegetables for lunch. Undertaking the chore offered Elen-ai a certain sense of comfort that she had never felt living in the Palace. Easy, casual chatter surrounded her. It was hard to reconcile the mundane harmony of the scene with the fact that all four members of the Family who worked in the kitchen had fought in the battle for Herran.

"Have you heard that cloth from the Fourth Country has doubled in price?" Elen-ai's Brother El-en said as he peeled a long mallenroot with deft movements.

"Mm. There's fighting there between six houses now. It'll be a wonder if we can get anything from the Fourth Country before long," their Father replied from his position at the stove. The finely diced moash frying there was the culprit of the smell that had sent Elen-ai's stomach into a flutter.

Her Sister, Tan-ai, heaved a lump of dough onto a countertop and began kneading it with rhythmic thuds. "There'll always be something coming in from the Fourth Country. It'll just be so expensive you'll have to sell yourself to buy it."

"Better ready yourself now, El-en. I know how much you love the candied nuts from the Fourth Country," their Father said.

"Who'd want to buy El-en?" asked Tan-ai, evoking a chuckle from everyone in the room.

Elen-ai chuckled along with them. It was good to be among the intimate banter, free from the rigid social mores of the Court. It was what she had known her whole life.

"What about my fruit seller? He seems to like me just fine." El-en put a hand to his chest in feigned hurt.

"Yes El-en, that's because he's blind," their Father said with exaggerated patience, eliciting yet more chuckles.

Once the meal was prepared, Elen-ai took a bowl of the stew and climbed up to the roof, easily balancing the bowl as she negotiated the climb. The weak sunlight offered a pathetic warmth that could not dispel the shock of the rooftop's cold. Despite the chill seeping into her backside, Elen-ai sat happily, enjoying looking at the sea of haphazard rooftops cobbled together in an unintentionally graceful array. It was a sight she had known and loved her whole life.

Mari-am's appearance by her side was announced by only the slightest whisper.

"Is it a nicer view from the Palace?"

"Nothing's nicer than this view." Elen-ai's answer came immediately.

"You don't have to lie."

"I'm not. No view of the city will ever be as nice as this one."

For many minutes after that, they sat in silence and ate, as they had done from the first time they both were able to climb to the rooftop. This was their spot, and everybody in the Family knew better than to try to claim it for themselves.

Finally, Elen-ai could restrain her curiosity no longer. "Why were you fighting for Gidyon?" She had glimpsed her Sister on the battlefield, handling herself with deadly grace. In the days since the battle, she had pondered Mari-am's motives many times.

She tore her eyes away from the view and looked at Mari-am. Her Sister's brown eyes were, as always, sharp with intelligence and consideration. "Gidyon was the better choice. A Katan on the throne would have been unacceptable."

"You still don't support Gidyon, then?"

"No man should ever sit on the throne." Mari-am's voice indicated this was not a belief she was willing to debate.

"I'm sorry that I hurt you," Elen-ai said after the silence between them had stretched for too long.

Mari-am dispensed with the spoon that she was using and slurped up the remainder of her lunch straight from the bowl. Elen-ai suppressed a laugh, imagining the expressions of horror the inhabitants of the Palace would wear if someone were to do that in front of them.

"Are you coming home?" Mari-am asked, ignoring Elen-ai's apology.

Elen-ai looked out over the city. This was the sight that she had known her whole life. Sitting on the rooftop next to her Sister was where she felt the most comfortable. More than anything, she wanted to hold onto the moment, preserving it in time so that she never had to move into a future full of unknowns.

"No."

Mari-am exhaled slowly. "I guess life in the Palace really is that good."

"I made a promise." Elen-ai forced herself to look at Mari-am, to etch into her memory the slope of her nose, the blush that spread across Mari-am's cheek in reply to the cold air, the way the strands of hair played across her eyes. If it was the last time she was going to be with her Sister, she wanted to remember everything.

"What will happen to your skills? Who can you train against that will actually push you? Who can ensure that you are the finest weapon that you can possibly be?" Mari-am paused for a moment, looking out over the city with a slight squint. "I was on that battlefield. I saw you. You were magnificent. Nobody who approached you was your equal. Do you really believe that if you leave, you'll be able to maintain that skill?"

Elen-ai said nothing. Mari-am was correct. The truth was uncomfortable to hear. "I suppose if I stay by his side, I can't be an assassin any longer. So perhaps it's right that I'm not..." She couldn't finish the sentence. Her throat constricted at the prospect of losing the edge that her whole life had been spent honing. It was almost as awful as the prospect of never seeing any of her family again.

"Do you really love him that much?" Mari-am asked. "I can't imagine loving anyone so much that I'd give away being a member of the Family." The obstinate certainty in her Sister's tone was so characteristic of Mari-am that the familiarity was like an iron band around Elen-ai's heart.

Elen-ai shook her head, buying herself some time to work past the tightness in her throat. "I don't love him in the way you think I do."

Laughter arose from the street below, incongruous with the moment between the sisters. It seemed they were at a total impasse.

"I'll miss you." Elen-ai offered that truth in place of all the other things that she wanted to say.

"I'll miss you, too." Mari-am's dark eyes were unreadable. "Here, give me your bowl. I'll take it down to the kitchen." She held out her hand.

Within the offer was the painfully clear message that there was no need for Elen-ai to re-enter the Family's home. Mari-am's rebuff made her chest ache. She wanted so badly to take it all back, to say instead that she was coming home. She did not know what she would be if she wasn't a member of the Family, if her skills became dulled. She desperately wished that she could simply come home. But she had promised Gidyon that she would not leave him.

She turned her gaze back to the rooftops. It really was a beautiful view. She took a deep breath. The cold air burned her nose and throat. When she turned her head back to where Mari-am had been sitting, her Sister was gone.

She couldn't remember the walk up to the Palace. Her grief and shock at the enormity of what she had done had numbed her far more effectively than the frozen air. Walking back through the Palace gates had felt surreal. No matter how long she lived in the Palace, she would never fail to find it unusual that the Guards recognised her, stood aside for her, greeted her with obvious respect. She had been trained to live in the shadows, to slip unnoticed from place to place. Such conspicuousness felt so wrong.

In the Palace's driveway, she stood for several minutes, not even really noticing the cold. Her first thought was to find Gidyon, but she was not ready to explain to him what she had just done. Then, she thought about going to her rooms. But that prospect was too much a reminder of the home she had just lost. So her feet took her to the stables and the comforting presence of the kittanae.

The stables were warm, and Elen-ai slipped into the pen where she was met with a slow blink from one of the animals. They numbered only four now. Gidyon's mount had died on the battlefield. There was something forlorn about the remaining animals. They curled even more tightly together now. Being close to them and their grief made Elen-ai feel less alone.

She didn't know how long she had been there before Gidyon found her. She was sitting against the wooden wall of the pen, the massive paw of one kittanae thrown across her lap when she recognised his footfalls. His face appeared over the wall. "I thought I'd find you here," he said.

"How did you know?"

"I know you," he said. He vaulted over the wall – less nimbly than she had. All four of the kittanae raised their heads at his entrance. Gidyon walked to the nearest kittanae, a beast with rich brown fur, and held out a hand for it to smell. Once it had satisfied itself that Gidyon was not a threat, the king ildy scratched under its chin, eliciting a purr of contentment.

"Are you going to go back to the Family?" he asked in a voice smaller than she thought possible.

She didn't reply. To that, she had no answer. With Gidyon's appearance, Elen-ai's grief had condensed and lodged itself in her chest. The realisation that she had would never again see her family was a weight that pressed down upon her. If she allowed herself to contemplate the enormous finality of her decision – of never going back to the home, of never laughing with her Brothers and Sisters, of never belonging so completely – breathing became difficult. She hadn't truly considered what it meant to never go back. Now, all she could think of were the things she would never get to do. Suddenly the rest of her life, devoid of any link to who she was, seemed terribly long.

The King left the side of the kittanae and came to sit next to her. The straw sighed as he sat on it. The solidity of Gidyon's presence next to her roused her enough to answer him.

"I'm not going back."

"Ever?"

She shook her head, too exhausted by her grief to do anything else.

"Why?" Even though she wasn't looking at him, she could feel the intensity of his gaze. It gave her the resolve to be able to speak in a full sentence.

"I belong here, by your side."

Gidyon did not try to comfort her with the lie that she was able to visit. She appreciated that. "But you're miserable. I don't want you to be sad."

She took his hand. "I told you I'd never leave you, Gid."

Instead of replying, he squeezed her hand. His eyes were bright with tears. "You would do that for me?"

"I would do anything for you, Gidyon," Elen-ai told him. And with that, somehow, the grief that had placed itself on her chest with what seemed like an immutable weight, shifted slightly, and she found that she could breathe a little easier.

The initial shock and grief evoked by the enormity of her decision gradually abated. There was an almost unsettling normalcy to life in the Palace that removed the edge from her despondency. Preparations began for the construction of the new wing, and Elen-ai was forced to vacate her old rooms. She could not help but notice that her new rooms were in the wing where Kaine's were, and she knew Gidyon was behind this. She and Kaine did not exchange more than a few words whenever they saw one another, which happened infrequently. Elen-ai worked hard to ensure she spent as little time near him as possible. She did not yet know what she wanted to say to him.

She shadowed Gidyon wherever he went, taking comfort from the presence of her friend. As Elen-ai had predicted, the legend that surrounded Gidyon as the Sun King meant that no objection was raised to his decision to claim the Katan holdings as sovereign land. When he privately suggested in jest that he offer the lands to the Family, Elen-ai had given him a stare that would have withered most people.

"You're the Sun King. The sun doesn't shine from your backside," she told him.

He threw back his head and laughed.

She liked that she could make him laugh. It was good to see the King smile. Among the shining gold of his hair, she sometimes thought that she could see threads of silver. He wasn't even eighteen years old.

A month passed. Elen-ai still ached for home but she no longer wore the sadness like a shroud. A great celebration was planned to commemorate the victory against the Katan insurgency. Gidyon invited the new heads of the Bertak and Rasatan families. It was a clear message that he considered the treasonous behaviour of their families to be decisions made solely by their elders, regardless of what the truth may have been. Nikalus and Kaine vigorously opposed their inclusion, arguing that Gidyon had imprisoned their family members and imposed harsh taxes against them, and so there was no way that they would be loyal to Gidyon. Silius and Gidyon countered that while that much was obvious, it was better to show that the crown was willing to pretend otherwise and offer them the opportunity to redeem themselves. Elen-ai agreed with Kaine and Nikalus. She had, however, thought that bringing them to Court meant that they could be observed, which might be useful. But she didn't say anything, seeking to draw as little attention to herself from Gidyon's uncles as possible. They all might have Gidyon's best interests at heart, but she still could not help but feel betrayed by the three men.

She was praying in her rooms before the grand party when a rap at the door roused her. She was glad for the interruption. There was no way that she could not pray to the Shadow God, but every time she did, it brought forth a sharp bloom of sorrow at the life she no longer had. She opened the door to find Gidyon flanked by a small army of people.

"Do you need something?" she asked.

His face was totally serious. "I have a debt to collect."

"A debt?" She made no effort to hide her bewilderment.

"If I recall correctly, I won a bet. Silius danced at midwinter. I have yet to collect my winnings." Gidyon linked his arms behind his back.

"Are you serious?" Elen-ai took a panicked step back.

"Deadly." Gidyon advanced on her. The people he had brought with him remained at the threshold. Uncertainty clouded their faces as they peered at her. While the truth behind her origins was unknown, rumours about Elen-ai, especially after her performance on the battlefield, were certainly rife. Fortunately, they were all too enamoured with the fact that they worked for the Sun King to be overly bothered.

"I fought on a battlefield for you," Elen-ai said with a fierceness that she did not feel. The prospect of him putting her in skirts was terrifying.

"You swore on your honour that you would wear skirts if I could get Silius to dance. You were so certain that he would not." Gidyon smirked, enjoying her discomfort.

"Please, Gidyon. Anything but this." Elen-ai was not one for begging, but here she threw away her dignity in a desperate attempt to avoid this impending torture.

"Do you really expect me to show you any mercy?" Gidyon grinned wickedly, indicating to the people he had brought with him that they should enter her room. They did so, with obvious trepidation.

"I hate you," Elen-ai told him.

His smile simply broadened. Gidyon slipped his hands into his pockets and tilted his head to one side as he examined her. It was a predatory sort of examination. "Hmm. What about a nice flared skirt? In a delightful shade of sky-blue?"

"I beg that you do not," Elen-ai said.

Gidyon laughed at the panic on her face. "Don't worry. I'll make sure it's tasteful," he said. Somehow, the promise did not reassure her.

It took three hours to prepare Elen-ai for the evening's festivities. Her hair was brushed with the finest comb she had ever seen. Any snarl or kink in the short strands was removed by the careful hands of the man who seemed blissfully unconcerned that

Elen-ai was capable of snapping his neck with very little effort. In fact, there were several points throughout the entire process when she considered exacting a bloody vengeance upon the people who pampered, plucked, brushed, and combed every part of her. All through it, Gidyon watched her, amusement making his blue eyes even more vibrant than normal. This time, however, she was not glad that she was making him amused. Elaborate silver cords were threaded through her short hair, her face was painted with a slender brush, and finally she was squashed into a dress of blood red. The colour, she could only assume, was Gidyon's idea of a private joke.

Finally, she was ready. A mirror was held in front of her and the elegant woman who stared back at her with enormous dark eyes seemed a complete stranger.

"What have you done to me?" She demanded, standing with no small amount of difficulty.

"I think I've managed to actually transform you," Gidyon said, resplendent in his own dress clothes. Unlike her, he looked totally comfortable in his garb.

"Shall we?" He offered her his arm.

Grudgingly, she took it and they left her room together. Her torture was complete when they came across Gidyon's three uncles, obviously waiting for the King before they entered the grand hall in which all of the Palace's guests were gathered.

Kaine glanced at her, looked away, then did a double take. Elen-ai felt profoundly uncomfortable in the tight-fitting bodice and flared skirts that Gidyon had chosen for her. She wished that more paint had been put on her face so that she was totally unrecognisable. But unfortunately for her, Gidyon had sat opposite while his own face was made up, directing the lines and colours that should be drawn onto her features, emphasising rather than hiding them. How he had picked up this interest in dress and fashion, she had no idea.

"You look—" Kaine's lips parted slightly as his eyes once more traversed her length, from the dainty shoes on her feet, to the way the low cut of the bodice emphasised the curve of her breasts, to the blood red that stained her lips.

"Yes?" Elen-ai put her hands on her hips and arched an eyebrow that, to her chagrin, had been painted so as to 'accentuate' her eyes. She had no idea what that meant, exactly, but the man who had done it had been very excited about it.

Kaine shook his head slightly as though to clear it. "You look ridiculous," he said finally.

"The Shadow's blessings be upon you. Can you tell that to your nephew!" she exclaimed.

"Oh, I'm sure that was exactly what he was trying to achieve," Kaine told her.

"The thanks I get. I fight in his Shadow-cursed army, I protect his secrets, and this is what he does to me? I could ruin him, you know." Elen-ai crossed her arms, awkwardly realising that that action pushed her breasts higher. She dropped her arms so that they swung by her side.

She realised that Gidyon, Nikalus and Silius were watching the exchange between her and Kaine with mixtures of undisguised amusement and curiosity. This was the longest exchange between them since the day the brothers had told Elen-ai she had to choose between the Family and Gidyon, and it was obvious that they all knew that. Elen-ai pressed her lips together in mortification at the spectacle that was being made of her.

"Shall we go in?" Gidyon asked once the silence had stretched longer than necessary. A slight smirk crossed his face as Elen-ai and he locked eyes.

"I'm going to get back at you for this," Elen-ai promised him.

His smile broadened into an outright grin, and he proffered his arm once again. She made a rude gesture at him that caused

Silius' eyes to widen with shock and Gidyon to throw back his head in laughter.

"I'm intrigued to see what you will do to me," he told her before the doors opened to admit them. Together, they stepped into the room.

ACKNOWLEDGEMENTS

Many of the things I wrong in the acknowledgements of Queendom remain completely true. Self-publishing is slightly less terrifying, but it is still an enterprise fraught with a myriad of choices the information on which is more often misleading than it is helpful.

Yet here we are with King successfully completed, and I have a great many people to thank, many of whom had an enormous helping hand in Queendom's creation.

First, to my family. Both of my parents have been enormously encouraging and supportive of this journey, and I cannot be more grateful to them for listening to me endlessly prattle on about my marketing ideas, the editing process, among many other book-centric things. But support now is only the tip of the iceberg. I don't think my father ever denied me a book that I truly wanted, and I can still remember my mother reading to me when I was very young. This kind of nurturing is quite foundational, and my love of books and stories was nurtured and encouraged by both of my parents in different ways, from the time I was quite young. For this, I thank you both from the bottom of my heart.

This was the first time I have worked with an editor, and I must say Jason did a fabulous job. His work was both quick and incisive, and I feel that I've come out of working with him a better writer.

Ellen, of course, for her beautiful illustrations. She is not only a fabulous artist, but a wonderful person, and I am truly grateful to have had the opportunity to work with her. But of course, illustrations alone do not make a cover, so thank you very much to Marcus to his wonderful work in creating a cover, which in my words, "was as far away from the clichés of fantasy book covers as possible".

Although this is the only one of my manuscripts she has not beta read, Jess should always have a place on this list. She is such a champion and supporter – and she is one of the most amazing people I have the privilege of knowing.

One more person deserves being singled out, and that is Mitchell. His steadfast belief in my success is a true ballast in times of uncertainty and self-doubt, and it means more than I could ever possibly say to have him by my side.

Finally, I would like to that those first readers of Queendom who have loved it, and whose praise has sung out across the internet. Elen-ai and Gidyon are as much yours as they are mine now, and I am so unbelievably happy to be sharing them with you. I can only hope that you have enjoyed the conclusion to this part of their story, and hang in there for the next part.

ABOUT THE AUTHOR

Alice Jane Boer-Endacott was born and raised in Melbourne, Australia. She does not have a pet kangaroo, and she certainly did not ride a kangaroo to school. She does have cats, however. From her first stories about fairy princesses, she has worked to refine her prose. Queendom of the Seven Lakes, her debut novel, was written while playing Dragon Age Inquisition. King of the Seven Lakes was not written while playing any specific video game, although she does recommend Borderlands for some light relief when a scene isn't quite working.

You can visit her website to keep up to date with books releases, or to read more about the Second Country at: www.abendacott.com
Alternatively, you can follow her on facebook (A B Endacott)
Or Instagram (@alicejaneboere)
Or Twitter (@ajendacott)

COMING MID 2018
THE RUTHLESS LAND

"Lying is not simply about telling a plausible story, it's about being able to tell what someone will want to believe"

To outsiders, the Fourth Country is an unforgiving place. Under the leadership of ruthless women, powerful families regularly wage brutal campaigns against one another to increase their land and wealth, and men live in a state of complete subjugation.

Lexana, heiress to the Farwan family, is sent to the Academy, an elite institution where the daughters of powerful families learn and refine techniques to maintain and gain power. There, she finds herself attracted to Jaxen, one of the teachers who defies convention and often goes about unveiled. His apparent disregard for what is expected of him leaves her both uneasy and fascinated.

Then the impossible comes to pass and disaster befalls the Farwan family. Lexa must leave the Academy to find her mother and help restore her family to power. Jaxen insists upon accompanying her, arguing that she cannot survive without his help. Lexa can't be certain that she can trust Jaxen, but she needs his help if she is to succeed.

READ ON FOR THE FIRST CHAPTER

ONE

Passing through the lightning storm made the skin tingle and raised the hair on the back of the neck. But Lexana barely noticed thanks to the forget-me-not. She lifted the long holder to her lips and inhaled, feeling the smoke coalesce in the back of her throat. She stared out the window of the carriage with eyes turned bright violet by the drug and watched the forks of lightning streak down to kiss the ground. It was beautiful in a terrifying way.

Lexana felt the fear that the magnificent sight inspired, but it was as though she was experiencing it from a distance. Like she was feeling the memory of that fear. Forget-me-not, when drunk in the forgetting dens by those whose purses heavy with worthless coins did not permit them the safer inhaled version, could be crippling. When smoked though, it was far less dangerous, offering a respite from fear or sadness, rather than the complete oblivion for which someone had ironically named the drug.

Lexa let her head rest against the cushioned wall of the carriage with a sigh. The smoke clouded the window ever so slightly. The streaks of lightning became hazy. Her free hand clutched the letters she had just finished reading. Even the drug could not entirely dispel the emotions that swirled within her at their contents.

She had read the letter from her mother first, knowing that whatever it contained, she would likely find it the most offputting. She had been correct. Her mother, Tanita, had told her in the direct brusqueness that she reserved for her immediate family members, that once Lexa returned from The Academy she was to take her first slave-husband. The prospect of such intimacy with another person left Lexa unsettled. She was already worried enough about what The Academy might have in store for her without the nervous anticipation of taking a husband hovering above her for the duration of her time there. Once more, she brought the holder to her lips and inhaled in a bid to calm her nerves. Her mother had deliberately waited until she was on her way to tell her of this. Tanita entrusted many things to her daughter and heir, but she kept a great many of her plans and thoughts to herself, too. Lexa chastised herself for not guessing this particular plan. The gentle way her father had held her as they said goodbye, his voice soothing and warm through his veil, should have been a giveaway that her mother had chosen a first husband for her quiet daughter. At the time though, Lexa had simply assumed that her father was going to miss her. She certainly was going to miss him.

The second letter had been barely any better than her mother's, despite Lexa's hopes. The husband chosen for her was the brother of one of her closest friends, Emi. Perhaps her mother had thought this a kindness, but Lexa could only see it as further cause for anxiousness. Elui - slave-husbands - were bound to the will of their wives. Lexa knew as well as anyone that while one could love their husband, they must nevertheless be treated with a firm hand. After all, the primary function of men was to serve the interests of women. Lexa did not feel entirely comfortable with the idea of commanding the life of her friend's brother.

Upon learning the news, Emi had immediately written to Lexa to express her excitement. Her letter arrived with Tanita's. Far from reassuring Lexa, that had made her more anxious.

Perhaps she had been travelling for too long. The journey to The Academy had been interrupted by visits to her family's friends and allies. She had spoken with some of the merchants who were openly known to be in the employ of the Farwan family's massive trade network also overseeing a few important shipments and handoffs. She had dutifully reported back to her mother that all appeared to be going well, detailing anything that had seemed it might require closer scrutiny. Nobody would ever accuse the Farwans of being lax, and the intimate knowledge of their various enterprises was a not insignificant reason their businesses were among the most prosperous – and far-reaching – in the Fourth Country. Being personally present to speak with business partners, and to inspect operations was crucial. But the one thing Lexa looked forward to when she eventually replaced her mother as head of the family was that she would no longer have to undertake such tasks. Speaking with so many people left her exhausted, as did the careful observation for any hint of treachery.

Life in the Fourth Country was characterised by families invading one another. Indeed, the route she had taken to The Academy needed to be altered twice in response to attempted takeovers. While the Farwan family was entrenched within the Fourth Country thanks to its wealth and huge trade network, it did not mean that there were not those who would seek to take advantage of any perceived weakness. There had been times, speaking to women who had appraised her with calculating eyes, when Lexa had wanted to scurry away from the women and hide. But she had stood straight-backed and stared those women in the eyes, letting them know that house Farwan was a force that would crush anyone who tried to hurt it. Only when she had been back in her lodgings had she reached for the forget-me-not, inhaling it with trembling fingers that stilled once the drug had coiled itself around her with soothing smoky tendrils.

She soothed herself now with the thought that she had several months at The Academy before she would be forced to think with any seriousness about the prospect of having to speak once more with the many merchants and so-called friends of her family, or indeed her marriage.

She did have a natural aptitude for figures that meant she loved the aspects of her family's business many others loathed. To her, there was nothing more calming than the mundane task of balancing a ledger, or of doing more complicated sums that tracked the costs and rewards of certain trade routes or goods. Her mother had always encouraged this, recognising it as a skill that could uniquely advantage the Farwan family and their business, securing their status as one of a handful of families everybody knew it was madness to try and attack.

Lexa took a final drag of the forget-me-not and then extinguished the little flame. Her eyes needed time to return to their normal brown hue. The vibrant violet shade that gave away the fact that an individual was deep in the throes of the drug's embrace would not be a good first impression to make on her teachers, or indeed any of the other students.

As the carriage continued its ascent, she glanced out the window at the lightning, still forking down around them. She wondered how the monks managed to maintain the storm. It ran in a full circle around the mountain top on which the Enclave, which housed the Academy, was situated, ensuring that entry or exit could only be undertaken on the one road. That way, nobody could approach without the monks being aware of it. Although, Lexa reflected, anybody who tried to ascend the mountainside would probably arrive at the Enclave desperately fatigued even without the barrier of the lightning storm. The terrain here was sparse and unforgiving. Still, it was an interesting mathematical problem to consider. For how long could any one monk sustain the lightning, and how much could they conjure at any given time? To ensure that the lightning was around the entirety of the mountain, the measurement of the area would need to be known, too. She successfully passed a few minutes contemplating all the ways the area could be measured. Taking into consideration a margin for error, too, would be necessary. Losing herself in the requirements of the task meant she almost didn't notice the warmth that left her as the forget-me-not fled her system. Not that the task was a particularly difficult one. But at least it occupied her thoughts, keeping them away from the subject of her marriage.

From there, she turned her attention to contemplating how many carts would be needed to haul away the parts of the mountain in order to build the road. She made several different calculations, varying the amount that a given cart could take and the weight of the soil. Factoring in the probability that several carts would likely break in some way, she then determined how much time it would take to complete the path, assuming that the dirt and rocks were deposited somewhere within a half day's travel. That was slightly more difficult to calculate as she did not note any of her sums down, keeping the various figures in her head. It was a pleasant stretching of her mind.

She was startled from her thoughts by the carriage coming to a stop. She realised that they had long since passed through the lightning storm and broken back into terrain under clear skies, just in time to see a magnificent sunset. There were some advantages to living on the top of a mountain, it seemed. The driver opened the door for her and she stepped out, cautiously sniffing the air. She saw the briefest flash of her reflection in the window of the carriage door. The violet was gone from her eyes, the irises returned to their normal deep brown.

After the long journey it felt strange to be fully stretched out. She reached her arms wide, enjoying the space. "Thank you," she said to the driver. He nodded, a pillar of cloth with a human form. He had served her well on the journey. Her mother's fifteenth elui, he was well accustomed to tasks such as this, and often took Tanita on business journeys. He had already taken Lexa's trunks off the carriage.

"You're welcome mistress Lexana. I wish you all the best during your time here," he replied, his voice clear despite the veil. If Lexana remembered correctly, he was nearing his fortieth year. He had been given plenty of opportunity to practice speaking through the fabric.

"Will you be safe on your return?"

"You are too kind to worry, mistress. I'll be fine," he reassured her.

She offered him a smile and put out a hand to rest briefly on his arm in a gesture of thanks and farewell. He was family, after all.

She realised that a greeting party had appeared in the cleared area which served as entrance yard. Three women stood outside the impressive doors carved with an inscription to the goddess Mawani. Unusually, one of the women was hooded. All three remained silent while the carriage drove back down the mountainside the way it had come. No man was permitted to stay in the Enclave unless they were swearing themselves to the order, or in the very rare case that a family's only child was male and he was a student at the Academy.

"Lexana Farwan. Welcome." Once the carriage had descended to the point that it was out of sight, one of the women spoke. Her voice easily carried through the still mountain air.

Lexa turned. She pulled herself up straight, tilted her chin slightly skyward, the very picture of a daughter of wealth and power. "Thank you. It is an honour to be accepted into The Academy."

The third figure pushed back the hood and Lexa realised the error of her assumption. In front of her were not three women, but two women and one man whose naked face was now on display for the world to see. She gasped at the unveiled man. Except for those times he was alone with her and her mother, Lexa's father had always worn some form of shroud. Even her two younger brothers would have always seen her father with some kind of covering. The only men they would have ever seen completely without veils would be their own fathers.

She felt a blush work its way up her throat and cheeks as she all too slowly averted her gaze from the man's bare face. In the time that she had gazed upon him, she had noticed he was most attractive. That fact alone intensified the blush and left her struggling to speak.

She heard a warm chuckle come from the man, but she still remained looking steadfastly at her feet, saying nothing as she fought her profound embarrassment on behalf of this unveiled man. She wondered what he had done to be so shamed.

"You'll get accustomed to seeing Jaxen's face," one of the women told her, warm amusement in her voice.

Lexa raised her gaze to look at the woman who had spoken, refusing to look at the man's face, even out of the corner of her eye. "Yes," she whispered. The mortification at seeing an unveiled man still robbing her of the ability to speak normally.

"Come, let us show you to your room," the woman said, green eyes crinkling with mirth at Lexa's obvious discomfort. The three turned and began to walk back through the opened door.

"My trunks?" Lexa had to struggle to ask the question. The presence of an unveiled man was so offputting.

To her discomfort, it was he who answered her. "Will be brought." He gave her a quick wink that sent the crimson flying back up her face.

Mutely, Lexa followed the three figures into The Academy, wondering to what exactly her mother had sent her.

COMING LATER: FREYA'S JOURNEY IN THE THIRD COUNTRY

DARK INTENT

"you can either live in the world that surrounds you, or you can fight for the world you want."

Many years after the brutal Kade takeover of the Third Country, Freya Kuch, a healer, has succeeded when many Pious have failed: she is a perfect Kade citizen. However, this life of willing subjugation is torn apart when is caught in an attack perpetrated by the anarchic followers of the Dark Gods and assigned to care for Zarech, their captured leader. Contrary to her expectations, he is not a raving madman but charismatic and quite rational.

Over the long months of his treatment she unwillingly becomes close to Zarech and she begins to reconsider everything, especially as he reveals the supernatural abilities bestowed upon those with true piety.

Her obedience to the strict Kade regime is further complicated by her attraction to Ashtyn, a member of the Pious Resistance movement. She tries to ignore her feelings knowing full well the brutal punishments for adultery and dissidence. But soon, she is forced to decide: will she maintain her life of careful safety, or give in to her heart's dark desires and join the fight against the Kade's regime?